Fiction Fru
Fruchey, Deborah,
Unwilling heiress
DOWNTOWN   ocm14875317

71019200070 683

T4-ADP-229

The Unwilling Heiress

The Unwilling Heiress
Deborah Fruchey

Walker and Company
New York

Copyright © 1986 by Deborah Lynn Fruchey

All rights reserved. No part of this book may be reproduced or transmitted in any form or by any means, electronic or mechanical, including photocopying, recording, or by any information storage and retrieval system, without permission in writing from the Publisher.

All the characters and events portrayed in this story are fictitious.

First published in the United States of America
in 1986 by the Walker Publishing Company, Inc.

Published simultaneously in Canada by John Wiley & Sons
Canada, Limited, Rexdale, Ontario.

Library of Congress Cataloging-in-Publication Data

Fruchey, Deborah, 1959-
  The unwilling heiress.

  I. Title.
PS3556.R76U5   1986   813'.54   86-13199
ISBN 0-8027-0913-3

Printed in the United States of America

10 9 8 7 6 5 4 3 2 1

Dedicated to Daphne Rose, for lots of wonderful reasons that are nobody's business but ours.

AUTHOR'S NOTE

There aren't a lot of "surroundings" in this book. Most authors put them in out of a sense of duty; but as a reader, I have never particularly cared what color the ceiling was, or how many knick-knacks stood on the mantle. If someone is going to trip over an end-table later, I am careful to put it in. Otherwise you're on your own.

People who are bothered about this are free to improvise. If you feel conscience-bound to put a cabinet in the corner, please do so. I promise I won't mind.

The Unwilling Heiress

1

SHE COULD HAVE done without the rain.
It was bad enough that she had been turned off without a character from governessing Mrs. Bostram's three bad romps of children. It was irritating to reflect that her sin had not been of her own doing. She had been forcibly kissed by that lady's unsavoury nephew, Tom Crowley. It was disheartening to find that she had nary a pound on her, her wages having been something delayed by Mrs. Bostram's perpetual improvidence. Worse still that she had therefore been obliged to leave with nothing but a portmanteau, her trunk being stowed in a dank wine cellar. Worst of all that she must now tramp the streets of London without the slightest notion of where to spend the night. That it should, on top of all this, be raining vehemently, seemed a gross and calculated insult. All in all, Lucy Trahern reflected, it had been a most trying day.

Any other young lady of twenty, possessed of a good education and genteel manners, would have called it an unqualified disaster. But Lucy was made of sterner stuff.

As she turned yet another muddied corner to see additional closed housefronts, Lucy made a concerted effort to count her blessings. She was, first of all, an old campaigner; and while the situation was decidedly uncomfortable, she did not yet find herself at a stand. After all, she had been abandoned at coaching inns, faced with irate landlords, left without a penny more than once. And she had always handled these situations with, if not cheerfulness, at least a great deal of common sense and despatch. Of course—Lucy set her mouth grimly—she had never had all these things happen to her *at once*. And heretofore, such scrapes had been her father's doing.

Mr. George Trahern had always been, not to put too fine a point on it, an erratic provider. He was a rather fey, feckless fellow, with the best good-nature in the world, and a happy confidence that the ravens would feed him. When Lucy's mother had been alive, this confidence had largely been borne out, for Mrs. Trahern was of a practical disposition. Gently but not nobly born, she had managed to sew a fine seam for neighbours and teach their daughters the pianoforte and other arts without ever feeling, or allowing her daughter to feel, that she lost respectability by so doing. With the result that Lucy, though she was not in the least afraid of hard work, had retained a well-oiled sense of honour and impeccable manners under even the most trying of circumstances.

And to give him his due, Lucy's thoughts went on, (while noting as well that her shoes would not take her much farther without developing a hole), her father had sometimes managed to keep them in the first stare of elegance when, on occasion, one of his inventions caught on well. At such times he denied them nothing; and had good enough taste to keep from earning the damning epithet of "encroaching mushroom" by bringing his wife and daughter only into such social circles as would find them quite acceptable.

But he had no notion of management. He was forever selling his patents at a lump sum that was a tenth of what continued production would have realised. So that no matter how Mrs. Trahern scrimped and saved, it was soon time to sell the paintings and the carriages and move along.

Being of a rather weak constitution, Mrs. Trahern had survived this way of life only until Lucy was seventeen. Unfortunately, her last, devastating illness was succeeded by another period of pennilessness; between them, they soon devoured the funds that Lucy's mother had carefully saved for her daughter's come-out and eventual marriage portion.

Thus, when Lucy's father had once more found his pockets to let, he had quickly come up with another of his "brilliant ideas." This one, as Lucy understood it—none of Trahern's schemes were ever terribly intelligible—involved sublets and tobacco plantations in America. Getting there necessitated his working his passage on a merchant ship, which Lucy naturally could not do. But with his happy knack for making and keeping friends even through his misfortunes, Mr. Trahern had found Lucy a place as governess to the widow of a Mr. Sydney Bostram—a connection of his. And confessing himself very well satisfied with her position, George Trahern had posted off to America.

Lucy had never liked the place above half. Mrs. Bostram struck her as just the sort of employer one would dread. A fat, self-indulgent lady with a face like a pug dog's and a mind no sharper, who was forever accusing others of responsibility for her own lapses. She had, on at least one occasion, dismissed a maid for stealing something, only to find a week later that she had misplaced it herself. The maid had not been hired back.

But Lucy had been in no case to quarrel. She had set herself up as a model of propriety for her mistress's delectation, and until this afternoon, had done tolerably well. It had irked her a bit, wearing ridiculously dowdy clothes when she had silks and satins packed away from father's most recent run of luck, doing her hair in an outrageously ugly style, and never, never giving vent to her considerable sense of humour.

But there had been rewards. She had become very fond of the children, one girl and two boys aged eight to twelve; and they had minded her, liked her nonetheless for her firm hand. They recognised in her a person who respected them quite as much as they respected themselves; and though she would brook no nonsense, she was sympathetic to the impulses which prompted some of their wilder escapades. She had possessed a happy way of suggesting alternate, unexceptionable amusements; and if she had to forbid something outright, she always gave them very good reasons, demonstrating why it would redound to *their* advantage to abstain.

She even managed to wean young Cecilia from using boyish cant. Lucy did not waste time pointing out that this was unbecoming to a lady—a fruitless exercise since the girl was many years from that state and was not treated as such by her own mother, and since her brother's slang brought only fond smiles from Mrs. Bostram. Instead, she gently pointed out to Cecilia that these expressions, as modish as they might be now, were bound to seem a trifle stale in a very few years. Nothing, she stated, looked more foolish than their elders' habit of trotting out phrases that had seen their heyday a generation ago. Cecilia had agreed that she most certainly did not wish to look *silly*, and the cant had shortly disappeared.

Mrs. Bostram had been properly thankful and appreciative, but Lucy rather regretted the lost and lively ejaculations. So she did not stop the children when they rhapsodized in broad terms about the impending visit of their uncle, who had a great deal to say in the affairs of their mother.

"Uncle Jasper," it seemed, was an out-and-outer, a top-of-the-trees, a Corinthian, and a Great Gun. He could be depended on to give sugarplums and rides in the park behind his carriage horses (eulogised by Master Hyde as "a regular pair of sweet-goers, complete to a shade!"). And though Mother, they informed her, thought he drew the bustle somewhat overmuch, indeed called him clutch-fisted when she was in high dudgeon, Uncle Jasper was absolutely first-oars with the children.

Lucy, who had been somewhat apprehensive about the appearance of this paragon, pricked up her ears at this. She gathered by careful questioning that "Uncle Jasper" had been appointed by the children's father to administer his diminished estate and his children. Since the former had dwindled largely through the offices of his shatterbrained wife, Jasper was to manage her funds as well. While Mrs. Bostram might bewail the iniquitous Will, and think herself very ill used when she was not allowed to refurbish her chairs of green twill with straw-coloured silk, Lucy Trahern had silently decided that this Jasper must be a man of sense—something sadly needed in the Bostram household.

Unfortunately, Cousin Crowley had arrived first. This was Lucy's undoing.

He had started immediately to pursue her, disregarding her stern setdowns with the single-mindedness of a born rake. Receiving no encouragement, he had become bolder, and had chosen to press his attentions on her unwilling person in the library that afternoon, not a moment before Mrs. Bostram herself had walked in. Not able to believe that her dear nephew could do any wrong, she had rewarded Lucy with the title of impudent hussy, and told her to be out of the house within the hour. It was only by appeals to her particular friend the footman that Lucy had been able to have her things stowed in a dark corner of the cellar, and not thrown into the street, as Mrs. Bostram maintained they deserved.

It was, taken together, a very odd episode. For Thomas Crowley (whom Hyde had dismissed as a "jackstraw" and a "curst basket-scrambler") was not one who would normally be supposed to notice a girl like Lucy. Crowley, an aspirant to the most ridiculous heights of fashion, was in hourly danger of having an eye put out by the extravagantly tall collar-points he affected. Whereas Lucy, even by the kindest, could not have been called a beauty.

It is true that her dark eyes were large and widely-spaced, her nose patrician—perhaps a bit strong—and her lips, though thin and firmly set together over a decided chin, were well shaped. Her hair was a shiny, glossy dark brown, and quite long, but it was scraped into unattractive braids looped about her ears. Her figure, though excellent, was far too tall, and her dress could not be described as anything but frowsy.

Yet she was not by any means ill-figured. Perhaps Crowley had been more discerning than was his wont. For an educated eye would have seen that her own large eyes sparkled with intelligence and lurking humour, that the white skin was perfect in its freshness and texture, and that the hollows in her cheeks, which now made her look slightly haggard, would give her whole face an exotic cast if only given the half chance of a decent coiffure. Hers was a face, in fact, that was meant to be arresting and full of character. That circumstances had conspired to make Lucy look plain was a very great piece of injustice.

Lucy was unaware of any of this. Crowley's motives for kissing her were given only the most unflattering construction, and she devoutly wished he had not done so. To have the wet lips of a ramshackle fellow intruded upon her notice had been distinctly nasty. She scrubbed her mouth stringently at the very memory.

But there was no time for considerations such as these. Glancing about her, she noted, with a mind becoming numb with fatigue and cold, that she could hardly look to help from the inhabitants of this exceedingly fashionable neighbourhood into which she had stumbled. But then as her mother's daughter, she had no taste for the kind of lodging which her two or three shillings could have allowed her. Perhaps, if her luck held, she could find a cozy stable and—who knew?—clean up and present herself as a maid of some sort the next day. It had now become thoroughly dark, and she was beginning to attract unwelcome notice from hack drivers and night watchmen. Just as she looked desperately for a stable or tavern, it began to thunder. Lucy stepped up her pace, expostulating under her breath, and tripped into an enormous puddle. She was spattered with mud up to her waist. And at last, she felt the threatened hole materialise in her unfashionably sturdy boots.

The good Lord in His infinite mercy chose that moment for a perfect torrent of hail. As the thunder redoubled and the hard balls of ice became larger, one vanquishing the brim of her bonnet and leaving a deep cut on her cheek, Lucy admitted that her case was now serious. Discomfort was one thing. But this hail was positively dangerous. And while, earlier in the day, she might have found some tavern or inn where she could work off her lodging, this now appeared impossible. Only a few little changes in the order of things would have made such a difference! If only Crowley had kissed her yesterday, when the weather was fine—or at least earlier today, rather than two scant hours before darkness fell. Or not at all! If only she were not in such a very exclusive part of London, where the friendly, plebeian inns she needed were completely unknown. Or if . . . but this speculation booted nothing. Shelter she must have—this instant!

Another flash of lightning showed her a surprisingly small and unprepossessing cottage on her right. Just the thing! It looked as if it might belong to a gatekeeper or some such. She guessed that such a person would be more open to her plea, perhaps aided by the payment of her mother's brooch.

Stamping her pride ruthlessly under her feet, Lucy walked to the door and beat a resounding tattoo. She must hope to God she had guessed correctly.

2

It took a very long time for her knock to be answered. As she waited, dripping and shivering on the doorstep, Lucy had ample time to assess her condition. She was sodden with mud and water, bleeding on one cheek, and undoubtedly looked a fright. She was wandering in the night without money, trunks, or any sort of chaperone. In fact, it was more than likely that the door would be slammed in her face. Even worse, the watchman might be called to haul her away as a public nuisance. *Then* what would she do?

A candle was making its way uncertainly through the house, lighting the windows down from the upper storeys to the front door. By the time it arrived Lucy had had time to become thoroughly frightened. But she was a sensible girl, and she had prepared a very rational speech which she hoped would answer. It had better—the door was swinging open.

Lucy gripped her case with hands shaking slightly despite her best efforts, and put her chin up.

An amazing sight met her eyes. Before her, candle in hand, stood the strangest woman Lucy had ever seen.

A pretty, faded blonde of perhaps forty-five, quite alone, no footman or other servant being apparent. There was nothing in this to make Lucy stare, however. It was more the woman's expression and her dress.

Lucy would have expected a look of outrage, or at least mild surprise or enquiry. But the face of this apparition was perfectly blank, almost vacuous. The woman had lovely blue eyes (which, though kindly, held no trace of intelligence), a beautifully sculpted nose, and pink, pouting lips, all contained in a symmetrical oval face with pink-and-white skin. The effect that a dozen tiny wrinkles added to this was rather macabre, like a child who has made herself up old for All Hallow's Eve.

Lucy took this in in a scant second, and in the next second speech died on her lips. The woman was attired in clothes that were screechingly modish and most expensive: a lovely long silk dress, with neat little sleeves made to the wrist, and an overdress of three-quarter length in the finest Brussels lace. Lace, too, adorned her wrists and throat, and matched the charming Alexandrian cap on her plentiful gold ringlets, while her lavender kid boots exactly matched the silk of her dress.

This was odd enough, for it was certainly not at-home attire, especially for one living in a tiny and slightly run-down cottage. Odder still, everything about her had an air of extreme neglect. The lace was rent here and there, the sides of her skirt were crumpled as if she had carelessly sat on them several days running, there was a smudge on one sleeve and a scorch on the other. And behind her hem trailed a quantity of dust—or perhaps it was hair. For all around her, row upon row, cats of every size and description were gathering like a feline bodyguard.

"Oh, dear, you have got very wet. You had better come in by the fire," said this apparition in a vague, breathy voice. "This is not a night for walking, you know," she reproved. And stood calmly aside, as if she had bedraggled strangers appearing at her door every night of her life.

Bewildered, Lucy did as she was bid, shivering convulsively as she at last came into a warm, lighted room. She clutched her bag to her and looked around.

"Oh, you have got a bag. That's good. You'll want to change out of your wet things."

Lucy tried to make a recover. "I am more than grateful

for your kind offices, ma'am. Please forgive my intruding in this fashion. It goes very much against the grain with me, but on such a night as this . . ."

"Quite right," the eccentric beauty approved. "It is the most *dreadful* weather, and most disagreeable of it to catch you out in such a way when I daresay you had other things to do. It is quite vexatious when one considers that this is only September. Or is it September?" The lady paused in childlike puzzlement. "I can never recall, for I have the most dreadful memory, and Natalie says I am quite birdwitted, so that she despairs of keeping me in order. But it doesn't signify," she went on with a happy smile, "for whatever time of year it is, and whether it was *supposed* to rain or no, which I am sure I don't know, it *is* doing so, and so of course one needs to seek shelter, which you did like the sensible girl I can see you are, and now you have found it!" She looked triumphant at having produced this awesome piece of logic. And then, as an afterthought, "Am I acquainted with you? I have the most lowering suspicion that I cannot recall your name."

Now Lucy was fairly in for it. "No, ma'am, we have not met. That is why I am all the more thankful for your hospitality. I am Lucy Trahern." She took a deep breath, preparatory to making a clean breast of it.

"Lucy. That's a pretty name," said the beauty, as if that explained everything to her satisfaction. "I am Almeria. I expect you would like some tea?" And she wandered off, presumably towards the kitchen, leaving Lucy gaping. "You can change to dry clothes in that little parlour, if you like," Almeria advised over her shoulder. "No one will disturb you, and it's quite warm in there."

Lucy was too bemused to avail herself of this invitation immediately. She stood stock-still by the fire for some five minutes. With half her mind she noted her surroundings. We will follow this half, since the cogitations of the other are beyond coherent chronicling.

The cottage was fairly small, comprising no more than

ten rooms at a guess, and quite as surprising as its mistress. There were the same paradoxes about it. The fireplace, where Lucy stood, was opposite the front door, and was made of Venetian marble cunningly carved. Yet it had cracks and chips, and appeared not to have been polished for some years. The elegant clock on the mantelpiece was covered with dust. To her left were a fine sopha and several deep armchairs, upholstered in heavy damask, but soiled and worn; the exquisite cherrywood table had rings from glasses on every inch of its surface, and on it sat, of all items, an enamelled snuffbox. Did her hostess add a habit of taking snuff to her other eccentricities? Lucy wondered. The fine, costly Persian carpet boasted several capacious holes, and a lovely harpsichord, to her right, had two keys missing. This instrument was pressed against the far, panelled wall, and was topped by a painting which she could have sworn was a Rembrandt. But how could it be? A little door had been let into this wall, its sill of plaster adorned with cherubs and pomegranates. It was through this that Almeria had exited. The cats had gone with her, but signs of their occupation were everywhere. In the wall opposite the fireplace, next to the front door, was the window she had noticed from outside. It was small—one might even say mean—yet flanked by deep velvet curtains of burgundy which echoed the similar shades in the room. This material, which most certainly must have been costly, had been used by the yard and covered almost all the wall. But no one had, it seemed, made the least push at stopping the cats' use of it as a scratching post.

Right of the hearth was a large doorway which led, as Lucy could see by peeking around the substantial oaken doors, to a steep carpeted stairway. Farther to her left, a half-open door revealed the parlour which Almeria had recommended. It was similarly small and elegantly furnished, the predominant colors green and white, and equally shabby. Lucy had a strange conviction, however, that all of these things were fairly new despite their unkempt condition. The pattern of the damask covering the loveseat, for instance, was in the very last scream of fashion. Everything spoke, in fact, of an easy competence, or at least a very tidy annuity.

Lucy could only conclude that she had fallen into the hands of a madwoman of noble family. But the prospect did not frighten her in the least. It seemed absurd to associate such words as "danger" with the sweet, drifting Almeria. Presumably her family had found her vagueness disquieting, and had set her up with her own little house, plenty of money, and a keeper. Her hostess had mentioned somebody—Natalie, was it? Yes, that must be the explanation.

Of course—Lucy abstractedly tossed a damp strand of hair off her forehead—she could not dream of taking advantage of this dear soul, who was so obviously no more, in understanding, than seven. She would just dry off, and perhaps beg a suitable head-covering, and be on her way. If there had been a stable, or servants' quarters, she might have pled shelter for a night there. But this was patently a house where no such amenities were available. Nothing for it. She would have to go look for other shelter just as soon as she was dry.

A shiver gripped her at this point, and Lucy decided she must at least change her dress. She could not very well forage for herself while in the throes of pneumonia.

She scurried into the parlour, and huddled into the only other dress in her portmanteau. It was of heavy brown worsted, quite unfashionable, and exceedingly crumpled. But, Lucy thought with a smile, Almeria would not care for that. She did not have another pair of shoes, which was going to make life difficult. But that was a problem for another day. Her stockings would soon dry by the fire; meanwhile, she donned a pair of soft slippers. A pretty little round looking glass informed her that her hair was past praying for. She pulled it out of its braids and let it fall to her waist, combing it briskly with no regard for tangles.

Her face, though white and pinched, was at least clean from the rain. She dabbed the scratch carefully with a sodden handkerchief, and called herself complete.

There was still no one in the drawing room, though a few cats had ambled back to make themselves comfortable on the hearthstone. Lucy settled herself in an armchair, combing her hair and looking into the flames with intense concentration, weaving her plans for the night. A glance at the clock told her it was already nearing ten. She was at the point of wondering if perhaps she could reconcile it with her conscience to remain just this one night—perhaps with a blanket on the kitchen floor near the stove—and tickling the ears of the nearest cat, when two women entered the room. One was Almeria, looking satisfied with herself for having managed to make up the tea tray. The other was, Lucy thought in awe, quite possibly the consort to God Almighty.

She was every bit as astounding as Almeria—but here the resemblance ended. Natalie, for so this must be, was at least six feet tall: robust, imposing, some few years older than Almeria, and obviously bad-tempered. Her features were craggy and strongly marked, and included a stern, pursed mouth, a pugnacious chin, and piercing eyes apostrophised by pronounced black eyebrows. Her hair was black as well, black as night itself; thick and coarse and worked into a construction of remarkable height. Her frame, held ramrod straight with the aid of a wicked-looking ebony cane, was encased in bristling, crackling satin to which not a speck adhered anywhere. All her clothing was rigidly in the height of fashion—but of twenty years earlier. She must, thought Lucy irrelevantly, take rigorous care of it, for the archaic skirts and their bustle looked very nearly new. As Lucy was to learn, this redoubtable old lady relentlessly bullied her long-suffering modiste into making up all her new fabrics into this style, not approving of "that fribble, flip-flap, French stuff they wear nowadays."

This personage gave Lucy one scathing glance, taking her in from her wet hair to her frumpy dress to her stockinged feet and then dismissing her. She next beat the cannonade of her eyes on Almeria. Lucy expected to see the other woman quail.

"What, may I ask, is this Young Person doing in our best armchair?" she asked in stentorian tones which would have done credit to a duchess.

Perhaps Almeria was too accustomed to her guardian's strictures to tease herself about them, for she merely answered brightly, "Oh, that is Lucy. She is having some tea with us, which I just made myself and without the least little difficulty," she said proudly. As she crossed to the fire and set her tray on the abused cherrywood table, she added thoughtfully, "Except for that pot I broke, but I daresay it can be mended, or at all events we can purchase another. And I am not altogether sure I did not let the tea steep too long. But Lucy won't mind it, will you, dear?"

Lucy indicated that she would not. She could not, for the life of her, speak. It was beginning to be borne in on her what a truly absurd situation this was. Her impulse to laugh could only be quelled by silence.

Almeria patted the sopha invitingly, for Lucy had risen when the ladies entered the room. Recalling that this was, after all, Almeria's house, Lucy accordingly sat beside her.

Natalie advanced into the room and stood menacingly over the teapot. "And when, if I may be so bold as to enquire," she asked in repressive accents, "did you meet this engaging baggage? I do not perfectly recall being acquainted with her."

Lucy bristled a little at being called a "baggage," but Almeria forestalled her.

"Why, just now, to be sure," she answered ingenuously. "Only think! The most *fortunate* circumstance! I was wishing for company, and thinking it quite odious that we could not stir abroad on account of the weather, and, I confess, becoming a trifle hipped. Why, I even considered reading a *book* for entertainment!" She made wide, kitten's-eyes at her keeper. "Which you know of all things I most detest. But happily, just at that moment, Lucy scratched on the door. In truth, I think it very well timed of her, for almost no one is about on such a night, and if she had knocked on any other door but ours, we should never have known her!"

This was not a speech calculated to put Natalie's doubts to rest. "Good God, Almeria! I have always said you never cut your eyeteeth, and I begin to think you never will! What kind of nodcock are you, to invite in every stray trumpery Cyprian comes to the door? Why, you don't know a thing about her, whether she is genteel or the merest vagrant!"

By this time, Lucy felt very far from laughter. But she would not lower herself by arguing with a servant, however coming or oddly dressed. She listened with tolerable composure to Almeria's next remarks.

"Why, I let her in because it was wet out. Don't be such a slowtop! Of course, I don't know all her history, for I went away to fetch the tea before she had time to tell me anything. But anyone can see she's a lady, just by the way she hold her teacup. And such a respectable name, Trahern, was it?"

Lucy agreed that it was.

"Why, I know him! The famous inventor! Only call to mind, Natalie, he is the nacky fellow who designed those bits Lord Morelock dotes on—the ones that are perfect for cattle who have had their mouths ruined but are otherwise perfectly up to the mark! He says they saved him a pretty penny, not having to dispense with his wife's breakdowns. And her mother—I do not perfectly recollect your mother's name. Did I ask you, dear?"

"No. My mother is dead. But her maiden name was Shrevecote."

"Dead! You poor dear!" She took on a melancholy expression, and patted Lucy's hand, dabbing at her eyes with a tiny lace handkerchief. "There, there," she said comfort-ingly to a Lucy who did not particularly require comforting, since her mother had gone to her grave some three years earlier. "But—one of the Shrevecote brood! I am sure they are perfectly respectable. Not in the first circles of the ton, perhaps, but a family with such principles and good taste as must command respect. Now I am *doubly* glad I brought you in out of the wet," she beamed. "For to leave a connexion of the Shrevecotes out in the night—and an orphan, too—is not to be thought of!

"Besides, I feel sure her character is just what it ought to be, for Wellington likes her, and Wellington is *never* wrong in his reading of character, *are* you, darling?"

The cat thus addressed jumped into Lucy's lap and rubbed itself against her arm.

"You see?" said Almeria victoriously. And with this clincher, she poured out another cup of the strongest tea Lucy had ever tasted.

"My dear sister," said Natalie in awful tones, "there is no such clunch in Christendom as you. If *you* mean to let yourself be imposed upon by every toadeating mushroom that shoulders their way into your living room, let me tell you that *I* do not!"

Lucy had given a little start at the word "sister." Now, with what aplomb she could muster, she rose to go. It was one thing to allow the kindhearted Almeria to take her in if she wished. It was quite another to stay in the teeth of the violent exception of her relative. Her heart sank, and she was very angry at the accusations levelled against her; but she was nothing if not her own mistress.

With quiet dignity, she faced the taller woman. "Certainly I would not consider remaining in the face of your opposition, ma'am." Her tone was polite but very cold. "I would have acceded to it before, save that I did not perfectly understand the nature of your relationship.

"There were circumstances which drove me to this strange means of finding shelter, which I would not have scrupled to explain, had anyone asked me. But I have not the smallest desire to *impose* on anybody. I had meant, perhaps, to beg a corner by the kitchen stove, no more than that. But as the case stands," and here, out of her anger, she allowed her glance to sweep comprehensively around the dilapidated room, "I am sure I can procure more *suitable* quarters. Would you be so kind as to direct me to the nearest respectable inn?" She could not afford such a place, of course, but she wasn't about to give this harridan the satisfaction of such an intelligence.

Almeria had given a little gasp of dismay, and made as if to stop Lucy from going. But Natalie, to Lucy's astonishment, gave a great snort of laughter and sat down at last.

"Well done, girl! Well done! If ever I got such a setdown from a chit! There, you needn't go. I was only testing your mettle."

Lucy looked down at her with impressive hauteur. "I would not dream of intruding upon you. Now, if you please, about that hostelry?"

"No, no, not at all the thing! You can't show up at a public inn without an abigail, ruin your reputation. And it's no night to be out, m'sister's right about that."

This was quite true, and gave Lucy a qualm. The repercussions of travelling alone, not in terms of danger but of reputation, had occurred to her before. But to stay was impossible.

"I thank you for your concern, but I shall manage," she said smoothly, and started to bundle her half-dry dress into the overnight bag.

"Tush, girl!" Natalie was smiling now and looked amazingly genial. "Don't get on your high ropes with me, it ain't becoming. And not necessary. I daresay I got your back up, and I admire your pluck, but I don't mean a thing by it. Got to understand," she went on in her gruff, mannish way. "M'sister's the greatest peagoose in creation. Has to be protected. My job, y'see? All I was doing."

Lucy looked at her consideringly. "My compliments. You do it to a nicety. I shan't pick her pockets tonight, you may rest assured." She continued packing, donning her still-sodden bonnet, broken brim and all, with a little air as if it were the very cream of Bond Street's creation.

"Come. Think a little, girl! I said all those things not because I believed them but to catch your reaction. If you had *not* taken umbrage, I'd have known them to be true. Obviously they're not, so I'm perfectly content with your company. Kiss and be friends, heh? After all," she said wisely, "a girl of your stamp wouldn't be traipsing about London alone except under the direst need. Stands to reason. Why not let us help you? We can, you know. Place may look tatty, but we're well to pass. Very."

"Oh, do stay!" Almeria entreated.

The olive branch of Natalie's admission that she believed Lucy to be respectable dissolved Lucy's anger somewhat. At last she paused, resting her hand on the back of the armchair, which Wellington, a fat grey monarch, was now possessing in all the magnificence of a vociferous purr.

"I shan't deny," Lucy said slowly, "that there is something in what you say. I . . . I am in unhappy case, through no fault of my own . . . but it goes very much against the pluck with me to take advantage of strangers. Indeed, it was just such considerations which . . ."

"Which put you into a pucker," finished Natalie. "*I* know. But think on this: it's eleven o'clock already, and even if you had a feather to fly with, which I'd go bail you don't, you couldn't find any hotel to take you in this time of night."

Lucy did not like to capitulate so easily. But she was uncomfortably aware that the storm had not abated a jot, and that her situation was unimproved. If anything, she was more tired and hungry than before. But it is probable she would have sallied forth anyway, if not for Almeria.

"Oh, but you *must* not leave. You've only just now become the slightest bit dry, and if you go out now, you will very likely contract an inflammation of the lungs. And public inns are so very horrid—they don't have mustard foot baths, or anything to the point, and their denizens are so very vulgar! Why, I don't doubt the sheets will be clammy, which would be *fatal!* And then, you see, I should be very sorry, for you could never come visit us again, and I should never hear your romantic history, such as I am sure it is, even if you *do* wear a hat a trifle dowdy," she finished hopefully.

Lucy laughed outright. "Indeed, how can I persist against such blandishments?"

"Yes, child, do sink your pride and stay," urged Natalie. "After all, to put it plainly, why should *you* mind if *we* do not?"

"Put that way, I suppose I must accept. But just for the night, mind! And I want to say this instant how very grateful I am, for truly—"

"Stuff!" said Natalie roundly. "Sit down, child—Lucy, was it? Abominable custom, nicknames, I shall call you Lucille—and stop acting like a regular jaw-me-dead with your pretty protestations. You can thank us all you like in the morning. And for the Lord's sake, take off that confounded bonnet. Sit down. There, that's better. Now we are more cozy, eh?"

Almeria, who had never doubted the outcome for a moment, smiled impartially round at her companions. "Another cup of tea?" she remarked brightly.

3

She had awakened refreshed after a night in a magnificently untidy room with a warm brick at her feet, both ladies having insisted that the kitchen was no place for a young woman of her gentility. The two older women had talked and argued far into the night, having mild spats that were not very equal, Almeria retiring from the lists as soon as logic was introduced, and prattling on in her own inimitable style as long as she was allowed. By the time she went to bed, Lucy felt she had their measures. Almeria was every bit a darling, and while she was not precisely unbalanced, she had no force of mind whatever. This was offset, however, by her diverting pronouncements and her innately affectionate disposition. Natalie was, in fact if not in office, her keeper.

Within an hour or so, Lucy had Natalie pegged as well. She was one of those crusty curmudgeons who liked to argue. She was never so happy as when she found someone up to her weight for the spirited crossing of swords. But she was not by any means cross-grained; she respected anyone who would dare stand up to her and under all that guff, was rather grudgingly kindhearted. Before long, Lucy found herself replying with a spritely sauciness that obviously delighted the salty old lady. In just one evening, Lucy felt they had completely taken her in and accepted her as a friend. She was going to be sorry to leave them. She hoped she could see them again.

Lucy told her mentors the whole story of her adventure

over breakfast. This meal, although badly prepared on chipped Sèvres plates by a grumbling Natalie, was perfectly adequate, as were their reactions to her tale. Almeria was gratifyingly sympathetic, and Natalie gave a low cackle from time to time.

It was strangely peaceful, sitting in the grimy, sunshiny breakfast room at an unsteady table in last night's crumpled gown, eating eggs and bacon with these two eccentric ladies. Almeria was dressed in a devastating, frothy, food-spotted negligee, while Natalie (whom Lucy had discovered was a widow and instantly dubbed The Dowager to herself) wore black wool and took snuff.

"And so what did you do," that lady asked pointedly, "when this infamous sprout started making up to you?"

"Why, I told him," said Lucy with a twinkle, "that I thought he was an infamous sprout! And an April-squire, besides."

"Using cant, weren't you, girl?" Natalie queried, with a complete disregard for her own lavish misuse of the language.

"I had learned a few things from the children," Lucy replied with composure. "And besides, if anyone ever more deserved it . . . but as luck would have it, my employer appeared at just this juncture. That's when I was turned off without a character. For naturally her dear nephew could not have behaved with *such* impropriety. She was *shocked* that her children's governess should prove to be a brass-faced—no, I won't say it!" Lucy ended her sardonic recitation with a wicked grin. Natalie brought out the wag in her. "She is probably burning my sheets at this very moment. And as for my bits and pieces, if she has discovered their hiding place in the cellar, there's an end to them!"

"But, my dear, how perfectly *horrid* for you. Why, the woman should be *shot!* Or, better yet, have her ears boxed. In Public!" Predictably, this was Almeria.

"I remember Maria Bostram," said The Dowager dourly. "Always had more hair than wit. And little enough of that."

"Poor Lucy, weren't you *frightened?* I should have gone into *hysterics!*"

"Well, it was a trifle stiff," admitted Lucy, chewing on her bacon. "But I was not *frightened,* no. Father is a dear man, one must own, but he was never of the most reliable. I had been in a scrape or two before."

"Do tell," said The Dowager, delighted at the prospect.

"Most of them were after Mother died, taking her common sense with her," Lucy obliged her. "Father is quite loving, but inclined to forgetfulness. One time in Bath, I recall, he left without me, paying our reckoning at the coaching inn and heading north. I had a roll of soft, and I knew he'd notice my absence in a day or two, so I had only to seek out a respectable inn. But without an escort, you know . . . it would have looked so *very* particular. Luckily, I remembered that a serving wench at the inn the previous night had been let go for some misdemeanor. I asked one of the stable boys for her direction, and she was perfectly willing to pretend to be my personal maid for one night. I think she enjoyed it, actually, pokering up and acting superior. I had enough cash to buy her what passed for a uniform, and it was only for one night as Father came back the next day—so everything was quite all right, you see."

"How *odious* for you!"

"Call it an adventure, rather."

"Game as a pebble!" chortled Natalie. "Told you so! What else did this diverting father of yours do?"

"More what he did not do," sighed Lucy. "That was always the root of the trouble. At one point we hired a furnished house in town, servants included. Only he rented it merely for the season, and neglected to tell me. So one day, when he had disappeared for a week for so—he does that, you see, when he's on one of his inventing starts—the owners came home plump in the middle of tea. They were excessively displeased to find me there, as you may well imagine. It was awkward. So I explained the situation, and proposed to remove myself immediately if they'd only allow me to send round for my things a day or two later. Then I packed a small valise and went directly around the corner. Some of Papa's oldest friends were staying there. They knew what he was, of course. They were uncommonly helpful. A message was sent round to Hookham's library. I knew he would visit there before he came home. And our friends collected our possessions. So it was really not the least trouble." Lucy's voice was calm and matter-of-fact, but there was an impish look in her eyes.

"You're telling us a whisker!" Almeria exclaimed in hurt accents.

"Indeed, I promise you I am not."

"Why then, I can only suppose your father to be the greatest beast in nature!"

"No, no, never think so. He is everything that is kind, when he can only remember to be so. Why, one time when we were all to pieces, I told him I wanted to contribute to our upkeep. He went to the moneylenders for some dreadful amount of interest the next day and got me a piano. And of all things, Father despises a cent-per-cent."

"That of course," said Natalie dryly, "was the greatest comfort to you, and solved the money problem nicely."

This caustic comment at last caused Lucy's unholy mirth to spill out. Almeria companionably laughed along with her, although she did not quite understand the joke. It seemed perfectly reasonable to her. If one *must* live impecuniously, why not have a few comforts? "I daresay," she remarked wisely, "that one more dun wouldn't make a difference when one was already in the basket!"

"You may well say so," Lucy replied to this artless remark with a trembling voice and a ruthlessly suppressed smile. "Nevertheless it did answer," she told Natalie. "Because I gave a great many piano lessons, you see, and we came right in a trivet."

Almeria returned to their first subject with surprising persistence. "But do you truly mean you were not daunted at *all*? Not the least little bit?"

"How unladylike of you," quizzed Natalie. "You should at the limit have had *one* mild vapourish attack."

"I daresay I should have, had I known how. For there is no fadging that my case was—not desperate, but difficult, perhaps. This time I had neither friends in town, nor a father any nearer than America, nor any money. Although I am of a saving disposition, Father had not left me any funds, and Mrs. Bostram had never yet paid me a groat, though quarter day had come and gone."

"Nip-farthing," said the Dowager disapprovingly.

"Just so." Lucy continued calmly. "Still," with her chin in her hand, "I daresay I should have contrived, if not for the rain and hail. But that made it so I couldn't see well enough to find a place. And even if I had, I should have looked so draggled they would not have taken me."

"What had you intended to do?" Natalie asked with interest.

"That is the question to hand, is it not?" She played abstractedly with her toast. "I am without references, which is rather ticklish." Her fine, wide brow furrowed and the shapely lips pursed. "Do you know, strange as it may seem to you, I have always been a lady. We may have been in Queer Street from time to time. And it is true that I have been reduced to some odd shifts. But they were never of my making. And they were never such as to put me in a —a less than *virtuous* position. I am not—have never been, and one can't wonder at it—in the first circles of society. But I may say I have frequently been in the second. For we have had several fortunes, you know, before Papa made ducks and drakes of them. I have been accustomed to have a lady's maid and an abigail and lord knows how many footmen. And if I have never attended a ball, I have helped Mama arrange several; yes, and presided over a large household, too." She was speaking almost as if to herself, and both ladies listened attentively, Natalie in particular. "Even when I was obliged to become a governess, that is an acceptably genteel occupation. But now . . . ," she shook her head, coming to herself with a start. She sat up and said with resolution, "That's all done. I can't be choicy. Nothing for it but to be a tavern maid. At least they don't ask too many questions about one's antecedents."

"Unthinkable!" cried Almeria.

"Preposterous!" snorted Natalie. "My dear twit, you can't have thought. What do you suppose the duties of such persons to be?"

Grinning at being called her "dear twit," Lucy replied, "Waiting on tables, bringing beer and such to louts. Oh, I know what you are thinking. Being pinched and ogled does seem part of the picture, and that's a lowering prospect. But at least I should be earning my keep and could hold up my head." There was a stern set to her mouth.

Natalie nodded approval but said, "Don't be such a slowtop, girl! Pinching is the least of it. What d'ye think happens when the gentlemen get bosky and ask to be taken upstairs? And who d'ye suppose takes 'em there? It's part of the job, my girl, and you'll not last out a night else."

Lucy had turned quite white. "You don't mean—good God, I had no conception!"

"Nincompoop!" said Natalie, but not unkindly.

But Lucy had recovered her equilibrium. "Well, that won't answer, I can see. Never mind. I shall think of another plan. It is nothing of your concern, however, since I leave this morning. Don't trouble your heads over it for a moment."

"Leave this morning?" squealed Almeria.

"Nonsense, girl. You're doing nothing of the sort."

"Ah, but I am!" said Lucy, a martial glint in her eye. "Whatever makes you think, ma'am, that you have any say in my affairs?"

"You'll stay because you have to stay!" thundered the Dowager, dashing her cane against the floor. "Damme, girl, you're no better off than you were last night. Did you find any letters of introduction under your pillow? Do you know anybody? Have you, overnight, acquired a pocket of blunt? Answer me that!"

"Of course I haven't," answered Lucy quietly. "But I am warm and dry and fed, and quite in spirits again. If you imagine that just because I was forced to beg assistance for one night, I have the least intention of becoming a charity case, you are fair and far off the mark."

"Fustian!" the Dowager bellowed. "You can't eat a principle, girl, and you had better do as I say! I may not be your guardian but I'm your elder, and I know what I'm about!"

"I am very sure you do," said Lucy. "And I don't wish to seem ungrateful. Truly I don't know what I would have done last evening without you both. But there's an end of it."

"You're not going." Natalie stood to her full, considerable height, flashing-eyed and quite purple in the face.

"I do not precisely see," said Lucy with a maddening grin, "how you can stop me."

There followed a loud and extremely animated exchange of personalities. During this Lucy was characterised as an ungrateful, impudent, saucy wench, a frippery, good-for-naught widgeon, and many other epithets of a similarly unflattering stripe. Lucy held her own by sitting silently. She drank her tea with an entirely unmoved countenance marked only by that same faint smile.

This infuriated Natalie. Waving her cane, she hurled one final shot.

"Goosecap!"

"Pokenose!" replied Lucy imperturbably.

Natalie looked for a moment as if she would fly into a hundred angry fragments. Then all at once she dropped into her seat and began to laugh raucously in a rusty, engaging voice. She wiped a suspicion of damp from her eyes and leaned her elbows confidingly on the table. "I haven't been so amused in a score of Sundays. My dear young nitwit," she smiled warmly, "can't you see that we *want* you to stay?"

There was a short silence after this frank remark. At length Lucy said in a shaken voice, "But I can't, you must see that. Really I can't."

Almeria, who had been watching all this with wide, anxious eyes, now tugged distressfully on Natalie's sleeve. "You mustn't tease her, Nat, really you mustn't. I own it makes me excessively sorry, and it would have been above anything to have her bear us company but . . . ," she twisted her ribbons between her hands, "we are just two scruffy old things, you know, and she mightn't *like* to stay with us."

Her sweet face was so woebegone that Lucy was betrayed into saying impulsively, "Oh, ma'am, it's not that! Indeed, indeed, I like you very much. Nothing would be more pleasant than to remain here. But—," suddenly realising that she had just spiked her own guns, Lucy folded her lips tightly over the next words.

"But what, dearest? I don't understand."

"Natalie does." Lucy looked at the Dowager with direct eyes. "You have rung a fine peal over me, and I am suitably cowed. But you can't gammon me into believing that you don't collect my reasons perfectly. I am persuaded that beneath all that bluster you approve. If I were a daughter of yours, you would wish me to behave exactly so."

"Yes," admitted that lady simply. "Damn your eyes for saying so." She drooped a little, and for the first time looked truly old.

"But that's famous!" cried Almeria, clapping her hands. "Now we shall be be comfy. For if your only problem is money, why we have pots and pots of that, and it will not be the least fuss to—"

"Hush, Almeria!" her sister said sharply. "You have put a spoke in her wheel very nicely. I'm grateful. Now don't spoil it by being a gudgeon. Let me think!" She paced back and forth briskly, tapping her snuffbox with one finger. "Obstinate chit!" she rapped out of the corner of her mouth.

"Now, ma'am, how can you say so?" Lucy coaxed. "It is only what you would do yourself."

"Whipstraw." But she said it without conviction.

"Oh, *don't* upset her Natalie, she'll leave!"

"Nonsense. Lucille knows I don't mean it. For I will say this for you, child, you've got a good head on your shoulders. Not like the frippery cawkers most mothers raise nowadays."

She continued pacing and muttering to herself, thumping her cane as she went. "As I see it," she pronounced at last, "the problem is that you need to make your own living for the sake of your self respect. Very proper, too, and only what I would expect from a girl of your breeding. After all, we ain't your relatives, which would be a different pair of shoes. However, without references you can't find decent employment. Oh, you might eventually, you're resourceful at all events. But how to live in the meantime? That's it, ain't it?"

"You have stated my dilemma to a nicety." Lucy's voice was discouraged.

"Buck up, girl. It's never so bad as that. What makes you think," she looked at Lucy with a sharp gleam in her eye, "that we couldn't give you a character, hey? Think we're too blue to do any good, do you?"

Lucy had the grace to blush.

"Thought as much. Odd fish we may be. But odd fish with friends. We can find you something in time. Lady's companion if not governess. Not immediately, mind you!" she cautioned. "But eventually I've no doubt. Meanwhile,"—she gave her roguish grin—"I've seen you looking around this place and thinking unflattering things about it. Think we need taking in hand, do you?" She cackled at Lucy's embarrassed expression. "You're dashed right. We neither of us ever learned to hold household—never had to—and Almeria *can't*. I try. No good at it. Makes me cross as crabs. Can't hire any servants, because Almeria's frightened of 'em and lets 'em bully her. But she wouldn't behave so with you. *Would* you, Sister?" She favoured this lady with a quelling glance.

Almeria did not even notice it. "Oh no, I could never be afraid of Lucy. I am quite attached to her already."

"Well, what do you think, eh? Willing to keep us from under the cat's paw for your board and keep?"

Lucy thought over this scheme in growing excitement. She could really find no flaw in it. She told them so, in simple words but with a glowing face; and was immediately inunudated in a wave of patchouli and stained lace. For Almeria ran to embrace her, crying and being incoherently happy and effectively preventing Lucy's own thanks from being anything but disjointed.

Natalie put an abrupt end to this scene by saying she despised ninnyhammers and watering pots. Almeria should rather apply herself to changing that disgraceful robe and Lucille should this instant do the washing up.

This broke up the tableau. Everyone departed out various doors, Lucy stopping only to ask Natalie what she was to call them.

"For I hardly feel proper using only your Christian names."

"Fiddlestick. If you must be so missish, call us Aunt Natalie and Aunt Almeria. Lord knows you're worth a dozen of any relative *I* ever was plagued with."

And with this deceptively curt dismissal she trod majestically up the stairs. While Lucy, generally not a girl of extreme sensibility, cried softly into the dishwater at their kindness and her good fortune.

4

THE RIGHT HONOURABLE Lord Hersington, Earl of Kentsey—otherwise known to a certain three nipperkins as "Uncle Jasper"—descended languidly from his travelling carriage. He eyed the house of his coattail cousin-in-law, Maria Bostram, with bored disfavour. His visits here, with the exception of the opportunity they afforded of seeing the aforesaid youngsters, were perfunctory and generally quite distasteful. For they usually embroiled him in some flap or other that a little management might have prevented.

Today things looked to be in more than usual disorder. The kerb had not been swept. There was no one to take the horses. A clear track of muddy footprints, which looked to be several days old, trailed up to a door hanging open. Lord Hersington shot his immaculate cuffs and was offended. He flicked an invisible speck of dust from his blue kerseymere coat (which clearly said "Weston" to the educated eye) and prepared himself for the worst.

"Morton," he addressed his groom in a cool, collected voice, "it would appear that your hostess is . . . otherwise occupied. I suggest you take the cattle round to the stables and make the best shift you can. Unhitch them and see they get a feed, but do not stable them as yet. Take Mr. Pannet and the chef Gascard with you. It is entirely possible we may have to remove to the Pulteney."

Inured to the problems of this particular household, his groom merely nodded and did as suggested. Lord Hersington ascended the sullied steps with the greatest of misgivings.

The entrance hall showed similar signs of neglect. Flowers drooped in their vases, dust lay thick on the table, and three days' newspapers lay untouched on a chest. He took in these signs with interest as he removed his curly-brimmed beaver and lay down his cane.

It was not many moments before a small thin gentleman of soldierly bearing appeared to greet him. This personage was the butler. However if Hersington had not known this to an indisputable fact, having hired the man himself, he would never have guessed it. The man's garb up to the waist was unexceptionable. But above this sat incongruously a patterned shirt clearly meant—and used for some time past—only for gardening; and he wore no coat whatsoever.

This very superior butler, however, seemed not to suffer the least loss of countenance. He bowed as correctly as if he had always donned paisley to greet members of the peerage, and gave his lordship a proper welcome as he relieved him of his driving cape.

"It is a pleasure to see your lordship, if I may say so. Your advent in this household is always a fortuitous one."

"Thank you," said his lordship imperturbably. "I trust I find you well, Pentworthy?"

"Quite, sir."

He cast an eye over Pentworthy's outfit. "You are not perchance suffering from a fever? One which necessitates the discarding of your jacket?"

"Not in the least, my lord. I am in perfect health. My appearance, which I hope your lordship will excuse, is occasioned by the fact that no uniforms are available at this present. They have been—ahem—misplaced."

"Misplaced by whom, if I may enquire?"

"By the children, sir. I ought perhaps to explain that madame found it necessary to dismiss, some three days ago, a governess of whom the children were markedly fond. They have chosen this method, among others, of evincing their displeasure."

Calmly he closed the door and put Hersington's cape over his arm.

The latter raised one slim honey-coloured brow. He showed no other sign of displeasure or ruffling. But then Jasper, Lord Hersington, did not often—not ever, some said—allow himself to be visibly ruffled.

He was an exceedingly handsome gentleman, lean and well muscled, with long legs encased in Hessians whose blinding shine was the toast of his valet's fame. His clothes were of subdued colour but excellent cut, and never less than meticulous in condition. His dark, slim-fingered hands were not detracted from by more than one signet ring, its amber stone nearly matching in colour his unusual shade of hair, somewhere between brown and blond. It was more straight than curly and tended to fall into natural, attractive ruffles that ladies found provocatively touchable, some wanting to smooth them down and some to dissarrange them further.

His face was much less approachable. The dark skin was complemented by the slanted, narrow bones accenting a stong, almost hawklike nose, and firm thin lips. Usually, as now, the large eyes, of a peculiar brandy hue, were hooded and evidenced detachment. A few intimates had once or twice seen this boredom banished, and an intense light of interest or puckish humor emerge. At such times he looked a good deal younger than his thirty-five years.

This was not such a moment.

"I collect you may consider yourselves fortunate that the uniforms were not cut up and strewn out the windows."

"Oh, no, my lord," answered the butler with a creditably straight face. "The closest we've come to that is madam's best hat."

"Hidden?"

"Dismantled. I believe the peacock feathers have been made into quite serviceable quill pens."

The earl's lips twitched, but his tone altered not a hair. "And what has been the result of this? Are the imps now locked in the nursery?"

"They have hidden the keys, my lord. Madam and the rest of the staff—what's left of it—have been searching, to no avail."

"Ah." The earl said nothing further for a moment, only allowing himself a small, rueful upturn at the corner of his mouth. "It seems that I am most timely arrived. How long has this situation prevailed?"

"Three days, your lordship."

"I see." He paused and then turned towards the hall. "Well. Under the circumstances I believe I shall make shift to announce myself, Pentworthy."

"Very good, sir."

"I gather the staff is . . . somewhat reduced?"

"Six maids, a housekeeper, and a cook, sir, have left in the last two days. Frogs in the larder, the cat let loose in cook's pâté, ghosts—small people in bedsheets—at midnight in the maid's room."

"How glad I am that I brought my own chef," murmured Hersington. And with no further comment, he sauntered into the hall.

He had not taken above seven steps before the object of his search approached him. Or perhaps "approached" is too civilised a word. Maria Bostram flung herself at the earl bodily, heedless of the careful folds of his cravat and his dignity.

In the moment before she was launched, Jasper had time to note with distaste that her bag-shaped figure was contained in a gown of the vilest pea green, her scant brown-grey curls frizzled into a style that had not been the mode for ten years (and never that for one of her uncertain years), and that her face looked more than usually aggrieved. Lady

Bostram had never been terribly steady or sensible. Three days of rebelling offspring had reduced her to alternate bouts of hysterics, vapours, faints, and palpitations. None of this had made the slightest dent in the children's sympathies. Bereft of her most powerful weapons, Maria could only cling to Lord Hersington and sob incoherently, alternately proclaiming him as her saviour, berating him for not arriving sooner, and vigorously bemoaning her fate.

After three minutes of this the earl decided it was high time to put a stop to it. He thrust her away and said sternly, "Enough, Maria! We have provided the servants with quite as much circus as they can stomach already. Now go into the parlour, like the sensible woman you are not, and try if you can to compose yourself."

This harsh speech had its effect. Maria straightened herself and stopped speaking on a convulsive sob. With her best imitation of self-control—she would have made a very poor actress, Jasper reflected—she conducted him into the first floor parlour directly behind the receiving room and shut the door.

"Now," continued the earl when she had seated herself. "Would you mind telling me what is the matter? I collect the children are in revolt, and it all seems connected with some governess that was turned away."

"Miss Trahern!" said the lady in passionate accents. *"Never* have I been so taken in. Only fancy, she came to me with the *highest* references, from one of Sir Sydney's oldest friends—her father, in fact, George Trahern. I daresay you don't know him."

"I fancy my father was aquainted with him a trifle."

"Then you can see why I placed the utmost confidence—and really until three days ago I thought I had truly stumbled on a gem. The children minded her beautifully, as they have never done for anyone before."

"I recollect," said his lordship dryly.

"And her conduct and manners seemed to be just what they ought. She was never saucy, nor snippy, nor did she behave above her station. In truth, I thought her the very model of propriety. And then, just the other day," Maria here had recourse to a lacy pocket handkerchief embroidered in a truly repulsive shade of yellow, "why, I caught her accepting a—a salute! In our own library! The most shocking thing! So of course I had to turn her off. Whatever my faults," she finished with a small dignity, "I certainly would not allow my daughter to be supervised by a—a *loose* woman!"

The earl was much inclined to think she was right. But placing no dependence on Mrs. Bostram's limited understanding, he felt in honour bound to explore the situation further.

"I imagine you have also dismissed the gentleman involved?"

"No, oh, heavens, no! It was *Tom*, you see. That is why—I was sure—my nephew would never *consider* lowering himself in such a way, and so it must have been her fault."

"Ah." This put a different face on the situation. It would not be the first time Maria had turned off a menial who was blameless.

But there were other things to be attended to first. "How is it that you have not contrived to bring order to the household by now? This sort of hobble is not at all what I am accustomed to, Maria, and I may say it doesn't look very good to your neighbours either."

His tone was scathing. Lady Bostram looked mortified. But she had her excuse ready. "Why, I am sure I have done everything possible! The children have been put on a strict regime of bread and water, and denied all their privileges and outings. But they say they don't care for *that*, as they are not hungry now Miss Trahern is gone, and wouldn't enjoy anything. I sent for my sister Augusta, too, the minute things got out of hand. But she cannot possibly be here in under ten days, you know."

"Do you have some reason to suppose," he asked mockingly, "that she will be any more competent to control them than before? Never mind. Don't answer, since you cannot. It seems I must talk to the children if I want to discover anything more."

The maid he encountered in the hall seemed to have no very clear idea where the termagants might be. Begging his honour's pardon, she was sure, but they were neither to hold nor to bind since Miss left and no fratching about it. He might try the library; there had but recently been a serious of ominous noises obtruding from that room. And she took herself off as fast as her spindly little legs would carry her.

She proved to be right, however, when his lordship extended his head cautiously into this apartment. The three enterprising truants were to be seen in various parts of the room happily engaged at their destructive tasks.

Cecilia, a fair-haired damsel who at the moment looked very much less than twelve, had her skirts hitched up and was concentrating on an ambitious work of art planned to grace the walls of the library. The execution was rather shaky owing to the fact that it was being completed on a large sheet of foolscap with unmended pens from her father's desk. Nevertheless it had the virtue of imagination; and was unmistakably a depiction of Miss Trahern being thrown to the lions by a Lady Bostram twice her normal size. Lindon, as flaxen as his sister but still carrying the touching pudginess of eight years, was energetically tumbling books from the shelves. Hyde, a dark slim lad with a clever face patently destined to break many hearts, was teetering precariously on a table by the window with a view to detaching the curtains.

All this activity ceased immediately when Jasper stepped into the room saying apologetically, "Pardon me for intruding, ladies and gentlemen, but I would like a word with you."

"Uncle Jasper! Uncle Jasper!" The children rushed towards him shouting and laughing, eager for his attention.

Cecilia danced in front of him. Hyde made him a fancy bow. And Lindon clasped his buff pantaloons and gazed up soulfully into his face.

It could not be seen that his lordship minded these demonstrations, though his valet would deplore the wrinkles in his artwork later. Rather he moved, despite considerable hampering, to a large armchair and sat down. Any of his cronies would have been nonplussed by the gentleness of his countenance. His face was suffused with that expression his friends had so seldom seen: a restrained amusement tempered by what must have been, hard as it was to credit, affection.

"May I ask," he said idly, "what is the meaning of this general dishevelment? You hell-born brats have reduced the house to a shambles, you know."

The trio took no umbrage. They tumbled over themselves to give him an instant explanation.

"We want Miss Trahern back!" Lindon told him.

"We're going to keep on being naughty till she comes," Hyde added.

"That chin of yours will set very impressively one day," commented the earl. "But at the moment I need more explanations. Tell me, why is it you feel so very strongly about this *particular* governess?"

"She was a Trump!" Lindon put in.

"Don't be a paperskull," his brother exclaimed with all the infinite scorn that only a ten-year-old can command. "A *female* can't be a Trump."

"Well, she *was*," maintained Lindon stoutly.

"I will admit that you seem to have liked her," said Hersington. "But I'm not sure that is necessarily a recommendation. You liked Miss Scabbert too—and as I recall, she had no control over you at all. Which is probably why."

None of the children seemed to think this at all insulting. He was addressing them as an equal, and they responded to it with a frank good sense which would have astonished their mother.

"Oh, but we always minded Miss Trahern," Cecilia responded.

"Always?" Their elder was doubtful.

"Always," she replied firmly.

The two boys nodded agreement.

"Remarkable. How did this come about?"

"Because she didn't treat us like—like loobies, like our other governesses did. She 'splained *why* we should behave. Just as if we were grown up!"

"It quite won our hearts," Cecy finished.

Lindon piped up. "She never, ever said 'because I told you so' or 'when you're older.' "

The other two agreed vigourously.

"Oh?"

"Miss Lucy never cut up stiff, or got up in the boughs," Hyde illuminated.

Hersington was suitably impressed. But he said only, "She allowed you to call her Miss Lucy?"

Lindon was trying hard to be as lucid as his siblings. "Well, only when she was having a special cose with you."

"Tell me, then. How is it that this paragon came to be turned away?"

Lindon said breathlessly, emboldened by the success of his last statement, "She was making advances to Cousin Tom!"

Hyde, abandoning his short attempt at maturity, kicked him in the shins. "Nodcock! You have it backwards! Tom made advances to her! I *know* Miss Trahern didn't like it, because she called Tom an impudent sprout."

"She said that to you?" Hersington was very far from being pleased or convinced.

"No, I just—just heard it." Hyde had the grace to look abashed.

"Cousin Tom had stopped her in the hall, you see. He grabbed her arm."

"And spilt milk all over her best dress!" Cecy interrupted indignantly. "And she only had two!"

"That's when she called him a sprout. *And* an April-squire."

"And a thatch-gallows," added Lindon hopefully. "I heard her!"

"But he paid no mind. He said she was a teasing minx, and he shouldn't regard it."

"I see." But Hersington was looking thoughtful. "But you know, a woman may say these things in a laughing voice when she really welcomes the gentleman's attentions."

"Not Miss Trahern," said Cecilia hotly.

"I know she did not like it," Hyde added. "The kiss I mean. Because when she came out of the library she wiped her mouth."

"*Did* she?" said Hersington with interest.

"Yes. And said something to herself."

"What did she say?"

"She said 'bounder!' " Lindon supplied.

"Well," concluded the earl. "This is all very interesting, and I see why you are unhappy. But I can hardly acquiesce in your scheme of turning the house topsy-turvy to remedy the fault."

"But it was so *unfair!*" cried Cecilia.

"And now mother has sent for our Aunt Augusta, and we never have fun when she's here," Hyde said disgustedly.

"I quite see your point," began Jasper, "but I can hardly condone—"

He got no further. The group was interrupted by one of the few remaining footmen. Begging his lordship's pardon, and not wanting to cause trouble, he craved permission to present several messages which had just been left by Miss Trahern.

"Miss Trahern was here?"

"She left a message!"

"For us?"

Indeed. It seemed that Miss Trahern, although directing

a note to "the children's Uncle Jasper," had written to the children themselves as well. There was a long, general letter and a separate squib for each of them. They took these up eagerly. There was silence in the library for a long while.

Hersington had long since begun to be convinced that Miss Trahern was a sensible woman whose loss was only to be regretted. So he perused his note with great interest.

> My Dear Sir,
> I hope you will excuse my addressing this letter so familiarly. But since I know you only as the children's "Uncle Jasper," there is no other way I could be certain this communication reaches you. I understand that since my departure a state of riot has obtained in the house of my late mistress, Dame Bostram.

How, he wondered had she learned of that?

> This is not at all what I would have wished, and I have written a letter to the children which I hope will appeal to their better instincts and keep them out of further mischief.

He glanced up and saw that the three were carefully perusing their joint missive. Cecilia was reading out the difficult words for Lindon's edification. All three were looking very serious.

> The children told me before I so summarily left that they expected a visit from you. My errand to you is simple, and I hope you will not consider it forward in one you do not know. I have every faith that my former charges—who have more common sense than they are generally given the credit for—will desist in their scandalous behavior once they read what I have to say to them.

What I very much wish is that once they have stopped they not be punished for their rash actions.

Hersington turned the page here with rabid curiosity.

I mean to invoke a spontaneous demonstration of conscience from them. And since I have every reason to believe that you are a man of sense, I hope that you will support me in keeping this demonstration from being undermined. If they act with goodwill and are subsequently reprimanded, they will probably "fall into a fit of the sullens," as Hyde would say, which would invalidate the whole. But if they see that their repentance is rewarded not with scolds but with appreciation, all shall be well.

Reposing on your calm management, of which the children have advised (and in whose opinion I place considerable confidence), I trust most sincerely to remain—

It was signed "Lucy Trahern."

After reading this remarkable missive, Hersington turned instinctively to the children to gauge its effect. White-faced, they were earnestly trying to undo the havoc they had begun to wreak in the library. Lord Hersington picked up the children's epistle. It gave him considerable pause.

Dear Cecilia, Hyde, and Lindon:

You know that I have always thought well of you and valued your opinions. Nevertheless, I am vastly disappointed in what I hear of your conduct since my departure. It is not at all the thing, you know. I have always tried to treat you as the sensible persons I know you to be. More, I have tried to convince your mother that this was so.

But how can she believe us when, the minute your governess leaves, you behave like schoolchildren? My dears, it is not worthy of you!

If you care for me as much as I care for you—and I harbour no doubts that our regard is as mutual as it is enduring—then you will not want to make a mull of my future chances. What must happen to me if it is known that my departure from a post caused only chaos? I know I need not say more.

I expect your actions are caused by a sense of injustice at the cause of my dismissal. True, I am not guilty of that of which I am accused. But the case is not so simple. I beg you will not blame your mother overmuch. It certainly looked bad to her, and we all make mistakes. We have each of us done things we would blush to own. I could tell you of scrapes of my own which would make you giggle!

So please, my friends, have a little charity. I have faith that you will heed me, even though I no longer have a right to call myself your preceptress.

With greatest love, always, to my favorite pupils,

        Miss Lucy Trahern

Hersington looked up from this letter, impressed, to find the library restored almost to order. The earl could only think that Miss Trahern knew her charges very well indeed to inspire such an immediate response.

The children straggled back to him with disconsolate expressions.

"To think we believed ourselves doing her a favour, and find it a disservice!" Cecilia said sadly. "What shall we do?"

"Restore the footmen to their uniforms, I should think," responded Jasper cooly. "And promise most faithfully to put up with whatever governess your mother and I can contrive."

"We'll try," said Hyde bravely. "But *nobody* could be as good as Miss Trahern."

"I am not sure you are not right," said the earl with a secretive grin. "But you must leave us adults to cobble that up as best we may."

"Oh, we trust *you*, Uncle Jasper," said Lindon fervently. "You'll do what's right. And get us off bread and water, too, which is a dead bore."

"I'll try." Hersington smiled openly now. "I promise nothing."

5

Lord Hersington did not go immediately in search of the children's mother. Instead, he trod leisurely up the stairs, noting as he passed the unmistakable signs of chaos. He directed his steps toward the room of the ultimate author of this confusion—Tom Crowley. He mused, as he walked, that he should have brought this pup to heel long before.

Two years ago, Hersington had become Crowley's guardian when the boy's parents—Maria's brother and sister-in-law—had died in a boating accident. But at that point, already encumbered by four unwanted wards who caused him infinite trouble, he had not had the stomach for further watchdog duties. He had allowed himself instead to be satisfied with Tom's attendance at Harrow, made him a decent allowance, and promptly forgot all about him.

It seemed that this had been a mistake. This latest prank, though it had ended in throwing a blameless girl on the street and a household out of order, was harmless enough in intent. But it was only one of a pattern of actions that added to a disturbing total. There had been numerous other minor run-ins over the fair sex, though so far as he knew this was the first one who had been unwilling. But Crowley had, in addition, become shockingly expensive and, it was rumoured, was fast developing a habit of drinking blue ruin and tampering with the peace of nightwatchmen. There had been disquieting rumbles from his tutors, as well. Yes, it was undoubtedly time he made Tom feel like the boy he was, and then led him by the nose to some more suitable diversions.

A marvelous sight met his eyes as he stepped over the threshold. Thomas Jarrett Crowley III was seated laxly before a mirror, ogling the beauty of his twenty years in great comfort. This was accomplished with the help of a bottle of brandy (which was half empty and had only recently become so). It is doubtful that he was admiring his person, although this was worthy enough: dark, curly hair, blue eyes, and a well-formed face which had not yet ceded to the effects of dissipation nor wholly lost its inherent good nature. Nor did his form merit scorn, for it was in its natural state both well-knit and neatly proportioned. But it is more probable that what he was studying with such rapt concentration were the clothes that encased that form.

Tom was attired in all the glory of a Mathematical-tied neckcloth twice the size of the usual and adorned with a number of showy pins; a billowing shirt of the softest dove-grey satin, lavishly ruffled and tucked and shirred; an extremely fanciful vest which, could it have been seen under its array of seals, watches and fobs, might have been graceful; and skintight trousers of the most delicate shade of salmon pink.

But the whole has not been told. We have not yet said a word concerning the invisible but obvious corset which exquisitely nipped his waist in to a remarkable size. Nor has mention been made of the black satin jacket carefully laid across the bed but not donned due to the absence of the three servants necessary to assist in this dangerous operation. And crowning all was the slightly precious, pouting configuration of the lips, specially adopted to complement the lisp which Tom had seen fit to painstakingly cultivate over the last three months.

Faced with this hallucination, my lord executed a slight bow and said in cool accents, "My pardon, sir. I was under the impression that this was the room of my nephew, Thomas Crowley. I must have been mistaken."

Childish delight at his uncle's arrival made Tom commit a serious error. Oblivious to his shirtpoints he swiftly turned his head, thus bringing about the collision that Lucy had been awaiting ever since their first meeting.

As a first utterance, "Ouch!" is hardly calculated to impress. But Tom did his possible, covering his smarting, watering eye and saying in his best fashionable manner, "That ith tho, thir. I *am* Thomath Crowley. But not, I fanthy, quite ath you remember him!" His undamaged eye gleamed proudly, and he unconsciously smoothed the folds of his Mathematical.

"I see," replied Hersington in amused accents. And before his nephew could well recover himself, he raised his quizzing glass. As this dread piece was levelled upon him, young Crowley's sentiments began to undergo a change.

Moments before he had thought himself supremely well dressed; a very Pink of the Ton and the most delicate Tulip of Fashion. Under that magnified gaze, however, he soon shrank to the merest fop. A moment more, and he could easily fancy himself a large, ugly toad, who had parked himself on the front-parlour carpet, to the owner's astonished revulsion.

His intention had been to astound his uncle. He saw now that he was far more like to revolt him. Tom had not seen the earl in two years. He had remembered him as extremely elegant, and had tried to live up to that slightly garbled recollection. Why, oh, why had his brain not registered the snowiest linen in London, arranged in quiet, precise folds, the minimum jewelry (but of unquestionable quality), the discreet yet unimpeachable cut of the unostentatious trousers? And how the devil had he gotten such a shine on his boots? His valet must be a genius! The deuce was in it that Tom couldn't even *find* a valet this morning, but had had to dress himself.

Crowley had sunk to a very cowed state when the earl finally deigned to address him. "Must you—must you really, nephew—wear quite that reprehensible shade of pink?"

"You're bamming me! They're all the crack!"

"I confess I find that a poor excuse for bad taste," returned his lordship ironically.

Another pause, while Tom searched vainly for an adequate reply. Hersington ambled over to the bed and sat upon it, giving every appearance of ease, swinging one leg to and fro.

"You know, my boy, if you want to set up as a dandy there are a few things you ought to consider. For one thing, the ladies don't like it half as much as you may believe. It gives them too much competition. For another, it's demmed expensive. As I understand it, you've outrun the constable three times already; and if you continue in this vein your pockets will shortly be not only to let but sublet. You can't borrow on your expectations forever, you know."

"But it's only one more year!" Tom cried, then hung his head guiltily. He had forgotten his lisp and was fast reverting to the rather silly, slightly earnest, and surprisingly engaging young man he had used to be. What the numerous beseechings and lectures of Maria had failed to do, Hersington had done just by being Hersington, and Tom's Model.

"And you think that covers all? My dear young sheepshead, at the rate you are going, you'd run through it in under a twelvemonth. It is not all that large a competence. It was never intended for a man on the go.

"And perhaps you are not aware," continued his lordship imperturbably as Tom slumped onto his dressing-table chair, "that I retain control of your principal even when you have attained your majority? I may release it at my discretion, when I feel you are ripe for it. At the moment, you look to be the greenest of apples."

This was a horrid surprise to Tom, and he straightened up and looked at his uncle in candid fear.

"You wouldn't!"

"Not if I thought you were grown serious," he answered, serious himself. "Come, Tom. Leave this foolish posing and let's be honest with each other. There is a great deal of good in you, although you're drowning it as fast as you can at the town sluiceries."

At this intimation that there was hope for him, the earl's nephew revived somewhat. But, "Dash it all!" he said in annoyance. "I bought this waistcoat only yesterday! Devilish expensive it was, too," he regarded it gloomily.

Hersington gave it another look through his glass. "Oh, I daresay the waistcoat's well enough. Only needs less adornment and a, er, quieter ensemble."

This reprieved Tom remarkably, and he sat up straighter and took another toss at his glass.

"Do you always drink brandy before noon, by the by?" asked Hersington casually.

"Oh, no," grinned Tom. "It's just that with the house at sixes and sevens there was no one to prevent me. Aunt Maria don't think I'm old enough to drink," he added morbidly.

"She will think otherwise when I invite you to sit with me over port this evening."

Tom's eyes were glowing, and he was now patently his lordship's slave. Jasper decided it was a politic moment to introduce the subject closest to his heart.

"Speaking of sixes and sevens," he started diffidently, "what of this governess whose going has reduced the house to such a shambles? Do you know anything about her?"

"Not really." Another tot of brandy, not so natural this time. Tom watched him warily from under lowered eyelids. "I was only here a few days when she left."

"I heard that she had been caught kissing you in the library?"

"That's right," Tom answered patly—too patly. "Been making advances to me. Not at all the thing. Aunt had to ler her go."

"The way I heard it," said Hersington deliberately, "you had been making advances to her."

Crowley gave a careless shrug. "Perhaps. In any case, she didn't seem to mind."

"She welcomed your attentions?"

"That's it," he said with relief. "She encouraged me."

"I have it on the best authority," said the earl levelly, taking a pinch of snuff, "that she called you an impudent sprout, an April-squire, and a thatch-gallows." He paused, putting his snuffbox away and casting one keen glance at Crowley's white face. "Are you in the habit," he asked mockingly, "of construing such statements as . . . encouragement?"

"Very well!" cried Tom. "All right! So I did . . . press her. Is that so very bad? A man's a man, you know! For all you may think me a sapskull."

"I don't," replied Jasper, smiling at him in a friendly fashion. "A man's a man, as you say, and generally likes to kiss the ladies—but not, I submit, against their will.

"Yet neither do I think you had considered the consequences. You are a young man of birth, with position and expectations, if not estate. She is an impoverished nobody, obliged to earn her living, with no family in the world but a father who as I recall it is a trifle unsteady. Your aunt had every reason to believe in you, and even if she didn't, she could hardly do anything drastic to you. But that girl has just lost her livelihood. She's going to have trouble finding another, with a bad name behind her. How do you like being responsible for that?"

Tom's eyes widened, then he drew a hand across his face. "I hadn't thought . . . I'm sorry now, truly sorry. You're right. I would make amends if I could."

"You can't. But I think the better of you for wanting to. Tell me," with a little smile. "I expect she was very pretty?"

"No," said Tom in a puzzled tone. "She wasn't in the least. It was the oddest thing for me to be drawn to her. Not at all in my style. But there was—I don't know—a certain look in her eye. A sort of—twinkle. She never turned it on me," he finished sadly.

"And you thought she might if you kissed her."

"But she didn't," Tom finished, grinning ruefully. "I guess I'm not such a bounder as all that! The real ones are successful!"

"Well, then," said Hersington, tucking away his glass and standing up, "I think I shall go talk to your aunt. The rebellion has been quelled, but there's the devil of a mess down there. It seems wise to try and reinstate Miss Trahern. I shall have to tell Maria something, you realise," he said kindly down to Tom's apprehensive face. "But I shall do your character as little damage as possible. It would help if I could inform her that I had undertaken the reform of your habits. May I do so?" he asked politely.

Tom nodded, enraptured. It never occurred to him that half an hour since he would have considered this the grossest impertinence.

"In that case," said his mentor majestically, "I believe I shall start by sending my valet to you. Your boots are badly in need of a shine!" And having conveyed this great favour as if it were a sentence, he swept out of the room.

He found Maria pacing distractedly in the parlour. "Well, well, *well?*" she asked in high, frenetic colour. "You were gone an age! What has happened?"

"The rebellion is ended," said Jasper, his collected manner posing a severe contrast to her disconnected style.

"Oh, I *knew* I could rely on you!" she replied in transports, and prepared to throw herself at him again.

He held up one slim brown hand. "Calm yourself," he warned. "It is not I, but Miss Trahern, we have to thank for the restored order. She sent them a civil note, and they halted at once."

"Why, of all the interfering—!"

"Myself, I thought it very kind in her," he commented. "It showed a most pleasing lack of rancour, and an admirable concern for her former charges."

"I still think it a piece of high meddling! We could have managed very well without her."

"I think not. The children are this instant quite repentant and will do, I fancy, anything we ask for the next fortnight. While I think I can claim that I could have stopped the revolt itself, such a thorough change of heart would have been beyond my powers. Truly, cousin, you ought to be grateful to her."

"I suppose." Grudgingly. "They always did mind her, I'll give her that. But I still maintain it would have been beyond all bounds to let my children have to do with a—a *flirt!*"

"If your thinking were correct, that would certainly be true," he said neutrally, seating himself by the cold fire.

"Why, what else can I think?" asked Maria indignantly. "Tom would never, wouldn't ever—"

"Oh, wouldn't he just?" asked Hersington musingly, raising his eyes to her flushed face.

"I can't believe it!"

His tone was bored. "Cast your mind back, dear cousin-in-law, to the last seven maids you have turned off on grounds of . . . brassiness. Is it not odd that these incidents all coincided with Crowley's advent upon the premises?"

Mrs. Bostram's pug-dog face turned first white, then red, then purple. Hersington listened unmoved to a long animadversion on the suddenly discovered evils of Crowley's character, ending with, "If only *you* had had the raising of him, cousin, things would be quite different!"

"If I had had the raising of him," my lord answered indifferently, "he would have been boxed on the ears just once too often, and died of concussion."

A servant entered at this point to report that the upper maid put in the housekeeper's place had been reduced to strong hysterics; she says it's too much for her and did madame have any instructions to give?

Maria was flustered. "Oh, oh, I do not know. I cannot think!" she wrung her hands and paced.

"Instruct my chef, Gascard," his lordship said smoothly

to the footman, "to take command of the kitchen for the evening. Tell him to order whatever is lacking; and so long as we are not obliged to drink lemonade, I shall pay the bills. Oh, and remove that lady from the kitchen with some hartshorn, or whatever. I fancy she would be very seriously in the way."

"Very good, sir."

"By and by, what is the latest count of deserters?"

"Twelve housemaids, two stableboys, three footmen, the housekeeper, and the cook, sir."

"I see. And who generally had charge of hiring replacements?"

"Miss Trahern, sir. The housekeeper was used to say she had a better eye for character than anyone of her experience. If I may take the liberty, your lordship."

"You have, and I am obliged. Be pleased to wait outside, my good man, after you have delivered my orders."

"Yes, sir." The door closed.

"Do you know," said the earl, "I begin to think that when you threw off Miss Trahern you did yourself the greatest disservice, Maria."

This lady was now sitting in a disconsolate heap on a loveseat, applying herself to her vinaigrette. Her high-pitched voice quivered with imminent tears. "Oh, yes, it is all *too* bad! I begin to think you are right, but what's *that* to the purpose? *I* don't know what to do about housemaids and uniforms and—and hiring people. Miss Trahern did, but she's gone and—and even my nephew has betrayed me!" At this, her self pity overcame her, and she bawled like the veriest child.

"Calm yourself, Maria," said his lordship in distaste. "Things are never so bad as that! I will take charge of matters myself."

"You will?" Maria looked up from her handkerchief, eyes suddenly bright. "Oh, my dear, *dear* Jasper, I *knew* I could rely on you."

"Under certain conditions," interpolated my lord, a hint

of steel in his voice. "If I am to extract you from this brummagem brawl, I will expect to be obeyed implicitly."

"Why, yes, of *course*, Jasper."

"Good. Then you will leave the brush-up of Crowley to me; and for starters, you will not say a word when I allow him to decant a glass of port with me this evening."

"But, Hersington! . . ."

"You may as well face the truth, Maria—whatever Banbury tale he may have told you—he *was* sent down from Harrow, or he'd not be here. The only thing for it is to cram him and send him on to Cambridge. But it cannot be done without his cooperation. I will treat him as the adult he believes he is, meanwhile keeping him always under my eye. Then, when he runs into deep waters—as he assuredly will—I will be there to give his thoughts a suitable direction and send him on. Trust me, he will be more than glad to escape to school."

Maria sniffed.

"Second condition. The children are not to be punished."

"But—Jasper!"

"Softly, cousin. Think a bit. If you weren't able to control them when they were running amok, what impression will it give to punish them once they are repentant? Right now they are very sincerely contrite and soft of heart. This would not, I submit, be precisely the moment to harden them. Do recollect that as yet we have no governess."

"Very true. But my sister Augusta—"

"Will never answer, and well you know it. No, what we need is Miss Trahern back."

Mrs. Bostram sighed. "I suppose you are right. Well, then, now that I have agreed to these conditions, what do I get in return?" A sudden sharpness in her voice brought an instant's smile to the earl's countenance. Not for nothing had his cousin-in-law been nicknamed the Pinchbeck of Bond Street.

"Why, I shall restore order to the house," he replied

soothingly. "I shall hire new servants, see that all the proper repairs are made, replace anything broken and, as I said, take young Crowley in hand. And stand the nonsense," he added dryly, seeing her expression become pinched. "What's more, I shall remain here personally until I see that everything is properly done." This was the supreme sacrifice, and it soured his stomach. But he had no more reliance on Maria's management than on that of an infant.

"We are agreed then?"

"Yes."

"Good." His lordship called in the servant he had asked to wait, and bombarded this individual with a perfect volley of orders concerning his horses, his servants, an omelette for the children, dinner for the household. A message was to be sent to his lordship's secretary in Kentsey; he should travel up in the second-best carriage bringing with him additional luggage for an extended stay in London and a list of persons suitable to fill all the posts recently vacated in this household. Furthermore, he should arrange for the London house to be open in two weeks' time. "For it looks," said my lord wryly, "as if I might remain some little time. Have you got all that?" The footman repeated his instructions back, letter perfect.

"Good fellow," said Hersington admiringly. "You deserve a promotion, I think."

"Thank you, sir."

"Maria," Hersington turned to her, "you shall this instant go to Bond Street and replace your bonnet. Send a Dutch reckoning to my townhouse."

Mrs. Bostram bustled out happily, and Hersington took the servant aside.

"The first thing my valet is to do is ascend to young Master Crowley's chambers and see to his boots. Instruct him to give many helpful and respectful hints concerning the gentleman's wardrobe. While Crowley is thus occupied, I have a task for you." He paused. "There is a certain bottle of brandy on the young man's dressing table. It would be convenient if it—vanished."

"I understand, my lord."

"You *shall* have an advance," approved Sir Jasper. "I'll see to it myself. Oh, one other thing. It will be my happy task to reinstate Miss Trahern. I assume she has gone to her father. Could you possibly give me his direction?"

"I'm afraid not, sir. Mr. Trahern is presently in America."

"I see. And no other family, I assume? Well, no matter. It should be a simple exercise to question the local inns."

The footman coughed deprecatingly behind his hand. "Beg pardon, sir, but I don't believe she could have put up at an inn."

"Oh?" It was Hersington's experience, however, that servants often knew nearly as much as children.

"Yes. She was without baggage or escort, sir, and, I ought to inform you, very likely without funds."

Hersington's brow lowered indeed, though his anger was directed elsewhere than at the man. "How comes this?"

"I hesitate to embark on such a delicate topic," the man began apologetically.

"Out with it, man!"

"To make a round tale, my lord, when quarter day came, madame found herself in . . . some difficulties. Since that date was to be Miss Trahern's first disbursement, I venture to say that at the moment she is penniless."

"Am I to understand that *none* of the staff has yet been paid?"

"That is so, sir."

"Good God. I had begun to think them a ramshackle lot for having quit in such numbers. Now I am beginning positively to admire their fortitude! I must look into this at once. But tell me, my friend, what *is* your name, by the by?"

"James, sir."

"Well, James, why no luggage?"

"Madame ordered it thrown out into the street, your lordship. I fancy, however," with a glint that might, in a less correct menial, have been construed as glee, "that it found its way to the wine cellar . . . by some means."

Hersington eyed him with respect. "What a resourceful fellow you are, to be sure! You may tell Pentworthy that the staff will be in funds tomorrow. And—thank you."

"You are very welcome, sir."

The earl strode off down the hall, a thundercloud building on his face. He caught Mrs. Bostram just as she was stepping out the door, nattily attired for shopping. "Maria, I want a word with you," he said grimly.

"But I am only this moment—"

"It will not wait," he said, in the most frightening accents she had yet ever heard from her protector. His hand gripped her arm and very nearly dragged her into the library, disregarding a most charming tippet muff whose tiny pointed ears (Maria thought) would not be enhanced by such handling.

"What—what has happened, Hersington, to put you in such a towering miff? I thought we had quite settled everything!"

"You did not see fit to tell me, *cousin*," he grated between his teeth, "that not only did you throw Lucy Trahern out without cause, but without her own trunks, or any escort, knowing she had not a friend in the world; nor that not only she, but none of your staff, have been *paid!*" His voice had been rising steadily until the last word was a shout.

"Why—why, I was going to bring it up, I am sure, only it seemed such a bad moment. And you know, Jasper," she said confidingly, "things are grown so dear these days, I declare it is most shocking! I am sure I have not had so much as a new ribbon this twelfth-month, and as for any luxuries . . ."

"Stow it, Maria," said his lordship shortly. "I am well aware of how you spend your money. And I am quite sure

I have never seen that appalling green monstrosity you are wearing before, so it won't fadge. I am paying your staff today, but you are not shopping for bonnets or anything else until I have been reimbursed for every penny. Perhaps in this way you will finally learn something about economy!"

At this pronouncement, his charge collapsed in tears, both chins quivering.

"Yes, you may well cry," he told her scornfully. "Sitting in your fine house with a parcel of servants, a half dozen horses, and a manager to whom you need only write one of your disconnected excuses for a letter to bring him loping in from Kentsey! But I do not see you shedding any tears for Miss Trahern."

"For Miss *Trahern!*"

"Yes, Miss Trahern! What do you suppose, ma'am," he went on in low, deadly tones, "is likely to become of a homeless, friendless young woman, thrown onto the city without traps, money, or character? What sort of people, do you think, would take pity and offer her shelter? The manager of a tavern? A footpad, perhaps, who needs another pair of nimble fingers to keep him in comfort? A procurer of women, think you? A delightful prospect, to be sure. I collect you need not have a care in the world about the fate you have assigned her!"

Maria had gone quite white.

"Oh, no, Hersington, you *can't* mean—why, it never occurred to me that—heavens, we must find her at once!"

"I am glad you think so, ma'am," he said, leading her back to the hall and retrieving his cane and gloves. His cold fury had abated not one jot; but was now transformed into determination and the promise of tireless energy. "For I am going to search for her now. And whatever her condition," he glanced down at her with burning eyes, "you will accept her, is that clear? Be she never so covered in dirt and shame—for it will be your doing."

Maria's limited stock of altruism seemed to crumple under these disclosures. "Oh, dear. I'm sure I hope you *may* find her—*and* that she will be all right!"

"You had better pray I do," said Hersington.

In the entryway, Pentworthy presented him with his cape.

"My lord," said that estimable servant, "am I to understand that you are preparing to search for Miss Trahern?"

"Yes—and as speedily as possible."

"The young lady is found, sir."

"What?" He took his hand from the knob and swung around, favouring Pentworthy with an incredulous stare.

"Quite so, my lord. When she came to the house, it was to call for her trunk. The notes, I may say, were an afterthought as it were, reacting to the state of the household, of which I made so bold as to inform her. She had the trunk sent to a most eligible address, sir. Staventry House, to be exact."

"I . . . see," said Hersington in a tone which clearly indicated that he did not. "Staventry House? The devil you say! Now how would she fetch up there?"

"I couldn't venture to say, sir. But Miss Lucy was always one to land on her feet, so to speak."

"Apparently. Very well, you may take my cape. I am not, after all, going out."

He stood ruminatively in the hall as the butler disrobed him, and noticed Mrs. Bostram drooping sadly down the corridor.

"Oh, for heaven's sake, Maria. Go do your infernal shopping. I can't stand any more of your blubbering today."

She followed this order with alacrity, and soon Lord Jasper was at liberty to ascend the stairs and visit the children. It was the only restful thing he could think to do.

These three were sitting listlessly in the nursery in clean, starched clothes, doing very little of anything. The two older ones greeted him with a pleasure that was somewhat subdued. Lindon, however, whose spirits had revived by the promise of supper, ran up to him crying "Uncle Jasper!" and launched himself into the air with every confidence that he would be caught. This confidence was justified.

"Uncle Jasper, we are to have an omelette! We are ever so grateful!"

"You are quite welcome, imp. Well?" he questioned, looking at Cecilia and Hyde. "Why so gloomy?"

Cecilia raised her lashes for a moment, then dropped them. "Are we—are we to be punished, sir?"

"No doubt you should be, but you are not."

"Hurrah!" cried Lindon. Hyde and Cecilia looked relieved, and thanked him prettily.

Hersington decided it was time to liven them. "What do you think I have found out?" he asked lightly.

"Miss Trahern is staying with some extremely old ladies in another part of town. They are very strange, but everybody likes them because they have so much money. I fancy she would like to receive letters from you."

"That's famous, Uncle. Now, could we go for a ride in the park?"

"I'm afraid not," said Jasper. "My horses have done quite a bit of travelling, you know."

"The zoo, then? The Royal Exeter Zoo?"

"My dear young jobberknoll, it is true that I've managed to keep you from being flogged—with the greatest difficulty, I might add. But if your mother sees you getting outright treats, she will very likely go off in an apoplexy, which would be a shocking thing for me to have done my first day in town. However, I don't think I'm so fagged that I can't give you a story. Did I ever tell you about the time," he began, perching in one of the absurdly small nursery chairs, "when I was nearly eaten by a South African wildebeest?"

He most emphatically had not. The children showed every desire not to prolong their ignorance for another instant. Lindon wanted to know what a wildebeest might be.

And Hersington, whose day had been taken up from stem to stern with Lucy Trahern, wanted to know what kind of woman this governess might be. What was she doing at Staventry House? Was there any way of finding out?

6

Lucy threw her bonnet onto the front-parlour sopha.

"Oh, ma'am!" she said to Natalie. "*Such* a kickup as I have seen at Bostram house. You'd hardly credit it!"

"What the blazes were you doing there?"

"I went to call for my bits and pieces," Lucy explained. "It has been over a week, and I was afraid they might be discovered and removed. And I own I had some thought of replacing this old rag." She shook out her skirts disdainfully. "Three days in it is the outside of enough, I assure you!"

Natalie gave a bark of laughter. "True enough, girl. So what was all the rumpus?"

"Ah." Lucy chuckled softly, sinking down onto a settee. "What a lark! Only think, ma'am, the children were in open revolt at my dismissal. James the footman—he is a particular friend of mind, you know—swore to me that they had been unmanageable since I left and no punishment would deter them. They'd even taken their mother's best bonnet to pieces! I can just imagine her face!" She giggled behind a hand, her countenance rosy, her eyes brighter than usual.

For the first time it occurred to Natalie that their "housekeeper" might have looks worth cultivating under that plain exterior. But she said only, "Shouldn't have thought any children of Maria's would display such good sense."

"Say want of conduct, rather." Lucy straightened up and composed her face. "Really I ought not to laugh. It is too bad in me. But they are such *inventive* children . . . I was just imagining . . .," a reminiscent smile curved her cheek. "At any rate, things are very likely in train now. I wrote them a note which ought to calm them down. I expect they are this instant clearing away the debris and feeling virtuous."

This earned her a sharp glance from the quick old eyes. "High opinion of yourself, 'han't you? You just write them a note, and they'll stop forthwith? Bah!"

"We understand each other," said Lucy calmly. "Also, their Uncle Jasper is with them, and I rely on his help in finishing the business. He sounds a sensible man."

"Uncle Jasper," muttered Natalie. "I wonder—no, couldn't be."

Lucy was pursuing some thought of her own. "Ma'am—Aunt Natalie,"—this title did not yet come naturally—"I wonder if I have done quite the right thing. I said my things were to be fetched to Staventry House. I took the name from the plaque on that gate that stands by the cottage. The one that seems to lead to a disused manor? The gatehouse of Staventry House, I told them. But they stared so. It put me quite out of countenance. Tell me, have I done anything amiss?"

"No . . .," said the Dowager thoughtfully. "Come, I have something to show you."

Lucy trailed her upstairs and into one of the several back bedrooms (Lucy's own overlooked the street). The Dowager brushed aside a dusty curtain that crackled with grime and age—Lucy's efforts had not yet reached so far—and pointed abruptly. A mellow brick dome, resting on graceful white pillars, peeked through a dense stand of shaggy firs. The whole area behind the cottage seemed almost to amount to a miniature park, overgrown now and laden with gold-coloured leaves. But it had obviously once been a fine and stately place. Here and there a chimney pot or cupola poked above the trees. Over to one side, Lucy could see an extensive stable, and the edge of an ornamental pond. "Staventry House," said Natalie shortly.

Lucy was mystified. "But ma'am, what is it doing here? I have never heard of a home having such grounds in the middle of London! And it looks very much disused. Why in heaven would its owners desert it?"

"Freakish, ain't it?" Natalie concurred. "Family rich as Croesus. Richer, maybe. What odds? Croesus's coin was all in Greek. Can afford any oddity they want, I daresay. House ain't to rack and ruin, though it looks it. Passel of servants, all times. We have use of 'em, on occasion. Reminds me." She dropped the curtain and favoured Lucy with a piercing stare. "Went out alone today, didn't you? Thought as much. Not to happen again, you understand me? Improper, and which I care for more, dangerous. Footpads out there. Worse things. Next time, hop over to the House and get a footman or something. Promise?"

"You are sure the family will not mind it?"

Natalie gave a strange, cut-off laugh. "I should just about think *not*! Now, girl, your word."

"Very well, Aunt Natalie, I promise. No more solo journeys."

Almeria wandered in trailing yards of soft rose muslin (along with the inevitable dust mice).

"Oh, *there* you are, dear," she said to Lucy. "I am sure I don't know what to do. There is a, a Young Person at the door who *will* have speech with you—yes, and he has brought a nasty black box that positively *reeks* of brandy, and set it on that floor which you cleaned so carefully this morning! I think it *most* disobliging of him. I only hope he may not be stealing our silver and eating our chocolates! Not that we use the silver," she added thoughtfully. "But I *would* grudge him the comfits."

"Never trouble yourself, Aunt. It is merely the boy with my trunk, I'll be bound."

It was, but she was surprised to also find a letter in the

small servant's grubby paw. "Shall I wait fer an answer, miss?" he asked politely, tugging his forelock.

"No . . . please convey my compliments to the sender, and tell him I shall reply when I have read his message."

"Right, miss. I'll be orf, then."

"Take a comfit first," Lucy urged him, having noticed the way his eyes kept sliding toward the plate.

"Thank you, mum!" He wolfed this and ran in his enthusiasm.

Both old ladies came up from behind as Lucy closed the door and absently leaned against it, reading. Almeria clicked her tongue and said reproachfully, "You see, he *did* take one of our sweets! I made sure there were twelve when I left the room. And now, look! There are only eleven!"

"No, no, Aunt," Lucy reassured her. "I gave it to him myself. I did not have any money for vails, you see," she apologised.

"Oh, how thoughtless of me!" exclaimed Almeria. "*I* could have paid him. Lucy, you must promise to warn me about such visitors from now, so that I may save you embarrassment. For you know," she went on earnestly, "we may not *always* have comfits to pay with, besides which, some people do not care for them!"

Lucy smiled at her fondly, stepping away from the door. "I do not think it will come to that, dear." She sank down gracefully onto an armchair considerably less grimy than it had been three days before, and tapped her paper with one forefinger. "I have received a very civil note from—what *is* his name?" She muttered, peering at the bottom of the script. "How vexatious. He signs only 'Uncle Jasper.' And I so particularly wanted to know his correct title. At any rate, the kindest of letters has come from the children's uncle. He thanks me rather lavishly for what he terms 'my fine generalship in outmanoeuvering as clever a brace of imps as ever he has seen.' What is more, he says he is convinced I am not at fault in the matter of my dismissal. He would be happy to reinstate me . . .," Lucy was rereading bits, and here turned the page, ". . . except that I seem to have established myself quite respectably without his help. He has been 'authorised to tender the abject apologies of his nephew Tom Crowley as well as Mistress Bostram'—how very mannerly of him, since I am sure it is not true!—'particularly the former's.' And," she finished, holding out a sealed packet triumphantly, "Only see! He has sent my wages along, with deep regrets for the delay. So you see, Almeria, there is no least need to worry. I shall be able to pay any vails for quite some time to come."

"Pretty manners, at all events," commented Natalie. "I'll warrant he don't like going to Maria's above half. Puts it off for ever. Can't blame him."

Three smaller squibs had fallen out of the other letter, and Lucy was reading these with misty eyes. "From the children," she explained over her shoulder. "They miss me, they say. Lindon wants to know what I can possibly be doing at that what's-its-name place that is more important than tending to him."

Natalie, foreseeing a long argument on this topic, forestalled it by saying, "Tending to *us*, that's what! Got us in hand for the first time in years. Don't know how we managed to live in such a pelter, before."

"Oh, my, yes," nodded Almeria. "Only to think, Sister, I was *convinced* I had bought the wrong damask for these armchairs, for I found it quite ugly after all. And you know, one often *is* deceived by the fabrics in their warehouses, and the salespeople are so *very* clever. In short, I thought I should have to replace them, which would have been quite shocking, as this pattern is all the latest stare. But now I see there was nothing wrong at all! They were only dirty."

"Which you would have known were you only half the peagoose you are!" sniffed her sister.

"True," said Almeria placidly.

"And now that this money is so timely arrived," summed up Lucy, "I believe I will go get some articles we need, such as coarse soap. There is a lot to be done in this house yet!"

"Oh, *no*!" squealed Almeria. "You must *not* be using your own money for such things! Unless—Nat, we haven't outrun the constable this quarter, have we? I rather thought the draft that nice lawyer, Felix, sent us—after all, it was—"

"More than adequate?" Natalie cut in ruthlessly. "You're right. Can't think how I came to be so shatterbrained. Forgot to give Lucille the housekeeping allowance and the books. Sorry, girl. What a bumblebroth if you had to run the house out of your pin money!" She handed over a big black key on a chain, instructing her where the cash box and ledgers were to be found. "And don't let Almeria touch 'em," she concluded. "Like as not, she'd borrow it all for a silk-straw bonnet, and forget to tell you."

"Very likely!" Almeria agreed. "I was *never* any hand at figures! But that puts me in mind, dear . . .," she paused delicately. "Are you, by any chance, planning to . . . well, to buy some clothes? I am sure your own dress becomes you," she went on doubtfully, wrinkling her pretty nose. "At all events you must be fond of it . . . but . . . I confess I have a perfect horror of *brown* things. Ever since I was sent away to school, where *everything* was brown, and one had to wear such tedious uniforms and scratchy flannel nightdresses—yes, and read reams of nonsense about people who died so long ago that they wouldn't be worth remembering even *if* they hadn't made such a tangle out of their lives, which it seems," she mused, "they *did*. Fancy marrying one's own mother! Even *I* would not be such a clodpole! And as for searching for a sheep with golden wool—and on the ocean, too!—all I can say is that shows a sad want of sense. They would have done *much* better to go to Bond Street. Which I hope," she finished anxiously, "you are planning to do? I am excessively sorry to discommode you, and naturally I don't wish to offend. But it is just that I get the most sinking *feel* from—from *brown* things!" She was plucking at her skirts nervously. Lucy laid a fond hand over hers.

"Dear Aunt, I am not in the least offended. Pray don't worry. What do you think is in this trunk that we just paid a comfit to receive? Clothes, my dear! All clothes."

"Oh!" Almeria clapped her hands. Then, apprehensively, "No dark colours?"

"No, no!" laughed Lucy, flinging the lid open. "No 'brown things'! Although I do think this dress I am wearing would be most suitable for housecleaning. Do you suppose you could bear it if I covered it with a bright apron? In yellow, say?"

"Oh, that would be cheery!" Almeria nodded. "What have you got?"—peering into the trunk with childish excitement.

"Nothing that isn't wrinkled, that's certain," muttered Lucy. "Bother that wine cellar! The dresses at the bottom are bound to smell of spirits! I had best take these up and tend to them at once. Then I can give you an exhibition."

"I'll be glad to press them for you, Lucy dear," offered Almeria generously.

But Lucy, surreptitiously eyeing the scorches on Almeria's exquisite Alençon lace cuffs, politely declined.

Half an hour later, she appeared again in her hastily ironed finery. Lucy was wearing a perfectly acceptable muslin in a flattering forest-green colour. The modest scooped neckline was complemented by demure cream lace ruffles, as were the fitted sleeves made just to the elbow from which frills fell away in an attractive cascade. The skirt slipped from its under-the-bodice waistline in slim pleats, swirling about her feet as she walked, and ornamented with a few small silk ribbons of a slightly darker green.

In a word, Lucy looked transformed. Almeria squeaked in delight, and Natalie gave a most unladylike whistle.

"Well, miss," she puffed. "That looks as if it were from a very different stable than the rest of your wardrobe."

"Just the opposite, Aunt Natalie. My other clothes are more in this style. But you see, it is not particularly *tactful* in a governess to be presentable," she finished blushingly.

"Especially at Maria's, you mean?" asked the Dowager knowingly. "Eh, well, I see your point. Hairstyle, too? Yours is horrid, y'know."

"Natalie!" Almeria exclaimed reproachfully. "Lucy, love, I'm sure she was only funning! But you know, I had meant to mention . . . well, has it been a *very* long time since you turned governess? Because I thought you might very likely not be aware . . . that is, I am sure it was very modish once, but *now*, you see, your tresses are . . . what I mean to say is that they do not precisely match the dress. I hope you will not mind my just giving you the hint," she finished meekly.

Lucy smiled and gave the blonde woman a kiss on the cheek. "You dear, sweet thing. Don't tease yourself. Of course I know perfectly well I have looked a frightful quiz these six months and more! I have positively dreaded looking in the mirror. The very first use of my pay will be to dispose of these tresses; for I vow that being a figure of fun is exceedingly tiresome."

Almeria was relieved and enthusiastic, and proposed to perform this task for Lucy herself. "For I am accounted something of a hairdresser, even if I am *not* French. Why, even Pierre admits that I am quite above his touch when it comes to the Brutus, which I think," she said, cocking her shapely head to one side, "would be just your style. Your features are buried in all of that hair. A pity, for they are so fine."

Here Lucy demurred, thanking Almeria but suggesting gently that perhaps she ought to go to this Pierre, just for the *first* time, you know. Natalie interrupted her.

"Know what you're thinking, girl, but it's not true. M'sister may be hamhanded, but she's no shabster when it comes to the scissors. You could do worse than put yourself in her hands. Makes all her own clothes, you know."

This was news to Lucy, who had assumed that Almeria's

exquisite but much maligned dresses were made by some extremely talented modiste.

"Very well," she sighed. "Have at me. But wait!" And she ran to fetch a chair and a number of sacks, which she placed before the oval mirror in the small parlour. She sat with a shawl round her shoulders. When Almeria, appearing with a comb and hand mirror and shears, saw these preparations, she marvelled.

"How clever of you! Usually when I cut hair the cats are tracking it around for ages."

This remark did little to reassure Lucy about the ordeal to come. In fact, she shut her eyes through the whole operation, following its progress only by the snip of scissors, orders to turn her head this way or that, and Almeria's soft murmurings to herself about what would most become Lucy's eyes or chin. Natalie had made no sound throughout this production. It was with the greatest misgiving that Lucy at last opened her eyes.

At first, she could not believe she beheld herself. Who was that exciting young beauty in the glass? She blinked, and looked again. No . . . on consideration, the woman was not a beauty. But she was striking. How could that be?

Lucy pinched herself, and carefully scrutinised the image in the glass. Certainly her face had the same wide forehead, the big dark eyes, the decided nose, the pointed chin, the firm set of mouth, and those hollow cheeks she had always considered such a liability. Yet with soft, dark curls—which seemed to attract the light now that they were not trussed into braids, or forced into ringlets, as they had been before she turned governess—the whole took on a different aspect. The "Brutus," modeled on the early Grecian, brought out all her features to startlingly good effect. There was simply no denying now that she was a woman whose face had character, humour, intelligence, and quality stamped all over it.

"What do you think, Lucy dearest?" asked Almeria anxiously. The girl's long silence had unnerved her.

"I never believed in fairy tales before," Lucy told her. "I

do now! You just turned me from a pumpkin into a princess!" She gave Almeria a heartfelt hug.

"Oh, I am *so* glad! For if you had not liked it, I care not whether every gentleman of the ton adored it, I would have felt a failure. Your sentiments must always be of the first consideration with me."

"How sweet. And . . . Natalie?" Lucy asked hesitantly. "What is your opinion?"

"Brings out all the best in you. Much you'd care. Convinced you'd as soon live your life under a cloud. Stupid thing to do," she grumbled crossly.

"Oh, my dear aunt," said Lucy, hugging her for the first time, "Compliments are hardly your metier, but thank you, just the same."

"All right, all right," Natalie's voice was grouchy with embarrassment. "Go make supper, can't you?"

After supper, however, there was a right royal row. Aunt Natalie had been so foolish as to suggest paying Lucy a salary for her duties.

"I believed we had an agreement, ma'am, and I trusted you would honour it. I was to keep house in return for my room and board."

"So it's 'ma'am' again, is it?" said The Dowager shrewdly. "Then I'll take leave to tell you, miss, that you haven't kept your side of the bargain either! In addition to keeping the house clean—which you do to a high turn—you have also taken up the duties of companion, gardener, butler, abigail, accountant, and if I mistake not, lady's maid. You have been making inroads on Almeria's wardrobe. Don't think I've not noticed. Suspicious lack of tears and spots about her. What's more, the burns are fading. Use lemon water, do you?" She fixed Lucy with a smug eye. "*Now* let's talk about not keeping bargains! Oh, and did I forget animal trainer? Yes, animal trainer. The cats have not been on my bed these ten hours at least."

"Oh, yes, is it not *clever* of Lucy? I was concerned at first, you know, when I saw her rapping them with the *Chronicle;* but she says really it is only the slightest *tap*, just to remind them. For she told them that they were not allowed the furniture unless they were on a lap—yes, told them all separately! And I am sure they *must* remember that, for it was only two days ago, and felines you know are *monstrous* smart!"

"I left out spiritual medium," said Natalie dryly.

But Almeria's artless speech had given Lucy time to recover her poise, which had been badly shaken by Natalie's counteraccusation.

"If I give something more than agreed, it is only from gratitude," she said quietly. "You know very well—though you may graciously choose to ignore it—that you and your sister saved me from the gutter. It is fruitless to try to convince me that I am doing you a favour. I know too well it is all to the contrary."

"Contrary! I'll give you contrary, you conniving little, clutchfisted, Friday-faced, squeeze-crabbing—" And as always when balked of logic, Natalie went off in a string of epithets as pungent as they were original. *How* did she do it? Lucy marvelled. Never a single repetition, ending with, "and if I *want* to give you money, you idiotish puss, I *shall*! I should just like to see you prevent me!" She flourished her cane a final time (it seemed to be more a weapon than an aid to walking—Lucy had never seen her use it except in debate) then sat and took snuff with a satisfied air.

"Finished with your jobation, Aunt?" Lucy asked softly. "Then I will take leave to tell *you* that, though you may give me as much money as you wish, you cannot make me spend it."

They glared at each other for a long time after this. It was clearly stalemate.

Finally Almeria asked wistfully, "But *why* don't you want any money, Lucy? Don't you *like* money? I am so very fond of it myself, for it allows one to have whatever one likes, *besides* making people toadeat one who would otherwise cut one's acquaintance, that I confess I am quite at a loss to understand you!"

This broke the tension. Lucy laughed and held out her hands to Almeria, who clasped them trustingly in her cool, fragile ones. "Ah, my *dear* Almeria, I wish I could explain to you properly! I doubt I cannot. But I shall try.

"You see, as things stand, you are giving me something and I am giving you something. So we are equal. Now, if you give me more, it would be charity. Like one of those wards of the parish. I could not bear to be an object of pity! And I have an utter distaste of being beholden. It is not becoming in a lady of quality. Do you understand?"

"No," she said simply. "Because I do not feel we are giving you anything. You live here, but so do we. We all sleep here and eat here. But *you* do more than *anybody*, so it seems you *ought* to get something more. Besides which, if you are going to prate about equality, it is *most* unjust that we have money and you do not."

Lucy rolled her eyes. But Natalie had new ammunition.

"Just a moment. Let me understand you. It is *money* that distresses you, is it not? If we were to offer you something intangible, say, for extraordinary services, you would not object?"

"I suppose not," said Lucy carefully. "However, I do not in the slightest find my services 'extraordinary.' "

"Poppycock! Don't you understand anything at all, you widgeon?" The hard line of her mouth was trembling a little. "What d'you think we were before? Couple of scrappy old women, pinching at each other, living like we'd fallen out of the ragbag. Frustrated. Lonely. Much better now. Food alone is worth it."

Lucy's heart softened at the tiny hint of wetness in the older woman's eyes. Almeria, as seemed to be her function in life, finished the business.

"Oh, yes, it is *vastly* improved! Why, it is a miracle, the things you cook for us. I am sure I could never before eat in this house without a bit of trepidation, for as like as not I would find a fishbone, or a splinter, or at the very least a cat hair!"

Natalie sniffed.

"Oh, sister, I am sorry! I am quite sure you did your best. Very likely these things creep in, when one is not attending!

"And, do you know, it is the most remarkable circumstance, but I never lose things anymore. When I want a teacup now, I know I need only look in the cupboard, where I was used to find them under the sewing box! It is most singular, but Lucy seems to know how to make the whole house just behave! I *wish*," she pleaded, turning to the girl, "that you would let us give you *something*. Just some nice thing that would help you get on in the world. Is it so bad of us to want that?"

Lucy had never been proof against Almeria's lopsided sincerity. She ducked her head and said in a small voice, "I suppose, if it would truly give you pleasure—but no money, mind!"

"Famous!" cried Almeria. "What would you like? A pretty carriage, perhaps, or a nice parrot to carry on your wrist? All the most dashing females do so now, I am told. Or, oh, I saw the nicest fur-trimmed pelisse at Picadilly t'other day. . . ."

"No, no, nothing so dashing!" laughed Lucy, holding up her palms. "If you must give a gift to me, let it be a character when I depart for my next position."

"You've already earned a reference, and you'll get it. Call that a gift?" Natalie was incensed. "Hornswoggle, girl, that's an insult!"

"I suppose you are in the right of it, ma'am," she capitulated suddenly. It must be remembered that Lucy was very tired. She had been scrubbing floors and beating rugs and washing down walls and mending clothes for three days straight, not to mention walking several stout miles and composing three difficult letters just today, before she even made dinner.

"Have I your word, girl?" the Dowager asked suspiciously.

"Yes, Aunt," she sighed. Then she sat up straighter, driving her own bargain. "You have my promise that *if* you feel I render you a signal service, I will not cavil at receiving some benevolence—*provided* it is not money or goods."

"Well enough." The Dowager seemed satisfied with this. Lucy worried a little at the wise look she wore, as if turning over plans in her head. But she felt she had drawn her conditions so as to avoid embarrassment. Neither money nor goods. That left them with little.

"Lovely. We shall be able to contrive something, I am sure. And *just* in time for Christmas!" said Almeria happily.

"Christmas!" said Natalie sharply. "Pray, dear sister, what month do you conceive it to be?"

"Isn't it September?" asked this lady doubtfully.

"Well, no, I am afraid it is March," said Lucy apologetically. "And the fag-end of March, at that. You must resign yourself to the fact that it will soon be April."

"What's come to you, Almeria?" exclaimed Natalie. "You are usually no more than three months out in your reckonings."

"Now that *is* strange," pondered the elderly beauty. "Unless I am in love, for I am often confused then. Am I in love?" she pondered, biting a finger. "No, I don't think I can be. For I have been eating heartily, and not watching the card rack for any particular caller."

"Hmph!" Natalie dismissed the subject easily, not noticing Lucy's barely concealed amusement. Years of living had inured her to her sister's vagaries. "What's to do this evening? Shall you play the harpsichord, Lucille?"

"Oh, I think not," she answered. "My fingers are quite worn, what with one thing and another. Shall I read to you?"

"I don't usually like books," Almeria demurred.

"Ah, but I think you would like this one," Lucy coaxed.

"It is by a woman author, and her sentiments are quite what you would enter into. In addition to which, it has a touching romance inserted."

"Oh, do let's have it!"

"Stuff!" snorted Natalie. "I'd rather hear a book of sermons!"

"Oh, but do only listen, Aunt Natalie. There is that in it which, though I believe Almeria might not notice it—forgive me, Aunt Almeria!—would delight you. For quite apart from the overt plot, it is a wicked satire on society and its foibles."

Natalie, declaring that this was something more like, adjured her to fetch it at once.

"It may take me some little time," Lucy explained, "for the novel is larded somewhere amongst my belongings."

"Begone, then!" Natalie commanded. "What is this piece of frippery, anyway?"

"*Emma*, by a certain Jane Austen," Lucy answered as she rose and prepared to ascend the stairs.

She heard Almeria say behind her, "March! Only fancy! Why, it is very near the beginning of the Season! We shall not be idle much longer. What a mercy Lucy has us in train, so that we may not blush to entertain guests."

It is a pity Miss Trahern was not of an eavesdropping habit. For she would have known enough, by this time, to be alarmed by Almeria's next, low-voiced words.

"That puts me in mind, Sister, of the gift we want to give to dear Lucy. I have come upon the *nackiest* notion!"

And together, while Lucy rummaged in her baggage, the two came up with a scheme that the girl was bitterly to regret for some time to come.

The nackiest notion, as Almeria would have it.

7

"THERE! I BELIEVE you will do," said Lucy with a satisfied air. She stepped back from Almeria's hair and regarded it from the side. "Yes. It wants only a little posy, thus," she tucked one in, "and you are ready to become the toast of this card party you and Aunt Natalie are attending."

In truth Almeria looked more than a little dazzling. Her usual fragile good looks were heightened by Lucy's deft hand with the curling irons. She was also amazingly free of splotches, rips, and stains. And most miraculous of all, on time.

" 'Faith, I declare I can hardly credit it. Here I am all prepared and it's still half an hour until we need leave. But will that be time enough for *your* toilette, Lucy?" Almeria looked at the girl's workday wool anxiously. "Even with the yellow apron, I don't believe that dress will pass for this evening."

Lucy raised her eyebrows. "Surely you are not expecting me to attend? Your housekeeper? Oh, I think not!"

Natalie swept in at that moment. "Hmph! I see you're ready. What a hum, Lucille. You're attending as our niece, of course. And I've already told them there were three of us coming. But me no buts. Go off and dress. It's only a few old-lady friends of ours, anyway. Do you good to get out."

"Well . . ."

"Stubble it! You've been here three weeks and not gone anywhere but the back garden. Becoming a bore, that's what. Bustle about, girl! Not going to have you a recluse on our hands. Two's enough , in this house."

Lucy grinned as she hurried along the corridor. Trust Natalie to make a gift sound like an insult!

She supposed—huddling into an attractive burgundy muslin picked out in gold thread at the bodice—that one little card party wouldn't hurt. Just a few friends, The Dowager had said. Come to think of it—she paused, patting at her hair—this was probably the "favour" they had wanted to grant her. Perhaps one of these ladies needed a companion or personal maid. Well. Lucy pulled on her tan kid gloves and donned an ivory pelisse. She would just be on her best behaviour, and hope that no one ever found out that she and these two engaging ladies had not a drop of shared blood.

Lucy was surprised at the elegance of the equipage that Natalie had commandeered from Staventry House for the evening. The coachman and footmen also seemed to serve her with extreme deference. But then she supposed that Almeria and Natalie were effectually their masters. No one else ever seemed to keep an eye to them. For the tenth time, she wondered about the large mansion and its mysteriously absent family. Then she shrugged. She would probably never know. It wasn't something either woman seemed inclined to talk about.

Lucy came out of her meandering with a start. The carriage had stopped before an extremely elegant townhouse. There were a goodly number of lights, and the outdoor servants were heavily pomaded and uniformed. This couldn't be their "small card party," could it?

It could. She was helped to alight and followed timidly in Natalie's grand progress up the stairs.

The three were led to a small but exceedingly sumptuous parlour, where a number of well-dressed women were engaged at cards and dice. A string quartet played discreetly in one corner. In another was a table laid out with a lavish array of meats, pastries and syllabub. One of the ladies, dark-haired and haughty-looking, approached them archly.

"Why, Lady Staventry," she said to Almeria in a deep, arrogant voice. "You have stolen a march on us all! We did not look for you this hour yet. Now none of us shall win so much as a pony at hazard this evening. It is very much too bad in you. I wonder the Duchess of Bucklass should have allowed it!" This with a thin smile for Natalie.

Lucy stood frozen in her place. Lady Staventry. The Duchess of Bucklass. *Almeria. Natalie.* What had she done?

She railed at herself bitterly. How could she possibly have been so stupid? Everyone had heard of the eccentric Lady Staventry, of the God-knew-how-many-thousand pounds a year. And her monumental sister, the Duchess of Bucklass! Whom everyone feared and respected! A snatch of overheard conversation from a long-ago dinner party came back to tease her. "Windermere—such a fool, my dear. He offended the Duchess of Bucklass, you know, so there's an end of his hopes of a fortune! She has plenty of other relatives happy to help dispose of it!" Lady Staventry—Staventry House—no wonder they would not talk about it! They had been pulling the wool over her eyes all this time. And she had been calling them "Aunt" Almeria and "Aunt" Natalie. Cleaning their house. Keeping track of their finances. Training their cats. Oh no, oh no, oh *no*.

But Natalie was replying to their hostess's sally. "Don't eat me! Blame our niece, here. She's taken us in hand, and we daren't put a foot wrong these days. "Lucille!" she raised her voice. "Come do the pretty to the Countess Lieven. And do it to a nicety, mind. She likes being fussed over!"

The Countess Lieven—society's reigning goddess! This got worse and worse. Lucy groped for her training and swept the countess a deep, graceful curtsey, murmuring how honoured she was.

"Miss Lucille Trahern," said the duchess.

"A fetching child," said the countess dispassionately.

"One of your connexions, I gather. 'Faith, Duchess, you have more relatives than ever you have diamonds."

"That's as may be," sniffed Natalie. "But she's the only one as is worth a groat."

"Oh, yes," chimed Lady Staventry, settling herself at a table with a pretty rustling of taffeta. "And to think all these years she has been positively *buried* in the country with that rustic father of hers, and none of us the wiser! I vow, I was never more vexed than when I discovered he had posted off to America without making the *slightest* provision for her come-out! Why, it is time and past for her to be presented."

"Come, now, Lady Staventry." Lucy made a gallant effort at normalcy. "I may be twenty and two, but I am hardly at last prayers yet. I would have been perfectly happy to bide until father returned."

"You bad child!" Lady Staventry playfully rapped Lucy's knuckles with an ostrich feather fan. "How many times have I told you to sink the title in 'Aunt Almeria'? But every time we are in company you forget. We have been most fortunate in her," she confided to the table. "For where we thought only to do the favour of bringing her out, we have gained a companion and housekeeper and cook besides! She is the greatest possible comfort to us, besides keeping us both up to snuff. Only look how she has bullied me into arriving at the appointed hour, a thing I am sure I have never done before. Although that was not entirely my fault," she went on, shuffling cards with bejewelled hands. "For I never could make out what hour it was, let alone when something was scheduled to happen at a *particular* hour. And now we are to have the pleasure of her company a whole year, till her father finishes his sojourn."

"Pray, who *is* her father?" the countess queried. "Did you not say Trahern? Not the inventor? I had no idea—he cannot be a brother of yours. Yet you call her niece."

"Oh, yes, George Trahern," said Almeria airily. "He married one of the Shrevecotes, you know. Quite unexceptionable, and related to us some way or another a dozen generations back. I am sure I can't recall; family trees are *such* a bore, and it doesn't signify because her exact title would likely be something odious like cousin-eight-times-removed, which I *cannot* be expected to compass! We decided best call her 'niece' and have done. Isn't that true, dearest?"

"Quite so," said Lucy faintly. The duchess's eye was on her, wickedly glinting. She wondered how she was to get through the evening.

For Lucy, that evening was nothing short of nightmare. She curtsied and smiled and mouthed pretty nothings, always painfully aware that she was present under fraudulent terms. This "small card party" had turned out to be a very select gathering of the patronesses of Almack's and their friends! What was she doing here? How could they have deceived her so? And why?

She listened with horror as Lady Staventry prattled away happily. Oh, yes, they were going to present their dear niece to the ton. And they really had the highest hopes for her. For even if she had no title and was only a distant connexion, well, she *was* her principle heir—yes, and Natalie's as well! And such a presentable child, didn't they think? Lucy could only be glad that she had moved to another table and been spared the direct scrutiny these remarks must have occasioned. She huddled in her corner of the carriage on the way home: miserable, frightened, and angry. Mindful of the servants, she said not a word until they were in their own front parlour. Then she stepped inside and leaned back against the door with her hands splayed across it. She took a deep breath.

"What—*what* have you *done?*"

"Why, introduced you to the ton, to be sure," Almeria said. "Just as we promised. Or, no, we did *not* promise—it was to be a surprise, was it not? Yes, that's it. And I must say, it went off as well as one could wish. One can't hope for much approbation from the countess, she is such a high stickler. But I thought Lady Cowper quite taken with her, did not you, Natalie? I expect we are perfectly safe now for vouchers from Almack's."

"Almack's!" Lucy was aghast. "Pray what makes you imagine that *I* will be attending *Almack's?*"

"But that is the present, don't you see? You *did* promise we could give you something intangible if we liked. An introduction to society is neither money nor goods, so it works quite perfectly. I must say, I am surprised at you, Lucy," she reproved. "You are usually quicker than this. I have never had to explain anything to you before!"

"Then would you care to explain," said Lucy in a dangerous voice, advancing into the room, "how you expect me to take a place in society? I am a *nobody*. My father is engaged in *trade;* my mother from a family that commands respect, but whose members were all born without a shirt! I have been a governess—and a discredited one at that—and now I am a *housekeeper*. Just what do you think would be the omnipotent Countess Lieven's opinion of that?"

"That was just the difficulty, of course, and why Natalie thought best to keep addressing you as 'niece.' For I don't know how it is, but any connexion of ours, it seems, *must* be acceptable."

"But I am *not* your niece!" Lucy cried in desperation. Was there no way to represent to Almeria the impossibility of this situation?

"Oh, I don't know about that," Lady Staventry settled down gently into a chair. "You very well may be some relation to us, you know. For as I was talking to the countess about being crossed by the Shrevecotes somewhere down the line, I realised that it was quite possibly true. They are a very good family, after all; and if I have heard Papa say once that we are related to every decent family in Britain, I have heard it a *dozen* times!"

"God give me patience! Don't you see that if I present myself as eligible, I shall be an *impostor!*"

"Get off your high ropes, Lucille," The Duchess of Bucklass entered the fray for the first time. She was still standing, her cane firmly wedged against the floor. She regarded Lucy's caged-lion pacing with a twinkling eye. "Even forgetting our supposed relations—and Almeria for once is in the right of it, they are more likely than you may guess," she said parenthetically with an odd, shrewd look on her face, "you know as well as I that girls of lesser birth are fired off into the Marriage Mart every year. The only thing you lacked was backing. Now you've got it."

"But to tell them I'm your *heir!*" Lucy wailed.

"Hmmm, yes, surprised me too. Your idea, Almeria?"

"Indeed, was it not the *nackiest* notion? For of course *anyone* with enough money is acceptable in the *first* circles. So that should do the business nicely. And it is not a clanker, not really.

"For I daresay I *shall* leave you something. After all, you are a very pretty-behaved girl, and I can see you shall be the greatest comfort to me. But it shan't be a great deal, I'm afraid," she added sadly, pulling at the plumes on her bonnet. "The truth of it is," she said trustingly to a Lucy whom she did not seem to comprehend was seething with anger, "I have so *many* relatives hanging on my sleeve. And it is unpleasant to refuse them, they badger one so, besides which, I do dislike to deny them, knowing that most of them are in circumstances which . . . in short, their lot is so straitened that—"

"A parcel of dirty dishes!" interrupted the duchess in disgust. This was obviously an old argument between them.

"Why, Nat, how unkind! At any rate, you must own that they are of the most deserving. Cousin Haythrem—"

"That Bartholomew baby!" scorned the duchess.

"No, no, he is only somewhat overfond of a well-cut coat. Indeed, the marvels he gets out of that tailor of his in Rye . . . If he could but be fitted out properly by Stultz, I am sure he would cut quite the dash."

"Huh!" Natalie snorted.

"Then there is the honourable Sedgewick. His morals are something of the most tolerant, but I cannot but believe—"

"A loose-screw, Sister, nothing more. Anything you leave him will be dropped at White's inside a month. What he doesn't spend on baubles for his latest bird of paradise! A complete rip, in fact."

"Nothing of the kind! If he had a little blunt of his own, and could once find himself out from under the hatches, I make no doubt—"

"He's always swallowed a spider! Best buy him a boat, so he can row more comfortably up the River Tick."

"And I must not forget my seventh niece, Maria," Almeria went on bravely.

"That ninnyhammer!" Natalie said dismissively.

"And Lucton, Jessamy, Brenda, Thomas, and—"

"Nodcocks, slowtops, and jackstraws, all of 'em!" Derisively.

"And Lord knows how many others. Which means, you see, that I cannot leave you much, Lucy dear. Certainly not above seventy thousand pounds. It is a very great pity, for I like you excessively, and should wish to see you *comfortably* established." She dabbed lightly at her eyes.

Lucy sank bonelessly onto a chair. Her temperature was at zero. *Seventy thousand pounds?* As a *small* bequest? She'd had no idea. She was struck absolutely dumb.

"Don't be such a watering pot," the duchess recommended crossly to her sister. "It's your own fault for being so soft-hearted. If you gave our unconscionable relatives a slip on the shoulder, you could easily leave Lucille three times that amount. I rather fancy I shall."

"Oh, no!" said Lucy in horror. "You can't—you *can't* mean it! Either of you!"

"Why not? Button up, girl. If you wanted it, you most assuredly would not get it. And you can't stop us."

Lucy's head was spinning. She clutched the arms of her

chair weakly. The only questions that occurred to her were irrelevant ones.

"But how—how did you come into the Staventry fortune and why—*why*— live like *this* if you needn't? I would never have guessed . . .," her voice trailed off faintly. "You had me gammoned so well with your shabby little cottage . . ."

"As to how," Natalie answered her, "*I* didn't come into the Staventry fortune at all. Younger sister, you know. Married Bucklass. Rich as Golden Ball. Didn't like each other. Had to pack him off to the Continent, he bored me so. But he left his money to me. Said in his will I could manage it better than a dozen lawyers. Handsome of him," she said meditatively, taking snuff. "True, too."

Under any other circumstances, Lucy would have laughed at the picture of an irate Natalie driving her dull husband out of the country neck and crop.

"Almeria inherited because she was the eldest, of course. No entail. Papa was indulgent."

"You're the eldest?" Lucy asked the petite Almeria in astonishment. She had quite supposed the small blonde woman to be some ten years younger than her formidable sister.

"Oh, no, not precisely," she answered. "It seems to me there was someone else. Do you recollect, Natalie? Didn't we have a brother at one time? I hardly recall, but it seems he was older than me by several years."

This was too interesting. Almeria *thought* they had a brother, but couldn't *remember?* Lucy sat up straighter.

"True. 'Queer George.' Dark horse. Rope-ripe from birth. Probably dead now."

"Probably? You mean you don't know?!" Lucy was utterly bewildered.

"Disappeared," said Natalie shortly. "Wandered off one day. Never came back. Left a note: 'I don't like it here. I'm going.' No idea what became of him. Looked, of course. Gave up eventually."

"And as to *why* we live as we do, well, we *told* you,"

Almeria said shyly. "I . . . I don't like large houses, I keep thinking there are ghosts, and . . . and servants are so sort of—overbearing. I cannot abide it when I say something, some perfectly normal thing, you know, and they look at me *so* . . . We decided it would be nicer to stay here all by ourselves. But of course, we haven't done a very good job," she finished ruefully. "That's why I'm so glad you're here."

Lucy collected her scattered wits and rose. "I am most gratified that you found me useful. However, now I am afraid that I must go. You have placed me in a completely untenable position. I cannot allow this to continue. Now that I have wages of my own, I have no longer even the excuse of need. So this is goodbye. Lady Staventry. Your Grace."

"What a tiresome creature you are," Natalie pronounced decisively. "In a grand fuss again. Ridiculous habit of yours; got to stop. Just hold still a moment, Lucille! Look at me." All of her duchy was in her voice. "You made us a promise. What was it?" The old lady held Lucy's eyes uncompromisingly.

Reluctantly she replied. "I promised that I would accept a gift if it was neither money nor goods."

"We have given you an important introduction. Is that money? Is that goods?"

"No." Her voice was low and upset.

"Are you a woman of your word?"

"But, Your Grace, you can't expect me to go on thus! Why, I would be a—a charlatan!"

"It's either you or us. Think. We've presented you as our niece. We've stated that you're going to be our protégé for the season. If you give that the lie, what d'you suppose will happen to our credibility?"

Lucy's head dropped. "I had not thought of that."

"No. I wagered not. So you'll do as you're told. You'll present yourself to society, have one social season, and we'll say no more about it."

"Very well, Your Grace," said Lucy in a leaden voice.

Natalie noted the ominously persistent formal address. "You have trapped me finely. I see that I must comply. But I shall not," she finished stonily, "forgive you."

She turned towards the door with a constricted heart, meaning to go to her chamber. But behind her she heard a tiny, muffled sob.

She swung around. Natalie was sitting with a defeated look, shoulders slumping, cane askew. And Almeria was crying into her handkerchief. This was not the usual affected, pretty dabbing at an eye. She was earnestly weeping, and trying just as hard to cover the sounds. Her fragile shoulders shook under the thin blue taffeta.

Lucy felt a pull at her heart. She went to Almeria at once, and drew the small hands into her own. "Almeria. Aunt Almeria, dear, whatever is it?"

"Oh, L-Lucy, dear!" she said through hiccoughs. "I am so s-sorry. It was my idea, not Natalie's. I thought you would *l-like* a Season. I thought you would have f-fun! When I was your age, I adored the balls and the pretty gowns and th-the attention of the gentlemen, and I hoped it would *p-please* you! And I was all wrong and I've spoilt everything again and now you—*hate* us! Please forgive me, Lucy. I didn't mean it! I am just so stupid, you know, and I never seem to understand what people need."

Almeria seemed truly heartbroken, and Lucy ached for her. She took the woman—so much older but so very childlike—into her arms.

"Oh, my very dear aunt, forgive me. Of course I don't hate you. I was only very angry because I felt I had been forced into it. And I really despise the idea of lying to anybody."

"C-couldn't we take it all back?" Almeria asked hopefully.

"No, dear, I'm afraid not. Your sister is right. It would make you look very bad indeed."

"Oh." Her face was bleak.

"Never you fear," said Lucy soothingly, applying a

hanky to the swimming blue eyes. "It's all going to be right now. I am not angry any more. We will go to all the balls together, and let those silly people believe anything they want."

"You . . . you forgive us?"

Lucy heard a tense silence behind her. Natalie. Awaiting her answer.

"Yes, I do," she said quietly. "You meant well by it. I understand that now. So I'll go along with this fiction. I daresay I shall enjoy it once I become accustomed.

"But mind," she cautioned, turning her head to a suddenly bright-eyed Natalie, "if I hear so much as another word about making me your heiress, I shall boil all the cats and put them in your evening stew!"

"You are a terrible child," said Natalie softly. "I don't know how I shall bear it."

And for the second time since they had met, they hugged each other.

8

On a certain mild evening in mid-April of 1818, Lord Hersington stood in the library at Bostram House regarding his nephew with an exacting eye. There was little with which even the fastidious earl could find fault. Crowley was a changed man.

Young Thomas's engaging smile and fresh countenance were once more visible, freed of the triple restraints of pout, powder, and prelunch drinking. His dark curls were carefully arranged in a moderate Windswept style. But everything else about him was discreet and tasteful: from the tiny diamond pin in his snowy cravat, to the cut of his dark-blue velvet tailcoat; from the cuffs out of which peeped the tiniest riffle of silver lace; from the blue and white striped waistcoat (impeded only by a very fine silver seal on a short fob), to the exquisite satin knee-breeches of elegant cut and pristine ivory colour. His white stockings were without clocking or other detraction, and his simple, buckled shoes were as quiet as they were expensive.

This ensemble represented the very cream of what could be salvaged from Crowley's former finery, plus a few carefully chosen pieces. The mixing and supplementing had been going for three weeks, as Jasper gradually reintroduced his nephew into social life on another level. Tonight he had intimated something special to the young man, who had made his very best efforts.

Hersington gave him an approving nod, and Tom smiled modestly. He had learned to be a good deal more humble in the preceding weeks. And had he but known it, he had therefore much more of which to boast.

"Well, Uncle, what is on the cards for tonight?"

"Almack's."

"No!" said Crowley in horrified accents. "The Marriage Mart? You're joking me."

"Indeed I am not," replied his mentor calmly. "You have comported yourself well so far, in coffee-houses, at card parties, in clubs, and at various smaller social functions of a casual nature. I am most pleased with your progress. Almack's, however, is the acid test."

"What! Stale cakes, simpering misses, and lemonade? I'd as lief stay home with my studies, thank you very much!"

His lordship languidly studied the nails of one immaculate hand. "Do you or do you not," he drawled, "wish to be admitted to White's?"

There was, of course, no such thing as a negative answer to that question. Hersington waited for Tom to swallow once or twice, and then continued. "Pass muster at Almack's, and I shall see you gain entrance there tomorrow evening."

"Lemonade is my favourite drink!" said Tom with charming promptness. And they promenaded to the carriage in very good charity with each other.

At first the evening seemed everything Tom had predicted: dull, stuffy, uneventful. Tom dutifully danced with a number of uninteresting maidens just out of the schoolroom, and except for one despairing glance at Hersington, accepted even the prosiness of Lady Prewlitt-Howes with a good grace.

He had just returned to the wall by his uncle, when a sudden stir at the door drew all eyes. Soon all the nearby young men who were not dancing disappeared in that direction as if by suction.

"What the devil has caused such a stampede?" Tom wondered aloud.

Lord Morelock, standing nearby, overhead this remark and chose to enlighten them.

" 'Evening Hersington. Crowley. That commotion yonder," he flicked a beringed finger toward the doors, "is the arrival of our new reigning belle. She joined the Season several weeks late, and has put quite a few noses out of joint."

"A diamond of the first water, I gather?" asked Hersington.

"Not precisely. She's—different. Refreshing. Never passes beyond the line, you know, but quite distinctive. They call her 'The Mysterious Original.' "

"Why mysterious?"

"Because she can't be drawn to speak of her background, which would seem to indicate shady antecedents. Not that that signifies. She came out under the aegis of Lady Staventry and the Duchess of Bucklass, which almost guarantees her success. Add to that the fact that they are gazetting her as their principal heir—both of them, mind you!—and you can see that nobody cares that her relationship to them is so distant that they don't even try to trace it."

"Intriguing," said Jasper mildly. A wild conjecture was forming in his mind. "I would certainly like to meet this enigma."

"It doesn't look as if you'll have much chance," said Morelock, patting his old-fashioned wig and scanning the moving, bobbing crowd that marked the Original's progress round the room. The center of this attention could not herself be seen. "I'm off to the card tables. Care to join me?"

"Not for the moment, I thank you," murmured Jasper. "You have most severely whet my curiosity."

"Don't blame you," puffed the man. "Taking little thing. Good stable, too. If I were your age, and single, I'd offer for her myself." And he rambled off.

It is fortunate that he did. For at that moment, the crowd parted slightly, and Tom gave a smothered exclamation.

"Good God!" he cried. "Lucy Trahern!"

Jasper, his unlikely guess confirmed, raised his quizzing glass and surveyed the girl narrowly. He was thinking at a very rapid pace, but said only, "Why, Tom, I thought you told me she was no beauty?"

"She wasn't," said Tom in a dazed voice. "At least . . . one couldn't tell under all the braids and that stuffy brown thing she wore."

"Hmmm." Jasper was noncommittal. He had half-expected a meeting of this kind someday, and the "acid test" he had referred to was about to confront his nephew. He watched Crowley carefully out of the corner of his eye.

"I must go to her," muttered the boy.

"Steady, my friend. To what purpose, pray? You surely are not going to tax her with your previous . . . acquaintance?"

Crowley looked affronted. "Nothing so shabby! I intend to solicit her hand for the dance and offer her a private apology. Moreover, if she learns I am here, it must cause her distress until she knows I do not intend to unveil her."

Jasper nodded approvingly. "Your sentiments do you credit. Congratulations, Nephew. You have just cleared the fence with flying colours. We are for White's on the morrow."

Tom beamed at him and made as if to hurry off.

"Stay a moment. Should you succeed in your aim, do be so kind as to make me known to Miss Trahern. I should very much like to meet such a sterling character."

"Certainly, Uncle."

"By the by, perhaps it would be best if you do not call me 'Uncle' in her presence. I wish to approach her quite without a history."

Tom looked surprised, then gave a sly smile. "Sits the wind in that quarter, does it?"

"Nothing of the kind," said his uncle reprovingly. "Do but consider her situation. Would it not put her out of countenance to meet me on the floor of Almack's as the man who once paid her wage?"

Chastened, Tom apologised and promised to do his best. Then he shouldered his way through the crowd toward Lucy's flock of admirers.

He was met on the way by another of the trials the earl had anticipated, in the form of a dashing group of dandies who had once been Tom's principal cronies.

The first notice Tom had of this was the drawling voice of Lennox Huston. "I'faith, methinks I see Tom Crowley. But no—I must be mistaken. 'Tis merely a parson. My glass must be fogged."

Tom turned around, stony-faced, to meet this attack.

"Ye Gods, it *is* Tom. Setting up for the priesthood, m'boy?"

"Not at all," said Tom, carefully polite, to the lavender-and-meringue exquisite who confronted him. "I am but adopting a new style."

"Style, he calls it! I say, that's doing it rather too brown, Thomas. Whatever are you about?"

"I am going to pay my respects to Miss Trahern," he answered patiently.

"Approaching the Original! That's rich! And what, pray, makes you think she would not shudder to gaze upon such rustic garb?" A small group of Tom's old circle was gathering. Though they had once called themselves his friends, none was above snickering nastily at this sally.

Tom was angry enough to play a dangerous card. "In my previous acquaintance with the lady, she gave me to understand that she preferred a quieter mode of dress."

"She's a flirt of yours, is she?" sneered Huston in patent disbelief. "Do let us accompany you, and see how this 'old friend' greets you. Perhaps you could give us some pointers!"

The gentlemen all thought this was famous sport, and

fell in behind Tom, affording him a quick passage to Lucy's side.

Tom was frightened now. He had set himself up for a serious snub if Lucy would not recognise him.

His hesitation gave Huston a chance to step forward. This coxcomb made a flourishing bow in front of Lucille.

"Miss Trahern, your most obedient. I beg to present a gentleman who claims some previous knowledge of you." He turned sideways and glanced mockingly at Thomas.

Lucy, ravishing in a gown of white gauze with silver and blue ribbons woven into it and trailing down from the white rosettes in her hair, gave him one bewildered look. Then she started, and said, "It cannot be—Tom Crowley!"

"The very same." He executed a bow of an equal mixture of grace and embarrassment, and was profoundly relieved when she held out her hand for a token kiss.

Lucy's circle moved in consternation. The dandies looked uneasily at each other. She did know him after all, did she? What if—awful thought—he had been right that she disliked dandies?

"Why, almost I did not know you! I vow you are a changed creature, sir!"

There was a question in her eyes, but she carried it off well, and Tom was admiring.

"My uncle has taken me in hand, Miss Trahern," he said gratefully. "I am quite reformed, as you see."

Before she could reply to this, Huston cut in with contemptuous ease.

"Mr. Crowley *claims*," he said knowingly, "that his manner of address will be more to your taste than ours. Come, Miss Trahern. The next set is forming—do enlighten us as to which style you prefer by selecting one of us for the dance.

"The cleric or the fop?" tinkled a sweet voice next to her shoulder. "Now there is a wager!"

This remark was made by Lucy's most constant—and unwelcome—satellite, a certain Miss Clarissa Stirlan. She had been all the rage before Lucy took the scene, and had attached herself to the newcomer to retain a bit of glory. Her ravishing pink-and-white looks and great fortune allowed her malicious comments to pass for wit. But she was known in many circles as Clarissa Cut-Tongue.

Lucy took in the ramifications of this situation with lightning speed. She could see that Crowley's appearance in the ton caused her the utmost danger of exposure. However, Crowley was in an equally tight place. He had obviously made a test of this meeting. If she refused him, he would lose face—and hate her. If she accepted him, she was still in a position of risk. But he might just be grateful enough to hold his tongue.

It would also be a good chance to snub Clarissa subtly—the girl showed a marked fancy for the dandies. Moreover, Lucy despised "Beau" Huston, as he had styled himself. In revenge for the insidious remarks he made in her ear and his creeping hands, she had dubbed him "Demi-Beau." This had only led him to step up his pursuit. To set him down once and for all would be a great victory.

Her decision made, Lucy smiled brilliantly around the circle and flitted her fan. "A most difficult choice, I vow. However, a lady cannot allow herself to be outshone by the gentlemen. And since Mr. Huston's perfume quite overpowers mine, I believe I shall take Mr. Crowley."

Then, leaving a number of hastily covered indignant looks behind her, she swept out onto the dance floor.

Lucy attacked as soon as they made their bows. "Now tell me, sir," she asked with a twinkle, "have I put my fingers further in the fire, or am I out of jeopardy?"

"You wrong me, Miss Trahern," said Crowley blushing. "I had meant to ask the favour of this dance only to apologise. Now I find I must thank you as well. I am so deeply in your debt that it puts me quite at a loss."

"Ah, let us not quibble over points. You are both forgiven and welcome."

"You are too gracious."

The movements of the dance parted them for a few moments. When they met again, Tom had a question of his own.

"Tell me though, most tolerant Miss Trahern—how comes it you are here? I had not hoped for such an opportunity to tender my apologies in person."

"La! A tedious story. You will not wish to be troubled with it."

"I understand you are in some sort related to the Staventrys. How comes it you made such a secret of the connexion?"

"You mean why be a governess when I had such high relations," Lucy said flatly. She was thinking fast. Whatever she told Tom would surely find its way to Mrs. Bostram. She took a breath and plunged in. "You are no doubt aware that they call themselves my aunts. But in fact we are the most tenuous of links. So distant, indeed, that I had not expected them to recognise me. Nor had I ever planned to apply to them for assistance, until I found myself in such exceeding dire straits."

"I know," he replied ruefully. "I have been pummelling myself ever since for being such a scoundrel."

She looked at him with a more friendly eye. "No matter. It's an ill wind, they say. For when I did approach them, almost by chance as it were (not knowing they were in town), they most kindly undertook my protection. And insisted on my having a Season. Which I cannot quite like, given my background," she finished quietly. "But they would have it so. I am hardly in a position to refuse them."

The music was finishing. "I am most pleased that they did," said Tom admiringly. "Forgive my saying so, but it is gratifying to see that you are cutting such a swathe. It validates my judgement in—in singling you out. I was brash, and vulgar, and I *am* very sorry. Yet I trust you understand me when I say that you certainly deserve the attention you have attracted."

"Bosh." Her colour was high as she curtsied.

"I'll say no more of it, 'pon my honor! I'm no hand at this yet, you know, though I try."

Lucy was touched by his boyish bashfulness. He seemed so much more appealing than the would-be roué she remembered.

"Compliment accepted in the spirit given. And may I compliment *you* on the new mode you have affected. It is very much more becoming to one of your birth."

They had returned to Lucy's coterie now, and further private conversation was impossible. But he pressed her hand lightly as he bowed over it, and asked that he be allowed to call and present his most humble respects. Perhaps, on some future date, she would give him the pleasure of driving her in the park?

"Call you certainly may—but drive with you I shall not! Not if you still sport those half-broken cattle you call carriage horses!"

"No!" laughed Tom. "I have bought a quieter pair."

"Afraid of a high-couraged horse, Miss Trahern?" Huston asked derisively. Her cuts had wounded his pride badly.

She looked him straight in the eye. "I trust I can ride and drive as well as the next, my dear sir," she told him. "But I will not be made a spectacle of by beasts that do not own their master."

It was a scathing reference to an incident in the park some two weeks prior. Huston's bays had taken high-bred exception to a pair of tall ostrich plumes, and had gone careening across the drive, leaving their owner dangling from a tree.

Incensed, Huston bowed stiffly and stalked away. There was a short break in the music, and Lucy was free to look about her.

Her eye was almost immediately caught by a tall, commanding gentleman on the opposite side of the room who was watching her with the utmost intensity. She had never seen anyone quite like him. He was somehow more than the sum of his parts. It was not merely the sleek silk pantaloons, white silk stockings, exquisite coat and elegantly subdued ensemble—snowy white and black, with just a diamond or two, all perfectly cut. Nor was it simply the pantherlike build, strong shoulders tapering to narrow hips and powerful but slim legs and arms. Nor even the languid, thoroughbred bearing or the arresting, fox-like face. The tawny colouring and touchable, ruffled hair, though fascinating, did not by themselves account for his magnetism. No, it was all these factors, coupled with his steady amber gaze, which made her catch her breath and look back for an instant with undisguised wonder. Something about that gaze was so personal and measuring that Lucy quickly looked away.

"Clarissa," she whispered out of the corner of her mouth, "who is that brandy-coloured gentleman who is staring so in our direction?"

Clarissa cast him a swift sideward glance, and grimaced. "Oh, that is my Lord Hersington. Don't set your cap in *that* direction," she warned. "Most handsome, I own, and quite the eligible *parti* these days with his fortune. But a most unsavoury fortune, to be frank."

"How is this?" Lucy asked faintly. The gentlemen was still staring at them.

"*Well*," breathed Clarissa with secret delight, "there is the most *scandalous* gossip about him, my dearest creature. He was a younger son with no prospects until only three years ago. And then, plump! He came into his brother's place under most *unpleasant* circumstances. The fellow died, and Hersington . . ." she paused, and continued with heavy meaning, "did not mourn overmuch. I am told it is only by stretching a considerable point he is allowed into Almack's at all!"

This was pushing the truth quite beyond its limits. But Lucy had no way of knowing that the fair Clarissa had herself thrown her handkerchief in that direction, and been ruthlessly snubbed.

"I see," Lucy replied thoughtfully. She was aware that Clarissa did not often let the truth stand in her way when she had it in mind to shred a reputation. Nor did Lucy miss the hungry glance thrown in his direction. But if Clarissa was brave enough to say such a thing outright, something similar could well be whispered elsewhere.

The music had begun again, and both girls were importuned with offers. But Lucy put it about that she was fatigued and wished to join her aunts for a while at cards.

Unlike many other young hopefuls at Almack's, Lucy had made a habit of leaving several dances on her card free every evening. Her reasons were twofold. It gave her room to breathe and discuss things with her aunts. And it was a break from the constant importunities of gentlemen that she well knew would never look at her twice if they had a whiff of her true circumstances. Lucy had learned to turn aside the rabid flirting with clever comments and light ripostes. She had even learned to enjoy it somewhat. But it made her tired. Sometimes she wished for nothing so much as to sit with the Bostram children and tell them a preposterous story.

She was unaware that this tactic only added to her cachet. It was a world where girls rushed to fill their cards and agonised over supper partners; where sitting out one dance was anathema. That she could, by choice, leave part of her evening free only added to her mystique.

So when she left, the men groaned; but Clarissa merely waved a cheery good-bye to her greatest rival and turned back to the eager gallants.

Lucy soon found the duchess in the card room. She waited for a pause in the game to whisper in Natalie's ear. "A word for you, Aunt. Only think who has just joined me on the dance floor. None other than Thomas Crowley."

"The April-squire?" The duchess smiled grimly. "Only let me finish this hand, girl, and I shall send him to the right-abouts."

"That is just what I wish you not to do," said Lucy earnestly. "I feared you would discover him and do so. But it is not in the least necessary. He has apologised, and promises most faithfully to keep my secret. Indeed, I think him quite reformed, and have given him permission to call."

"Have you?" asked the duchess with a sharp glance.

"You must own it would put a better face on things."

"Well, it's your lookout, girl. I'll bide my tongue. But let me know if he comes the pretty. I'll flay him!"

"I've no doubt," smiled Lucy. She strolled off to join Almeria on the other side of the table. She did not rejoin the dancers for some time.

Meanwhile, Tom had returned to his uncle and was regaling him with an account of their meeting.

"She was everything that was kind, sir," Tom told him. "She forgave me most graciously. I am much obliged to her. Believe it or not, she even contrived to do me some social good in the process."

"Oh?"

"Yes. Well. Ahem." Tom looked embarrassed. "Some of my old friends were there and—made game of my attire, sir. I'm afraid I lost my temper. I told them Miss Trahern had given me to believe she preferred such a style. They made rather a test of it, and asked her to choose between us. She chose me."

"You surprise me. One would have thought that you represented only danger to her."

"She said as much herself."

Jasper raised an eyebrow.

"But you know, sir, I have the strangest feeling she was way ahead of us all. She sized up the situation in the moment of our meeting. And—and made use of it!"

"You mean," the earl replied carefully, "that even if you had meant to do her a mischief, you could hardly do so once under an obligation to her?"

"Yes. Just so."

"I see." He paused. "Tell me. Did she ever give you an explanation for her sudden appearance in the ton?"

"Yes, she did. I must say it makes me admire her the more. She is not the type to beg, you see." And he told the story as he had heard it.

"Do I understand you correctly? She said she 'could not quite like' being constrained to present herself, but felt she could not refuse?"

"Yes."

"Hmmm."

"Only fancy her being a niece of the Staventrys, sir, and us never tumbling to it! I cannot imagine how the resemblance escaped me before. She is the very image of the duchess, you know."

"Doing it very much too brown, Nephew," Hersington smiled tolerantly. "Or do you tell me that you have become intoxicated from drinking that lemonade you so favour?"

Tom cocked his arm and pretended to stumble woozily. "Oh, no, my lord," he said in die-away accents. " 'Twas the orgeat!"

"True. It is agreed among experts that orgeat and stale cakes are a fatal combination."

Tom grinned back at him, perfectly understanding the double entendre. "But truly, Uncle, *everyone* is remarking on Lucy's resemblance to the duchess. My eye isn't out!"

Lord Hersington, Earl of Kentsey, lifted his glass and surveyed the sparkling, dark-haired girl as she whirled by in a rondel (she having returned to the floor with Lord Morelock). He dropped the lens again and shook his head. "Sorry. I just don't see it. And I beg you won't mention such a thing to your aunt. She would very likely be carried off with a spasm. And no telling how she would queer things for Miss Trahern. Somehow I find myself disinclined to puncture the progress of this intrepid miss."

"Oh, I am of your mind, my lord," nodded Tom enthusiastically. He was secretly relieved. There was much in this episode that could not redound to his credit. "Particularly after I promised discretion. It would hardly be the action of a gentleman."

"You," said Hersington with mock severity, "will never be a gentleman in any case. I had your sacred word that you would introduce me to our Cinderella. To deprive a gentleman of a lady's company is a very serious breach. I feel much inclined to call you out." He took snuff with a serious air. "I shan't, however. You would probably forget it and sleep in. A pretty fool I should look, winning by default over a suckling."

Tom was laughing openly. "If ever I heard such a bear-garden jaw! You terrify me, Uncle. I shall fetch Miss Trahern at once."

"You are not to introduce her to your uncle, mind," he warned.

Tom made a practised bow. "I should never dream of it, your lordship. Why should she wish to meet my uncle when she *could* be presented to the Earl of Kentsey?"

Lucy was surprised when Master Crowley approached her again, and even more surprised when he asked for a second dance. She pretended to rap his knuckles with her fan.

"And here was I all agog at your reformation! Stuff! Your uncle would not be pleased, I trow, if he could see you asking for two dances so close together."

"Why, he *can* see me," Tom said, defending himself. Then, realising his error, he stammered, "That is—he was here a moment ago—I, I cannot spy him now."

Lucy's eyes lit up with girlish glee. "You don't mean 'Uncle Jasper' is here tonight? Famous! I have been wanting to meet that man and give him a thank this age!"

"We can't—that is—he may have stepped out for air, you know, or left. And—and besides, there is someone else I promised to present to you. The Earl of Kentsey. Do step this way."

"Oh, pooh. I don't wish to meet another earl. All they ever do is ogle at me through their odious glasses and ask each other if it's true I'm an heiress."

"But, Miss Trahern, I did promise—," Tom tugged on her arm. He felt he was sinking faster and faster into a mire of misunderstandings and mistakes. Whoever heard of a woman who did not want to meet an earl?

"There seems to be some contretemps here," came a cool voice at Crowley's elbow. "Could I be of assistance?"

Lucy looked speculatively up at the tawny stranger who had drawn her notice earlier. She liked what she saw. Behind all the slim elegance, she was positive she detected a strong hint of humour.

Lucy could not know that she was seeing something unique. Hersington had been the bafflement of his contemporaries for years, and had only become more so at his ascension to the title. He was correct in every way; he pursued all the accepted interests of a gentleman; and he was known in White's as one who rarely lost his bets and never his temper. And yet something always seemed lacking. He was somehow innately detached from all that went on about him. As one *prieux chevalier* had grumbled, "His company's like a pane of glass—perfectly polished, and no way to get a purchase on it."

Perhaps it was merely the experience of being a younger son. For when he had first come out, the polite world had taken but scant notice, deeming him of little importance. His sudden elevation to the title had brought him many fawning attentions, particularly from hopeful mamas with daughters to launch. But it could not be seen that the earl felt it incumbent to respond—with gratitude or anything else—to these sudden, spurious overtures. This coldness, in the end, convinced his cronies that he would never marry. And it produced in large part the fiction that he had some sinister part in his brother's death. It is interesting to note that this story was current almost exclusively among the aforementioned disappointed matchmakers.

But Lucy was never to see this immobile face. He approached her from the first with interest and curiosity. He was ready to be amused; he was disposed to be helpful. Boredom was the furthest thing from his mind. He looked upon the events of the last several weeks as a vastly entertaining play to which only he knew all the script. And here, at last, was the leading lady—all gauze and silver and fascinating contradictions.

It was this amused involvement, seen lurking in his lordship's eyes, which emboldened Lucy to respond saucily. "Oh, yes, it is most vexing," Miss Trahern said, dimpling. "Here is Master Crowley bound and determined to present me to an earl. But I think it disobliging of him to press me. For I am heartily sick of earls and should far liefer meet his uncle!"

"The best solution to delicate diplomatic relations of this kind is compromise," suggested Hersington with an appreciative glint. "May I present myself as such? While I am most unfortunately an earl, I do have the redeeming grace of being Crowley's uncle. Hersington, Earl of Kentsey, at your service, Miss."

Tom looked at him, stricken.

"His *other* uncle," my lord added helpfully.

Lucy smiled at him. "Well, I suppose I shall just have to make a go of it. Miss Trahern, my lord, at yours. Though I *should* have preferred to meet Uncle *Jasper.*"

Hersington responded with a perfectly straight face. "What a pity. Do you know, I could have laid oath he was over there just a moment ago." He waved an arm in the direction from which he himself had just come. "But I must confess that I do not see him anywhere now." Wickedly amused, he pretended to search around the room.

"Tell me then," Lucy asked eagerly. "Do you *know* Uncle Jasper?"

"Indeed I do," said Hersington imperturbably. "In fact, I may say I know him better than anyone." Foreseeing difficult questions ahead, he quietly turned the joke around. "Do you have some particular reason for wishing to make the acquaintance of this gentleman? You have, I collect, never seen him."

It was Lucy's turn to be embarrassed. She could hardly tell a stranger that she wished to thank the man for paying her stipend.

"No—that is, Crowley has told me so much about him. Almost I feel that I do know him," she prevaricated hastily.

"Ah. In that case perhaps you would be pleased to pump me for information as we dance?"

"Indeed, my lord, I would be delighted." And she swept him a graceful curtsey before allowing herself to be led to the floor.

As it happened, this was a waltz. Lucy was uncomfortably aware of the closeness of this elegant gentleman. As she had expected, he waltzed beautifully. His steps were light, unconcerned, and perfectly harmonious. For some time she simply enjoyed this. Then he startled her.

"I have been acquainted with Lady Staventry and the duchess for some years. How is it that we have never met?"

"Oh, I have been rusticating," she told him airily. "They have only but recently extracted me from the wilds and insisted on giving me a come-out."

"Yet it is surprising that I had never heard of you. I believed I knew all their relatives."

She could not know that the smooth voice held gentle teasing.

She laughed up at him rather nervously. "That falls under the category of 'leading questions.' Do you suppose, my lord, that I have evaded the questions of the cream of society these three weeks only to impart the secret to you?" Her smile was arch.

"If I did, I can see I was mistaken," he murmured self-deprecatingly.

The waltz ended. Lucy was both sorry and relieved. This fellow fascinated her—but he made her uneasy too. She was casting about for an excuse to leave him when

Almeria came bustling up. Lady Staventry looked to be more than usually flustered and breathless.

"Oh, dearest, *here* you are! I hoped you would be able to bear me company, for I truly *cannot* abide the card tables another instant!"

"But, Aunt Almeria, you adore playing for pound points!"

"Not when everybody insists on talking politics! Of all the useless subjects . . . I think it most disobliging, for the chief tenet of polite conversation is to keep within the scope of the interests of one's partners. And if there is one thing I understand even less than figures, it is politics. I daresay I could run the Royal Treasury for a year with better success than listen to a state-dinner speech for two minutes."

Beau Huston had approached and was regarding Almeria with barely suppressed contempt. "No doubt it is difficult for such matters to keep your attention," he drawled.

"Yes, that is precisely it," said the blonde, cherubically unaware she had been insulted. "I like to compass *one* activity at a time, and I like it to be something—well, something *immediate*. I have never been *exposed* to politics, you see, for they have nothing at all to do with me. It has always been my way to attend to the matter at *hand*." She smiled and waved her pretty hands. "When I am in the milliner's shop, I think of bonnets, and in Picadilly I think of ribbons; in the kitchen I think of food, and in a ballroom, of dancing. At a card table," she finished repressively, "I should *like* to be allowed to think of cards! That does not seem to me so great a request. And I daresay," she added with a judicious expression, "I shall think of politics if ever it should chance that I am in the House of Lords."

There was good-natured laughter all round at this. Huston cut in.

"Under the circumstances, we must consider ourselves lucky that you never shall be. The country is in bad enough case already."

The sneer in his voice was so pronounced that even Lady

Staventry could not fail to notice. She looked first confused, then hurt. She cannot even defend herself! thought Lucy hotly. That rogue! I'll school him to insult a lady!

She drew herself up just slightly; her smile was cordial but there was a dangerous flush to her cheeks. "My dear Sir Lennox," her voice was deceptively calm, "you are a connoisseur of political personalities, I take it? Then perhaps you will consider this. My aunt's philosophy may be novel. But as she is neither as miserable as Mr. Cobb nor as dead as Mr. Pitt, I expect there is something to be said for it."

Lucy's eyes held an unpleasant glitter which grew more pronounced as Huston hastily took himself off. Who would have ever guessed the little Original read the papers?

Lucy breathed deeply to compose herself while Hersington digested this new aspect of her character. And Almeria, as always sublimely unaware of the receding storm, stepped up and put her palm on Lucy's wrist.

"Dearest, I am glad that fellow went away, for I have a favor to ask you. No, don't go, Hersington. You are an old friend.

"Lucy—the silliest thing. I have contrived to win very too much money at silver loo. For the talk distracted me so, and I always win when I am distracted—so I did not pay heed, and now I can't fit the coins in my reticule! Which doesn't signify because in fact I have managed to *lose* my reticule! That is something I cannot like at all, for I had a particularly devastating cologne in it that I intended to loan you for Lady Cowper's rout, besides my favorite French handkerchief that you mended so beautifully just yesterday.... In any case, I mean to say, could you just carry my coins for me awhile? They are all *over* the table, which I find a most *vulgar* sight and like to make me sink. Furthermore, if I give you the funds, I shall very likely forget them, and you will keep them for me. Whereas if *I* had them, it would all be spent by tomorrow, very probably on something I shall find a month hence that I don't like at all, and—oh, *will* you?"

Hersington was vastly amused by this artless recital. But for some reason, Miss Trahern seemed perturbed. Evidently she did not like the idea of husbanding Lady Staventry's money.

"Perhaps I could help you ladies by . . ." He had been going to suggest calling a menial to transport the coins. A sudden beseeching look from Almeria made him change the end of the sentence smoothly to "escorting you to the card room."

And he did so in great style, with a lady on each arm. On one side he received a battery of grateful glances from Lady Staventry. On the other, through her conventional chatter, he could sense Miss Trahern's well-concealed agitation by the occasional trembling of her fingers against his coat. As they regimented a truly astounding pile of guineas, the earl received their assent to his intention to call the next day. They departed soon afterwards.

After that, the evening held no charm for Hersington. He was more interested in Miss Trahern and her story than he had been in anything for years; so much so that Tom Crowley was reduced to running after my lord's carriage, so as not to be left behind.

9

HERSINGTON ARRIVED THE next day at the gatehouse of Staventry. At first he thought it a wasted errand. Miss Trahern was receiving, to be sure. She was in fact surrounded by a bevy of the fashionable, the foolish, and the merely lovelorn. But her manner was listless and her greeting to him rather lacklustre.

Almeria, doing honors as chaperone, greeted him kindly, however. So he elected to remove himself to the furthest armchair and look about him.

The Earl of Kentsey was agreeably surprised by the changes in the house. He could not help contrasting it with the state of Mrs. Bostram's after Miss Trahern's departure. Everything here was clean and orderly, the cats were not in evidence, and even the tea had altered for the better. Lady Staventry was of course as witless as always. But she was unwontedly neat in her person, and addressed Miss Trahern with the greatest affection. He was also amused to see that Tom Crowley was present. The boy had insinuated himself near Lucy's side. It seemed he was earnestly entreating her to take a turn with him in the park.

"I say, Tom, that is too bad of you!" protested one fellow. "You have stolen a march on us by your prior knowledge of the lady. And now you are going to elbow us out because your greys are the most bang-up set of blood and bone represented in this room!"

"Coming it rather strong, Freton," said the earl goodnaturedly. Everyone in the room looked around. "I picked those horses for my nephew myself. And I know for a fact they are not the match of the blood chestnuts I have standing just out of doors."

There was a good deal of chaffing and joking at this, and Freton admitted he must consider himself rolled up. They might as well take their leave and have done, he said.

Hersington approached Lucy's chair and stood smiling over her. "What say you, Miss Trahern? Shall I depress these striplings' pretensions and drive you round Hyde Park?" And then, as she hesitated, "But no, I had forgot. You do not care for earls."

At this, her lassitude vanished and she smiled. "You wrong me, sir. I find lack of variety of all things most tedious. It is *uncles* that bore me today."

The earl turned his head to his nephew. "Do you hear that, Thomas? You may henceforth consider yourself cast off!"

"With pleasure," said Crowley. "How should I want to be attached to someone with so little conscience? You are not being at all sporting, you know." Shortly thereafter, the visitors, collectively, took their departure, until only the earl remained.

"Well?" He grinned down at Lucy quizzically. "I have thrown off my relations for your sake, Miss Trahern. Am I to be rewarded?"

She consented and followed him out the door, stopping only to don her pelisse and bonnet.

The horses were indeed a very fine pair, and Lucy halted to admire their points at length. " 'Complete to a shade,' " she quoted under her breath. " 'Slap up to the echo.' " And she hopped up on the perch of the phaeton with no help from her escort.

Hersington followed rather more demurely, smiling to himself. She gave herself away in a fashion, this woman. He distinctly recognised that phrase as being one of Master Hyde Bostram's.

He was fully occupied with the reins as they negotiated

their way to the park. Lucy seemed to have fallen back into her abstraction. Her face had relaxed into sad, thoughtful lines. Having gained the carriage ways in the park, Jasper decided to recall her from her distance.

"We are now in Hyde Park proper," he declaimed, "where it is considered bad ton to indulge in a brown study. It is obligatory that we make light, frivolous, thoroughly inconsequential conversation." He now had her full attention. "What shall we discuss? The weather, which is boringly beautiful? The crowd, which is uniformly dull? Your bonnet, which you are probably well aware is fetching?" She chuckled. "No? None of these? Suppose I start then by complimenting your rout of the odious Huston last evening? I was pleasantly surprised, you know. You rolled him up horse, foot, and guns!"

She arched one eyebrow. "You are pleased to make mock of me, sir. Nevertheless, I may not be sorry. I cannot account that as wit which depends on the outfacing of others."

"I am quite in agreement with you," he said seriously. "I intended no mockery, please believe me."

"I am glad," she sighed. "For truly, I could not keep my tongue between my teeth when he lit on Aunt Almeria that way. She cannot defend herself, you know. And she is the dearest soul, however totty-headed. I could not see her so insulted."

"You love your aunts," he observed.

"More than that." She turned her palms over and studied them. "I owe them everything. I would be—I do not like to think where—without their kindness."

"Was the country then so intolerable?" he teased gently, reminding her of her story.

"Oh no!" She regained her bantering tone. "Aunt Almeria and Aunt Natalie have some maggot in their heads that I was becoming too old to marry. I am all of two-and-twenty. An ape leader, you are thinking?"

"Quite," Hersington replied in kind. "You must accept any offer that is forthcoming; even if it is from an earl!"

"A fate worse than death. No, it is all very silly." She shook her head. "Why should I tease myself whether I marry this year or next, or indeed at all? A woman can surely find other occupations, even in the country!"

"So you are not bowled off your feet by the cream of society? I should think a country girl would be dazzled by the endless amusements and the glittering gallants."

"Perhaps I would be, had I found any sincerity or intellect among them. Bunch of fribbles," she said darkly. And then, recollecting herself, "Oh! I beg your pardon! I am being very uncivil, am I not?"

"Not at all," said Hersington calmly, hiding a smile. "I collect I am excluded from the list, since I am your auditor. Where," he asked wickedly, "did you pick up a word like 'fribbles'? And I am certain you characterised my cattle as 'slap up to the echo'?"

"Oh!" She coloured. "Am I doing it again? It was the children. I picked it up from them."

"What children do you mean?" he asked softly.

She shifted her seat uneasily. "Oh—that is—in the village, you know. Sometimes I used to mind them for their mothers, and. . . ."

"The village of . . . ?"

"Winton. In Shropshire." She invented hastily, acutely uncomfortable and quite red.

His voice was exceedingly gentle. "Do you know, I find it most reassuring to find out so early in our acquaintance how impossible you find it to tell a lie with any conviction?"

She stared at him in consternation.

"Please don't be alarmed," he went on, taking a corner with practised ease. "Nor tax your imagination further by thinking of other details. I'm very much more than seven, you know. I was aware, when you were pointed out to me as 'The Mysterious Original,' that there was more to your story than you cared to tell. I don't think the less of you for it. I expect, in fact, that you are protecting somebody, and I honour that."

She was still silent. Bemused.

"Nor do I intend to press you. You need never tell me anything. I merely wanted you to know that, should your situation become untenable, there is one person willing to count himself your friend. You need never cut a wheedle for my benefit."

His voice was so assured that there seemed no point in denial. "Thank you," she said faintly. "Does, does everybody know? I confess I thought I had covered my tracks rather finely."

"No." He gave her a mischievous grin. "And you mustn't insult me so! I preen myself I am uncommonly clever, Miss Trahern! I doubt anyone else in London has looked past the fact that you are a reputed heiress!"

This had the desired effect. Miss Trahern sat up and said in tones of outrage, "They are *not* still saying that!"

"To be sure, they are," he replied affably.

Lucy started gripping her hands and muttering under her breath. "Pickled," she said at last. "That's the only solution. I shall *pickle* the cats and put them in an *omelette!*"

"Excuse me, but do you intend to feed this novel breakfast to *all* of London?"

"No," she said savagely. "Only to my aunts!"

"Ah, I see." He nodded. He was incredibly diverted, but chose not to show it. "I am afraid that would be a miscarriage of justice. It is not your aunts who are bruiting this story about, you see, but the whole of the upper class. I believe it started with the Countess Lieven, however. You might try your gourmet ideas on her."

Lucy made a little, choked sound. Then suddenly burst out laughing. "Oh, *do* give me the reins, your lordship! This conversation is not going at all as I expected, and I do not know if I am glad or sorry. But I am sure that if I do not have an occupation—and speedily—I shall fall neatly off this seat and into a bramble!"

Obligingly (and to the astonishment of everyone in sight) he handed her the ribbons. Such a thing had never been seen in Hyde Park. The Earl of Kentsey had always been markedly jealous of his driving skill, never entrusting his horses' mouths to anyone but Morton.

They took another turn round the park before he decided it was time to start back.

"You handled them very creditably," he told Lucy, surprising himself further. "By the by, what upset you so about doing Lady Staventry that small service last night?"

Lucy scowled. "It was a ruse. They keep trying to give me money. I have told them and told them that an introduction to London is quite as much, and a good deal more, than I should accept. But they keep trying to foist cash on me, not very subtly, or with any great result. Were Almeria to look for her winnings six months hence, she would find them intact to the penny. She is already upset that I will not let her buy me clothes, but insist on wearing my own."

"And very becoming, too," he said with approval.

"They are from my father's last run of good luck. Long over. If my suitors knew, they would disappear in a trice! And I should miss them most pleasantly. I tell you, you can have no idea how despicable it is to be pursued only for one's wealth."

"Strangely enough," he said with a grim smile, "I rather think I know *exactly* what that is like."

They alighted at her door nearly an hour after they had left. Lucy's goodbye was rather tremulous and uncertain. He saw the doubt under her thank-yous, and stilled her hand in his own.

"Please don't be afraid," he said. "I merely wanted you to know that you are not alone. We need never speak of it again, if you wish."

"You are too kind." Lucy dropped her eyes. "I—I do not know what to say."

"Then don't say anything," he counselled. "Go back inside, sit down, have tea, and tell amusing stories to your Two Graces."

"My—what?"

"Oh, did you not know? You are not the only one in London with a colourful nickname. Brace yourself, Miss Trahern. Your two kind patronesses are known throughout the fashionable world as 'The Terror and The Twit.' "

And on a wave of laughter as warming as it was relaxing, Lucy abandoned her fears and stepped inside.

However much the earl might know, there was one fact of which he alone in London was ignorant. That fact was his own nickname: The Enigma. All the while that he had tooled Lucy through the park, he was being discussed by this sobriquet, and his nephew Tom became the target of his companions' disgruntled questions.

"What on earth does the Enigma want with the Mystery?" Freton demanded hotly.

" 'Faith, one must admit 'tis poetic justice," commented one young blood.

"It's no sort of justice at all!" Freton countered. "He could have any female he wants, and has refused them all these last several Seasons. Why should he suddenly try to attach Miss Trahern? It's passing strange, Tom. I wish you will enlighten us."

"Oh, there's nothing to tell," said Tom cautiously. "I'm sure his interest is strictly,"—he groped for a word—"avuncular."

"The Devil you say! The way he looked at her—well, I only hope you may be right. A fine thing it would be, if he carried her out from under our noses. *He* don't need the money!"

"Is that all your interest in Miss Trahern?" Tom asked distastefully. "I doubt that wouldn't recommend itself to her, you know. She is a very plain girl, when all is told."

"Plain!" It was Havenham, the young man who had

spoken before. "Well, I like that! She's the prettiest piece I've set eyes on this year! Not but what, if you mean she's simple-spoken and don't put on airs, I agree with you."

"That's precisely what I do mean. And I know for a fact she doesn't care two pins for money, or people who chase it."

"Easy for her to say," Freton scorned. "With how-many-thousand pounds and a mansion back of her. Oh, you needn't look so Friday-faced, Crowley. It's the way of the world after all, and how's a man to raise the wind 'thout an heiress or a repairing lease? And come to think of it, becoming tenant-for-life is both!"

He laughed long at his own mild joke, then went on when he saw no response. "Besides, I like her well enough. By heaven, I do! I daresay if it weren't for this damned spider I've swallowed, I'd have her even if she was penniless. She's something above the common cut," he said with unusual thoughtfulness. "Still the question is not whether I'll have her, but she me. Tell, Thomas, it ain't true she don't like dandies?" He was anxious. "I heard some Banbury tale that you changed your cloth for her, and now she likes you the better. It's a clanker, isn't it?" he beseeched.

Havenham laughed. "It's true enough, man. I was there. You might as well throw away your pretensions to the fair Original's hand unless you also throw away your ornaments."

Freton looked down wistfully at his accoutrements and sighed. He adored his one silver spur, his fantastical silk waistcoats, his intricate ties and the life-saving buckram wadding. It would go hard with him to give them up.

"You don't think it's too loud?" he asked plaintively, glancing sidelong at Crowley's modest assemblage.

"I don't, but Miss Trahern will," Tom answered uncompromisingly.

"I must go see my tailor at once," said Freton sadly. And he minced off, prepared to martyr himself for what he was pleased to call Love.

* * *

Meanwhile, Lucy had returned home and was sitting cozily with Almeria.

"Well, and did you have a nice drive with Hersington? Such a *fine* young man, with such address! I am very pleased that he came to call. He always was a well-favoured boy. How nicely he's grown up!

"You must tell me, when he proposes to you, whether he presents you with a rose and drops to one knee. His father did so. I expect they are much alike."

Ignoring the impropriety of discussing Hersington's possible proposal, Lucy latched onto the latter part of Almeria's speech. "His father—but my dear ma'am, I had thought you and Hersington of an age!"

"Goodness, gracious, *no!* Lucy, how unkind. Hersington is a very *adult* sort of person, I own. But to say that he looks all of sixty is a monstrous plumper!"

"Pray, Almeria, why should I think the earl sixty?"

"Why, because *I* am sixty, and you said we were *contemporaries.*"

"Here's a lookout! I have been paying the windiest compliment all this while, and all unknowing! My dear Aunt, I had made sure you were forty or forty-five at the best of it!"

Almeria turned pink with pleasure.

Natalie strode into the room here, and commandeered the entire loveseat for her voluminous black velvet skirts. "What's all this about the Earl of Kentsey?" Natalie was a shameless eavesdropper and never made any bones about it.

"Oh, the most *exciting* thing!" Almeria replied. "Lucy has been driving out with Hersington, who stole her right away from her admirers as if they had been so many strawmen, and kept her above half an hour. It is the most *distinguishing* attention, and I have great hopes of it. Except, excuse me, Nat, but Hersington said the oddest thing before he left.

He said to Lucy that she probably would not drive with him as he knew she did not like earls. Do you know what he meant?

"For if it's *true*, Lucy dear, I know not what to say. You are a sweet child of course, and I suppose may look as high as you like with our backing, but do you really wish to dismiss earls out of hand? Some of them are rather nice, you know; and we do not *know* that a duke or a marquis will offer for you. Indeed, I believe you ought to reconsider," she ended anxiously.

Lucy stifled a giggle. "Never trouble yourself, Aunt. It was a jest, merely. However, you had best dismiss your notions of matching me to an earl or anybody else. It is most lowering," she said wryly. "But any fool could see that the bucks dangling after me are to a man interested in my supposed fortune rather than my beautiful person."

"I don't know that," Natalie averred. "Did you mark how Havenham toned down his dress this morning? As I read it, that's a direct reaction to your set-down of the dandies last night. Family's pretty well set up, too, y'know. Shouldn't think he'd be wanting for the ready.

"And I'd lay odds he's not the only one. How many swains have you got, my girl? Knocker's never been still since your debut. Can't all of 'em be rakes and rattles. Must be someone in there you like. Mind, I ain't pressing you to get leg-shackled. But what's to stop you if you meet a good honest man?"

Lucy turned sober brown eyes on her. "Even if I were to become attached to someone, ma'am, I could not in all conscience agree to an engagement. What would he think when he found my true estate? How much regard could such a man as you describe retain for me?"

"There you have it, girl," the duchess cackled. "The perfect way of separating the wheat from the chaff! If the fortune hunters press you, you have only to tell the truth and they'll do a bolt. But a man who's sincerely attached won't give a snap of his fingers for it."

"I can't agree. I find all these attentions highly awkward."

"Bah! Quit quibbling, Lucille. You are in the best of all possible circumstances. You know how to tell the bad'uns apart, and can snap your fingers at the lot of 'em. *We're* not going to throw you off, so you won't starve. And when the Season's over, if you're still of the same mind, your father will be back to carry you off.

"All this puffery about you being a governess! Nobody's guessed it yet, have they? So what're you worried about!"

"Actually," said Lucy slowly, playing with one dark curl, "someone has." She gave a nervous laugh. "Well, not the *governess* part, precisely. But that I am not quite what I seem."

Natalie's brows snapped blackly together. "Who?" she rapped out.

"It was the Earl of Kentsey, actually," Lucy said reluctantly. She had not really meant to tell her aunts this.

Natalie drummed her fingers on her snuffbox, muttering about "inside information," which made no sense to Lucy.

"That coxcomb! Throwing it up to you! I'll see him hung!"

"No, you misapprehend," said Lucy, quick in his defense. "He was very civil and asked no questions whatever. He merely told me that he could see I was in an unusual situation. He wanted me to know that if things became difficult he would stand my friend. In truth, I thought it most generous. He could, instead, have ruined me."

"Hmmm." Natalie digested this. "Still don't like it. Hersington. Not a good stable, with that queer brother and the mother that ran off to the Continent and was never heard from again."

"Oh, Nat, how can you say so?" Almeria protested. "Why you *know* that the elder Hersington was one of my own suitors, and Papa approved of him excessively."

"And we know what came of *that!*" said the Dowager sarcastically. Catching Lucy's questioning look, she said,

"But that's neither here nor there. Truth is, I have no opinion of the current earl. Next time he calls, I want to speak to that young whelp."

"I wish you will not," said Lucy. The idea of Natalie grilling her kind friend filled her with dismay.

"If wishes were horses, all men would ride," replied Natalie loftily. And nothing else could be got out of her. So Lucy sighed, shook her curls, and went to prepare nuncheon.

To Lucy's dismay, Hersington did call the next day. Most unfortunately she and Natalie were alone in the parlour to receive him. Natalie did not even wait for the amenities, but attacked directly.

"Young man, I have a bone to pick with you, and I want a straight answer. Did you kill your brother?"

Lucy was relieved to see that Hersington did not seem in the least affronted. Instead, the laughter she already recognized bloomed in his eyes.

He made the Duchess an elegant bow, and said in the most affable tones imaginable, "No, ma'am, I did not. It was quite his own idea, I assure you. However," he added consolingly, "if he had possessed your manners, I might have."

There was an instant's silence as they faced off—the one cool and elegant and masculine, the other slightly taller, but raddled. Lucy knew her Aunt, however, and she burst into peals of laughter.

"By God, he's done you, Natalie! Picqued, repicqued, slammed, and capotted!"

Natalie tried to hide her smile, and failed. "No respect in my own house," she grumbled. "Get you gone, Lucille. His lordship and I have things to discuss. Oh, no need to fear for him," she warned as Lucy made to protest. "He's not a coward, at all events."

She stood up uncertainly. Hersington smiled down at her—one of the few men who could do so, for she generally towered above her partners. "Do you be easy," he reassured her. "I have survived rakings aplenty in my time."

And with that she had to be content.

They were closeted well over an hour. Lucy was relieved to see when Hersington emerged that he seemed to be in good humour. She could not forbear going to him and asking him how he had fared.

That tawny face looked down at her with an enigmatic expression. The sculptured mouth was firm. But demons were dancing in his eyes again.

"You wrong your aunt, surely, Miss Trahern? We dealt extremely, I assure you. Having decided that I am neither a fribble nor a thatch-gallows, the duchess is quite satisfied that I should call."

Lucy had no trouble recognising these epithets as a direct quote. A slow smile swept over her face. Hersington could not help thinking her countenance particularly ravishing when writ large with mischief.

"I can see she was on her best behaviour with you! You handled her very well. She is not bad at heart, you know. She merely likes to spar."

"Never fear, Miss Trahern. My father knew these women well. He coached me as to their characters. Indeed, I think rather better of your mentors after this interview than the reverse. They are so careful for you! But tell me," he said, ruthlessly changing the subject. "Do you attend Lady Huntingdon's ball tonight? Good. I look to see you there. And perhaps claim the honour of the first waltz, since I was cheated of my intent to speak with you today?"

Miss Trahern assenting, Lord Hersington took his leave. And Lucy was left to wonder, all the rest of that long day, what on earth the pair had found to talk about for so long.

10

Lady Huntingdon's ball was destined to be a memorable evening on more than one count.

First of all, there was the entertainment, which was lavish and lengthy. A very superior orchestra played for the dancers, who covered every inch of the polished marble floor. Festoons of lilies bedecked the pillars and twined up the walls on artificial trellises, kept fresh by man-made pools at their feet from which an ingenious device sprayed a soft stream of droplets upwards (these being lighted from behind to ethereal shades of blue and pink and lavender).

Nor had the comfort of non-dancing guests been neglected. The library had been set aside for the gentlemen and supplied with fine cigars and brandy. The card room was spacious, with resources for every conceivable game of chance. Lady Huntingdon had even provided her own bank, a bold move which met with raised eyebrows and, perversely, almost universal approval. There were, in addition, several retiring rooms for ladies of limited stamina, liberally stocked with hartshorn, feathers for burning, vinaigrettes, lavender water for migraines, and, for the more intrepid, a supply of pins for defecting flounces.

There was also to be a lavish supper later in the evening. Further, guests were invited by the open terrace doors to stroll out into the garden, charmingly lit by Chinese lanterns, and lose themselves in the shrubbery if they so desired. More than one practiced roué eyed with approval the tiny pagodas and secluded alcoves dimly visible in a light low enough to encourage blandishments of the most improper sort.

With a genius that had her aunts nodding approval and her rivals grinding their teeth in rage, Lucy managed to stand out even in this lush setting. The types of female dress around her divided into two distinct categories. The young hopefuls were all attired in variations of the theme of muslin, pastels, and innocence; the daring ones might wear a gauze overskirt. They wore ribbons, flowers, perhaps pearls; but never, under any circumstance, jewels. The married or widowed ladies had considerably more freedom (their morals being presumed, though often unjustly, to be above question), and most of them took this license to its extremes. Some of them were only saved from vulgarity by the fact of their indisputable wealth. This was the demesne of satins, brocades, velvets, alarmingly low necklines, ostrich plumes, garish jewels, and—if one would but admit it—paint! Not all the women dressed so ostentatiously. And not all the misses were bland. But the line was there, and none dared step across.

Except Lucy. Wouldn't you just know it? thought Clarissa Stirlan viciously. That *fiend!* Lucy had dared to wear silk, with an overskirt of silver threads so loosely woven as to almost seem a shawl. The silk, on a less clever woman, would have damned her as fast. But the cut of the dress was utterly simple, the neck high, and the hue a most delicate, virginal lavender. Moreover, she had taken care to wear not so much as a ribbon or a rose. Only two tiny pearls in her ears, peeping beneath her ringlets of dark hair, gave her ornament. Her gloves and shoes were both a plain, simple white. Lucy had managed, in fact, to be devastating, bold, and absolutely unexceptional. It was too provoking! Clarissa greeted her with a sugary smile and fervently wished her at Jericho. She cursed the impulse that had made *her* wear white muslin, believing she would stand out with refreshing innocence from the modish throng.

If Clarissa imagined that her chagrin had reached its

height, she was soon to be disillusioned. She had only just soothed her feathers with a few veiled comments about silk and loose women when the Earl of Kentsey came up to Miss Trahern and claimed his promised dance.

She did not, of course, (Clarissa told herself) care two pins for his enigmatical lordship! True, perhaps she had once fancied him a trifle, but she had been very much mistaken in him. She had soon shaken off the toils of such a mésalliance. No doubt Miss Trahern would find this, to her cost. So saying, with a notably set smile, she accepted the first offer and joined the floor.

Meanwhile, Hersington was laughing down into Lucy's upturned face. "Why so grave, Miss Trahern? You see that I survived whole and sound from my encounter with your fearsome guardian. Should I be insulted? Have you so little faith in my ability at tilting swords?"

His light tone put her at ease, and she smiled back. "I see no reason why you should be able to oppose her when her husband could not!"

"How is this?"

"Oh, 'tis a most diverting story. I only wish I knew the whole. But it seems that Natalie, having no fortune of her own (it all being left to Almeria) was obliged to marry money. What transpired, however, was that she found His Grace the Duke of Bucklass prodigiously tedious. So she had to, and I quote, 'pack him off to the Continent' because he bored her so!"

Hersington gave an appreciative grin, and whirled her around with greater vigour. "One can easily imagine it! If I did not know the Terror, I should think him a weak sort of fellow. After all, he held the purse strings. And a lord's rights over his lady."

"She must have made it worth his while to leave," Lucy concurred. "Only consider, my lord. At that time Napoleon was surely still at large. What inducements must have driven him to Europe!"

"I imagine," he said idly, "that you could answer that as

well as anyone. Yet you are still here. May I congratulate you on your bravery, Miss Trahern."

"You may not!" said Lucy tartly. "For you survived her yourself. And I positively *will* not be caught exchanging compliments with an earl all evening!"

He removed his hand from her waist for a moment to playfully flick her nose. "Very well, termagant! Let us pick another topic."

Lucy, not sure what to think of this fond gesture, decided to ignore it. "Ah, but you have not heard the cream of the jest, sir! The sequel is almost better than the story. For at the vanquished duke's demise, he left her all his money to the last shilling, because 'she was better able to handle it than anyone.' Is that not the crowning absurdity?"

The music had ended. He held her in the crook of his arm a moment longer and agreed. "I cannot conceive a more abject admission of surrender."

Lucy's court was forming already, Clarissa among them. She overheard the last remark. "What, prating of surrender already? Lucille, surely you cannot fall so readily to our careless-hearted Hersington? I had thought you made of sterner stuff!" The teasing note was underlaid with a trace of lemon.

The earl replied for her. "Nothing so fortunate, Miss Stirlan. I would not dream of besieging Miss Trahern, vain as it would be. She does not like earls, you know." And with this, he took himself fairly off, leaving Clarissa gaping.

"What on *earth* did the odd creature mean?"

And Lucy, liking her shadow less than ever, said sweetly, "Why, only what he said. I have no taste for earls. I intend to hold out for a marquis at the very least of it." She turned to her admirers, leaving Clarissa flabbergasted.

And angry. That little *nobody*, jumped up from God-knew-where, hanging out for a coronet? Preposterous! The *effrontery* of the creature. No, this could not be borne. She would have to find some way of cutting Miss Trahern's traces. Permanently.

124

* * *

Miss Trahern was unaware that she had just made an enemy. And if she had known, she might not have cared. She had always realised that Clarissa's regard was spurious, holding more than a little jealousy and spite. If she had thought about it, she would have said that between the Staventry backing and Crowley's silence, Clarissa could not possibly harm her.

This may have been true. But Lucy was about to acquire another enemy, a much more powerful one. And while she could not be held accountable for Clarissa's hatred, for this latter Lucy was more than a little responsible.

First, however, she had to run a gauntlet as touching as it was amusing. For it was at Lady Huntingdon's singular ball that Lucy received her first proposal.

This came about in a surprising way. Lucy was dancing when Lord Freton, oddly heavy on his feet for such a noted Tulip, trod on her flounces and tore them. He insisted on accompanying her to a retiring room to repair them, and as soon as the business was done, astonished her by sinking to one knee and making an offer in form.

It was not of course unusual in that day and age for a young man to take such a resolve after a mere three-and-a-half weeks of acquaintance. However, as Lucy had never made any distinguishing returns in his direction, never once riding out in his curricle, she was a good deal taken aback.

What she did not realise was that Hersington's advances had considerably discomposed Lord Freton, and he meant to take his chance before her head was turned. He would never have understood that such measures as Hersington's higher rank would never have weighed with a woman such as Lucy.

Thinking quickly, and rather ruefully, Lucy decided on the best tack to take.

"My dear Lord Freton," she told him gently, "I think perhaps you had better be standing for my reply."

She gave him her hand and he did rise, saying sadly, "I suppose that means your answer is no."

"Well, I would not have put it so bluntly. Indeed, I am most honoured and moved by your regard. But I think, on balance, that we should not suit."

Freton looked balefully down at his waistcoat. "I *knew* it was too loud," he muttered. "But I could change for your sake, my heart. 'Pon honour I could! I do not even think I should mind it . . . much."

Lucy concealed her smile and answered with aplomb. "It is generous of you to say so, sir. I doubt it would not be worth your while. There is—" she turned her back and paced the room, wondering how to approach this without offence. "There is a fact perhaps I should apprise you of. You had no doubt heard the rumours that I am—forgive me for broaching such a delicate subject—a very great heiress. This is, how shall I say, not quite the sober truth?"

"Do you tell me it's all a hum?" Freton's jaw dropped.

"Well, no, not precisely." Lucy hurried to assure him. She well knew what would become of her if such a tale made the rounds. "But the mere fact of a marriage between us, however happy it might be, would not automatically make all high tide with you."

"Are you saying that your prospects have been . . . exaggerated?"

"Just so," she said with relief. Then, as his face darkened, "Understand me. I do not by any means imply that you are a fortune hunter. I am sure your regard is sincere and deeply rooted. But you are a man of the world," she went on conspiratorially. "You know, as do I, that mere sentimental considerations cannot weigh against the practicalities of a lifetime. I would not, for any cause, wish to prejudice your chances. In future, I think, you will yet thank me for this relinquishment."

Deeply grateful for his timely rescue, Freton sank to one knee again and kissed her hand. "Dear—dearer than ever Miss Trahern! Your candour and nobility move me more than I can express! I need not tell you my heart is broken. But you are right—we must not let the fleeting spectre of a present happiness blind us to the vast horizon of the future."

"Precisely so," she said approvingly. "I knew that you, of all people, would understand. And that is why I ventured to speak so boldly to you. I do you the honour, you see, of assuming you will be as careful of my prospects. For I need not tell you they would be sadly damaged were this tale to get about."

Much struck, Freton rose and exclaimed, "Why, of course! My wise mentor, take no more thought about it! I shall be as silent as the grave!"

"I knew I could rely on you," she sighed languishingly. Inwardly, she was giggling, but no trace of this appeared on her face. "I feel sure that our regard, though thus prevented from becoming something warmer, can ripen into an easy friendship."

"I am yours to command," he bowed with a flourish. "Only tell me how I may serve you."

She removed herself to a nearby couch, patting the opposite seat invitingly. He complied.

"You may do so easily," she said, "though I would ask it of no other."

He beamed at this mark of intimacy. "Only name it."

"I have it in mind to set up my own stable," she told him earnestly. "And you well know that the best place to start is Tattersall's. Equally, however, no lady may go there. And as my aunts do not keep servants, there is no one else I may send. Do I dare trust you to look out a suitable riding horse for me? Not a 'lady's horse,' mind, for I should detest a spiritless nag, and I know you would not hold me so cheap. But it must be trained to the sidesaddle, and not broken in wind or mouth; a Mamaluke-trained gelding, perhaps? But, there. I need not, I am persuaded, school *you* on your eye for horseflesh."

"Nothing easier done!" He was immensely flattered that

she should trust him on such a mission. "How much had you in mind to spend?"

"Oh, 150 pounds or thereabouts, I was thinking. Or is that too paltry a figure?" Lucy said this with an inner qualm. She knew her aunts would never begrudge the expense. Indeed, they had been teasing her this age to buy a horse. She had not intended to be beholden to them for such. But Lucy could think of no surer way to convince Freton (and thus the ton, for she had no reliance on his discretion) that her fortune, though smaller than gazetted, was quite real. She did not care for herself but for her aunts.

They discussed various points of horseflesh for some ten minutes and then returned to the dance floor. Freton reflected to himself that it was an odd thing, but he thought more highly of her than if she had actually said yes. If anybody was going to malign Miss Trahern, he decided, it would be over his dead body.

Well, maybe his slightly *wounded* body.

Lucy's adventures for the evening were by no means ended. After her interview with Freton, she danced until her feet were aching and the ballroom seemed too stuffy to bear. Suddenly the artificially watered lilies seemed not charming but cloying. She wanted nothing so much as to escape, if only for a few moments.

Accordingly, she sent her current escort off to get her an ice, and absconded to the terrace. No one was in sight. It was a simple matter to slip into the garden and lose herself in the sweet-scented, deserted walks.

The solitude was delicious. Lucy took deep breaths and long, slow steps. Oh, how crowded she had felt since the beginning of this interminable Season. How did people stand it, rout after rout, year after year? Well, she conceded wryly, it might not be so bad if one were really what one appeared to be.

At the thought, she stopped at the foot of a small lilypond. A sudden longing swept her to see the children again; to be with them in the nursery and explain patiently why they really must not build castles out of the crockery. Even with its exigencies, life had been rather simple when she was plain Lucy Trahern, with her bread to earn. It was not that anyone had been unkind. Indeed, they were far too kind, for all the wrong reasons. The honest snobbery of a Maria Bostram would be welcome now. She sighed, and twirled her silvergilt reticule on its chain.

"Dreaming, most beauteous Miss Trahern?" came an unwelcome voice from behind her. She whirled to confront the insinuating smile of Beau Huston.

"No. Merely escaping," she said coldly. "I needed a breath of fresh air and a respite from my pressing court."

"But how can you wish to elude them when they all admire you so sincerely?"

She was not in the mood for this pretty fencing. "Oh, if I could believe they meant a word of it!" she scoffed on a bitter note. "But I am no fool, my lord, whatever you may think me. I see the clink of coin in their eyes."

To her distaste he moved closer, his breath brushing her face. She smelled cloves and pomade and brandy.

"Not all of them are of that stamp, surely," he purred. "Some, as I, must surely admire your person to the exclusion of your other attributes."

"Do you? That's refreshing," she said lightly. She was beginning to wish she had not come out alone. She could see Beau Huston's face quite clearly in the moonlight. Strangely, that half-light seemed to reveal things about his character that she had only sensed before.

She had never liked Huston, and not just because he was a fop. He was handsome. He had a title, and a respectable fortune. But he was arrogant and rude. Now, his long, elegant face seemed to evince only the most trivial boredom with yet one more idle flirtation. But under those sleepily drooping lids, the grey eyes glittered in a disturbingly predatory way. Beau Huston was a man who believed in conquest, not love.

"You do not sound as you much believe me, Miss Trahern. Allow me to prove myself to you." And so saying, he seized her and tried to kiss her.

Lucy had not been quick enough to elude his grasp. But she deftly turned her head to one side. Unwisely, Beau Huston persisted, releasing one hand from her waist in order to try and imprison her chin.

Lucy had only been annoyed before. Could the gentlemen of London think of nothing but forcing kisses on her? When Huston persevered, however, she became frankly angry. "Oh, really!" she ejaculated in disgust. And with a mighty heave, she pushed him into the pond.

His shrieks and ungainly flounderings soothed her soul, and she broke into peals of laughter.

A cultured voice broke into her amusement. "I think this most uncivil of you, Miss Trahern."

Looking behind her, Lucy spied Hersington sauntering up the path towards her, twirling his quizzing glass.

"Well, I do not!" she told him roundly. "It serves him richly right!"

"I could not agree with you more. It was not Huston's punishment to which I was referring. I have always had a fancy to rescue a damsel in distress," he said musingly, "which is what you seemed to be a moment since. I was ready—nay, eager—to come to your aid. But you have extracted yourself most capably. I take it ill of you, Miss Trahern," he said severely, "since this was very likely my only chance."

"Oh, I do beg your pardon," Lucy said contritely. "If I had known you were hanging about no doubt I would have constrained myself; even if it did mean he would have actually kissed me," she added magnanimously.

"That is a very handsome apology. I believe I will accept

it if you will also do me the honour of escorting me back to the ballroom."

They paid no attention to Huston, now climbing soddenly and with many an oath out of the muddy pond.

"With pleasure, my lord," she responded, making Hersington a curtsey. He took her arm and began to lead her off. Stopped, looked over his shoulder.

"A word of advice, Huston. Next time you want to assault a lady, make sure she is willing. A lady compromised against her will is not compromised at all." They strolled towards the sound of music.

Hersington looked down at Lucy's pure, strong profile. Her dark curls shone in the moonlight; her determined chin and flashing brown eyes belied a certain dangerous innocence. He felt moved to give her a warning. "You realise, don't you, that you have made the most sincere of enemies tonight? Huston will never forgive you for dunking his waistcoat."

"But it had coquelicot stripes!" objected Lucy.

"Precisely. If you had ruined his *lemon* waistcoat, he might, perhaps, have forgiven you."

"Much I should care! I hardly fear the enmity of that—that—park-saunterer!"

The earl hid a smile above her head. "You may have no opinion of Huston, but he could do you a mischief."

"Well now," said Lucy in hurt tones. "I vow I am mightily deceived in you, my lord! I had thought your credit high enough to extricate me from almost any scrape." Her voice was injured. "In fact, I was going to get into a few, just so as to avail myself of this license!"

"My *dear* Miss Trahern," he answered admiringly. "*That* was very well done. One would suppose you had been in the ton forever instead of a mere few weeks."

"Sometimes," Lucy groaned, "I feel as if I had!"

"Except for the small matter of your wandering about unescorted in the dark," Hersington reminded gently. "You really must not, you know. It gives rise to all sorts of unpleasant gossip, besides laying you open to just such attacks as Huston's. Forgive my strictures," he said kindly down to her indignant face. "I am only taking the privilege of a friend because I have your best interest at heart."

They had reached the edge of the terrace now. Lucy sighed and hung back. "I suppose you are right. No, I know you are. But must we return *just* yet?"

He gazed at her doubtfully for a moment. They were standing before the flagged stairs that led up to the terrace, which in turn opened into the ballroom. Large squares of light were laid over the garden from the French doors, and the music swirled and ebbed sweetly in the background.

Hersington led her to a stone bench only a few feet off the path. Since they were in full view, such a position was unexceptionable. Lucy would have preferred not to be so easily visible from the house, but she acquiesced, knowing this was the biggest concession she would get.

He saw her discontent as she settled herself, violet skirts softly rustling, and felt both concerned and touched. There she sat, in her fashionable gloves and reticule, her head, with its gleaming dark curls, lowered to let her stare into her trim lap, and probably a hundred desperate swains looking for her this very moment. Yet was she happy? He doubted it. There had been a glitter of moisture in those large eyes before she lowered them. Any other man would have thought her a very great fool. But the earl thought he understood. After all, what had this to do with any life she had ever known? Who here knew who she really was, or could enter into her sentiments? How could she really enjoy being petted and flattered when she knew herself to be living a lie? He suspected she would very much rather be wearing brown wool and bullying Maria's outrageous children. The earl was weary enough, himself, with insincere flattery to sympathise deeply. He felt very much drawn to this lonely girl—and admired her.

"Do you find it so very irksome, infant?" he asked softly.

She dashed a tear from her cheek surreptitiously and sat up straighter. "Oh, no! That is . . . I do not want to appear ungrateful. And it is a great opportunity for one such as myself, having a London Season, is it not? I only wish . . . that it had come about differently. That I could have appeared in my own character. Oh, I would have attracted a great deal less attention, no doubt. But I should have preferred that. At least it would be honest!"

"You are seeing the underside of the beau monde, rather," he admitted. "But don't you think you're underrating yourself a bit? It is true that a lot of the men are hymning your money rather than your beauty. However that does not, by itself, turn you into an antidote."

His rallying tone made her smile a little. "True," she said. "And it is not as if I dislike parties and society functions, although I believe," she went on thoughtfully, "that a little goes a long way with me in these matters. And you must admit," she teased him, "that Lord Freton would never have proposed to me in my natural person!"

"What? Never say so! That young dog? When?"

"Why, only tonight, to be sure." Lucy's brown eyes were dancing. "He was most excessively relieved when, after revealing that my fortune was not as large as he might have supposed, I graciously declined his flattering offer! I cared too much for his happiness," Lucy pronounced, striking a noble pose, "to wish to damage his future prospects."

A low chuckle escaped the earl. "Allow me to tell you, Miss Trahern, that you are the most complete hand!"

"Yes, and *you* are inconsistent, sir!" she countered. "For after telling me that I deserved some approbation from society, you are surprised that one of its members actually offered for me!"

Hersington arranged himself in a despondent attitude, hand on chin, and gave a deep sigh. "It is not that, oh estimable Miss Trahern—if only it were! You see before you a broken—nay, a destitute—man!" He returned to his normal pose, and said matter-of-factly, "I had placed a bet with Crowley that Freton wouldn't come up to scratch inside a week. I made sure he would wait for the new clothes from his tailor, you know. Now I am undone."

Lucy laughed heartily, but she was mildly shocked. "You do not tell me you lay wagers against your nephew? I am hardly in a position to lecture you, my lord, but only think how shocking if you had won. It would be said you were fleecing your own relatives."

"Nothing of the kind," said Hersington cheerfully. "It is merely strategy, my dear. We have agreed between us on a certain game. Bets are to be made on any suitable subject, no money to change hands but a record kept. A particular sum—which I will not divulge to you—is the final object. When Crowley owes me that sum, he is to go to Cambridge. If he wins first, he becomes a man of the town. It is amusing, and makes him feel he has a sporting chance; I shall never allow him to beat me, however. You have set me back several weeks, Miss Trahern." He looked at her quizzically. "Your charms for the dandy set must be even greater than I had supposed."

Lucy was greatly diverted by this odd scheme. She had been thinking carefully, though. "No. Do you know, I rather think you have beat yourself this time," she said consideringly.

"How so?"

"I should have agreed with you about Freton. I knew he was bound to propose, some weeks hence, but could not quite get up the courage. Then you appeared in my drawing room—and not twenty-four hours later he is brought to the sticking point! In fact," she ended, satisfied with her logic, "the dandy set see you as the greatest possible rival. It's all humgudgeon, of course. *You* haven't been trying to kiss me in out-of-the-way nooks. Indeed," she added with twinkling eyes, "my feelings are deeply wounded. I am not sure I shall not go into a decline."

He reached up and playfully pinched her chin between his thumb and forefinger. His voice was lazy and teasing.

"My dear Mystery, you do yourself a sad injustice. How do you know I have not been wanting to kiss you this hour and more? Just because I am a gentleman of scruples does not mean I am any less a man. And that you are a different woman than you seem does not make you any less a woman."

To her relief, he suddenly dropped his hand and regained a matter-of-fact voice. "Besides, I am in mortal fear of that horsepond! You had better stop blushing this instant. Miss Stirlan is approaching us, and she would surely notice. I fancy she would be only too happy to ruin both our reputations."

"Oh, does she hate you too?" Lucy made a game attempt to pretend nothing had happened. "I must congratulate you on your choice of enemies. I have been cordially disliking her ever since we met."

"Then she is a friend to neither of us," said Hersington with a quick, unreadable glance. "You because you stole her thunder, I collect. And I . . . because, when she set her cap at me, I knocked it over."

"Did you! Famous!" Lucy was delighted. So when Miss Stirlan did come up to them, little brown eyes darting suspiciously from face to face, she found only the friendliest laughter on either side.

"*There* you are, my dearest creature!" she effused. "Why, you have been gone quite this age. Your swains were despairing, and I have been in the most *dreadful* anxieties. But here you are with my lord Hersington! Only fancy! Quite the naughty girl as you are! I expect you have been wandering in the shrubbery, letting him turn your head."

"Nothing half so exciting," said the earl dampingly. "She was wandering in the shrubbery, certainly—and quite alone. I have been taking Miss Trahern to task for it this good long while, but I cannot knock any sense into her head. She will only laugh, and make jokes about it." This was to cover that last burst of chuckles Clarissa had witnessed.

"Indeed, he has been giving me the most dreadful scold," Lucy said with irritation, picking up his cue. "I am quite out of charity with him, for I had expected more out of the Wicked Earl. Instead, he says nothing but that I must go back to the dance, and not disappoint my partners."

"I think you ought," said Hersington repressively. "Pray, join your persuasions to mine, Miss Stirlan, so that I may stop playing this tiresome game of chaperone."

"Oh, yes, you *must* return, dear Lucy," she cooed. "It is *very* much more the thing. And we miss you quite sadly."

Lucy stood and shook out her skirts. "I do not see how I can refuse such a civil request. Let us, by all means, return."

Hersington gave an arm to each lady and this ill-assorted trio returned to the ballroom. Their appearance *in toto* scotched the tattle which was, indeed, beginning. Lucy had been missed. But Clarissa was not fooled by the seeming coldness of the couple's parting. Seething, she silently pledged vengeance.

Two miles away, Beau Huston, dripping in his carriage, was similarly occupied.

It remained only for these two newly vowed enemies to join forces. This happened almost immediately.

11

DURING THE SEASON, it is not unusual for the social elite to attend not one but two or three parties in a single evening. Many of these parties have substantially the same guest lists. Therefore it should surprise no one that our mismatched foursome—Huston, the Misses Trahern and Stirlan, and the Earl—were all present the next night at the soiree of His Grace the Duke of Parture.

Not that most of the guests cared a fig for the famous diva who had been engaged for the evening. Far from it. This was merely a cover for the animated scandalmongering which was the event's chief, if unmentioned, entertainment.

Clarissa had taken a leaf from Lucy's book and worn her mother's unexceptionable pale-green watered silk. She was certainly ravishing, the green a splendid foil for her Dresden face and fairylike silver-blonde hair. But the effect, which the evening before would have constituted a major triumph, was all too patently lost in light of Lucy's previous toilette. This was only exacerbated by the fact that Lucy had chosen to switch tactics tonight. Perhaps she was being excessively clever and squelching any lingering doubts about her virute. Or perhaps she was merely tired of her experiment and the comments it had engendered. In any case, she looked the complete miss in ivory muslin cut with a frothy, flouncy skirt and an enticing V neckline made acceptable by quantities of ruffled Brussels lace at hem and sleeves and bodice. Her Brutus had been allowed to fall free, with only a tendril or two pulled back about the ears to secure two perfect white rosebuds. Little satin ribbons trailed from her sleeves in knots, and she sported an exquisite sandalwood fan looped on one slender wrist. In short, she outshone Clarissa completely. This fact was borne in on Clarissa forcibly during the break (which had come, she felt, not a moment too soon!).

Lord Freton came and sat beside her, offering a glass of iced punch. They chatted desultorily for a few moments, and then Lord Freton revealed his real purpose in joining her.

"But where is Miss Trahern? I had made sure to find her somewhere in your vicinity."

Hiding her fury, Clarissa waved a hand airily. "Oh, she is about somewhere. I doubt she could not tear herself away from her numerous admirers."

"That is hardly a surprise," responded the young Tulip. "Your friend looks particularly *ravissant* tonight, do you not agree?"

"Of course," snapped Miss Stirlan, goaded beyond endurance. "When does she not! And I must own," she added slyly, regaining her control, "that she is very wise to do so, considering that shocking display last evening."

Freton's eyes went cold. "I do not perfectly understand you."

"Well!" A brittle laugh and a great deal of pretty play with her fan. "One must own it was vastly becoming to her, and I have even made so bold as to follow her lead tonight. But I cannot help reflecting that being the first debutante in the ton to wear silk—and in her first season, too!—is just a bit beyond the line of being pleasing."

"Miss Stirlan," said the man, very icily indeed, "Since I know you to be Miss Trahern's *friend*, I will not be so foolish as to take that remark in the spirit in which, from other lips, it would seem to have been uttered. I hold the highest possible esteem for the lady and should feel bound to issue a set down to anyone who held her otherwise."

The long flowing periods and serious censure from this milksop made Clarissa forget herself. She snapped her fan closed.

"Hold her in high esteem, do you?" she said venomously. "No doubt, since it is all Lombard Street to a China orange you mean to offer for her—or more exactly for her purse! You'll catch cold at that, I warn you! She means to hang out for a marquis at the very least of it. She told me so herself."

He looked down at her in tolerant contempt. "Shooting for a coronet, you think? My dear Miss Stirlan, if you were as well acquainted with the facts of her case as I am, you would drop that notion. I've no doubt Miss Trahern was bamming you.

"The aspersions on the sources of my own regard I shall pass over in silence. It may interest you to know, however, that I have already offered for her hand and been refused. And I may say that I hold her in somewhat higher regard than before." He paused to let this sink in, then bowed slightly. "Your servant, Miss Stirlan."

She watched him disappear towards the refreshment room with heightened colour, unconsciously crumpling her napkin in her hand. She did not notice when Beau Huston slithered into the gilt chair beside her.

He noted the direction of her eyes, and remarked lightly, "Are you admiring Miss Trahern's fetching rig?"

She turned sharply to him and spat, "The Devil fly away with Miss Trahern! I am heartily sick of her!"

"Can it be?" said Huston in mock surprise. "I had thought you the very picture of bosom beaus. No, no, do not fly out at me!" He held up his hands in self-defense. "I must say I am as pleased as I am surprised. It is refreshing to find that there is one person, at least, who has not been utterly taken in by her wiles."

It was Clarissa's turn to be surprised. "Why, I had thought you one of her most constant admirers!" she cried. "You are for ever hanging on her sleeve."

"One must observe the social niceties, must one not?" he

said smoothly. "Miss Trahern is all the rage, and one must make one's bow or be supposed an outcast. And perhaps I did fancy her at first," he said as Clarissa looked skeptical. "However, I soon found her not at all to my taste. I found on closer acquaintance that she is not at all the sort of female I admire."

"Nor I," nodded Clarissa eagerly, glad of a sympathetic ear. "As you say, one can hardly cut her acquaintance. But I cannot help feeling there is something about her that is ... not quite the thing. Hard though it goes with me to say so about anyone Lady Staventry and the Duchess of Bucklass choose to vouch for," she finished righteously.

"I could not agree with you more," he murmured, leaning closer. "It is amazing, is it not, how she has managed to fool them all to the top of their bent? One would think, as shady as her antecedents seem to be, that the leaders of society would have smoked her long since."

"Oh, yes! And some of her behaviour, I may tell you, is of the most questionable. Why, only last evening I found her sitting in a secluded alcove with Hersington, *quite* unaccompanied. He told me some Banbury tale of having found her pacing the grounds alone, and trying to represent the impropriety of such actions to her. She had been gone a good half hour and more, however, so I hardly believe *that*."

Her eyes were flashing. Huston took on an amused expression. "To think I had credited the earl with more imagination! He was only stealing my own story. It was in fact I who found Miss Trahern in the gardens—unchaperoned as you say—and tried to convince her to return. So far from listening to my importunities, she—but, stay! I should not say this to a lady." He paused expectantly.

Clarissa, breathing eager poison, urged him to tell her the whole. With a show of reluctance, Huston told her, "I ought not. Still, knowing so well your discretion, I shall say merely that she invited my attentions in the most brazen terms. I was quite at a loss when Hersington appeared, to my relief, and carried her off. My perturbation of mind was great, as you may imagine. I found myself quite unable to rejoin the festivities." This in case she had noticed and commented on his absence.

"No!" said Clarissa in tones of delighted revulsion. "One can't wonder at it if Hersington had greater success in that quarter, so bold as he is!"

"Do you know," he said with crafty strategy, "I have at last the answer to something that has puzzled me greatly. Not so very long ago, you yourself were going along prosperously with the earl."

Clarissa stiffened. Was he, perhaps, hinting that *she* had thrown herself at Hersington?

But Huston knew his business. He had put her in this pucker just so he could relieve it, simultaneously putting her in charity with him and giving her a new target.

"Indeed, we all believed he should settle down at last. But nothing came of it." He forestalled her angry words by saying, "I see now why. You are not—shall we say?—just in his style. It is obvious that he cannot appreciate a woman of taste and sensibility. He prefers, instead, the looser charms of such as Miss Trahern!"

He watched her narrowly after this stroke, and had the satisfaction of seeing her breast heave and her eyes sparkle.

"My lord, you are most perspicacious. That is just how it was! I may tell you that I was excessively relieved to be rid of his attentions, which were becoming too warm. Though Miss Trahern does not think so, they are not at all what would be acceptable to a lady of any breeding!"

"Just so," he said insinuatingly. "May I say that it is gratifying to at last meet a lady as intelligent as she is beautiful. It is the greatest pity that such as you must be forced to associate with . . . such as she. I do so wish there were some way to remedy the fault."

"Indeed," said Clarissa warmly. "It is a shocking take-in, and the haute monde would be very well shut of her. Why, she had the effrontery to tell me she held no brief for earls, but must needs look higher! Only to think of that bold piece in the nobility!"

"Do you know," said Huston as if suddenly struck, "I think we would be doing the highest favour to society if we could rid it of her presence."

"I have often thought so," Clarissa sighed. "But I do not see how it can be done. She is so firmly entrenched."

"It is merely to open their eyes to her true character," he suggested murmurously.

Clarissa drew herself up. "Surely you do not suggest," she said haughtily, "that I be involved in the blackening of a character?"

"But my dear lady, no! Nothing could be further from my meaning! I merely suggest that we tell the truth in certain quarters where it would be . . . appreciated."

"Not Freton," Clarissa remarked, falling into the spirit of this. "She is all in all to him, despite the fact that she has refused him. And indeed, she has not committed a major indiscretion."

"But she will," said Huston positively. "And we are bound to see it, if we keep our eyes open."

"I expect you are right," said Clarissa primly.

"Make sure I am. I believe we understand each other very well." He lifted her hand and kissed it. "Divine Miss Stirlan, please accept my compliments on your high principles and excellent grasp. May I hope to see you soon? Perhaps, if you would not mind it, I shall do myself the honour of calling in Berkeley Square."

Clarissa assented, thinking that really he was a most handsome and amiable gentleman. Odd that she had never thought of him in this light before. And the Huston fortune was not to be sneezed at, either.

Lucy, watching this exchange from across the room, thought that they would probably make a match of it. It had never struck her before she saw their shrewd, conspiring expressions, but they were quite remarkably alike.

* * *

Meanwhile, Lucy and Hersington were sitting out the break in a secluded corner. There was no impropriety in this, as Almeria sat in plain sight. Nor was there any surprise at their aloneness. Lucy's admirers had swiftly seen how the wind—as they thought—was blowing, and abandoned her as a lost cause when the earl was about.

After an animated discussion of the soprano, whom both of them, almost exclusively among the guests that evening, had enjoyed, Lucy had been so bold as to ask him about his brother.

"There are rumours that you were concerned in his death," she said frankly. "I know, of course, that *you* did not kill him, but what I cannot imagine is how such flummery came to be repeated in the first place."

He gazed at her quizzically. "I know your mystery and now you want to know mine, is that it?" He laughed at her confusion. "Very well, it is only right. Though I caution you it is a far from edifying story."

He gazed downwards, and his face became troubled. "My brother and I were much alike," he began, taking a deep breath. "We had a fatal propensity for wanting the same things. We often fell out over a horse or a particular pair of duelling pistols. Being the eldest, he usually won. And I never grudged it, until I met Peggy.

"She was the tiniest thing," he said sadly, "all rose and pink and dimples. Very lively. Too lively. That was her undoing. She insisted on flirting with the both of us, playing one off against the other. I think she liked me rather better. But looking back, I believe she was hanging out for a title. At the time, I couldn't see that. I could admit no faults in her."

He paused, turning his hands over. Lucy looked at him with a pucker between her brows, aware of the unmentioned pain despite his matter-of-fact telling.

"One day," he stopped, swallowed, went on, "one day I came back from hunting to find that Peggy had called. She had left with Justin, walking alone with him in the woods.

Ostensibly she was going to accompany him pheasant-shooting. This would have been thought strange in another woman, but Peggy was fond of sport. I should not have been worried. But somehow my heart misgave me. Justin was fond of the ladies, and not too nice in his standards. I feared the worst. I crept to a hunting shack in the woods where I knew he sometimes took his ladybirds.

"Nobody seemed to be about, and I decided my misgivings had been premature. I had just turned back into the trees when I heard the door swing open. I looked behind me.

"My worst fears were realized. There in the doorway stood my Peggy. She was dishevelled and weeping. It was obvious what had happened. I will not repeat their conversation. Suffice it to say that she upbraided him, and he made it clear that marriage would not be the reward of her sacrifice.

"And then—I hardly dare repeat it!" His hands clenched. Lucy laid her own on them. "I suppose Justin had let her carry his guns. Or perhaps she had a pistol. I don't know. I can't remember. It happened so fast. She raised it—and—she shot him, and—," Lucy gripped his hands tightly. "Before I could move, she shot herself as well. . . ."

His voice trailed off. Lucy, horrified, realized his shoulders were shaking just slightly.

But then, she cautiously looked at his face—and was undeceived. His lips were twitching irrepressibly, his eyes dancing.

She flung his hands away and exclaimed indignantly, "You're roasting me!"

"To a fine turn," he admitted. His eyes were entirely unrepentant. And seeing them twinkle in that tawny face, she could not resist laughing herself. "Oh, you odious, *odious* man!" she cried. "What a wretched trick to play on me! I should not forgive you."

"I hope you shall, however."

"I suppose I shall," said Lucy, wiping her eyes. "Though why you should treat me so I cannot imagine."

"Forgive me. I could not resist," he smiled. "You seemed so *very* concerned." Then the smile faded. His voice became quite gruff. "The truth is worse, you see. I shall tell you.

"My brother shot himself."

Lucy drew in a breath.

"It was not an accident. I could have done nothing to prevent it; and I never knew why." His tone was very clipped and brusque.

"Oh, my poor friend," said Lucy softly. "That is the hardest part, is it not? Never to know."

His eyes focussed on her again. "Yes." Quietly. He shrugged, as if to shake off the story, and finished in a businesslike manner. "I was out hunting. That much is true. Came back to the house, not knowing what had happened, laughing at a joke the gamekeeper had made. The servants were shocked, not knowing my ignorance. That's how the rumour started."

"I see," said Lucy gently. She felt deeply for him, but did not want to make a gesture that might endanger his stiff control in public. And how could one possibly react appropriately to such a story? Especially when he had done his best to make light of it? Lucy could see, now, that that was what the original faradiddle had been intended to do—smooth the way and take some of the sting out of an incident that could not be easy to tell and must surely still be haunting him.

The intermission was ending. People were abandoning the punch room, reclaiming their seats.

"Thank you for telling me," she said quietly.

"I have never done so before," he confessed.

"Then I am all the more honoured," said Lucy, rising and giving him her hand. "Though why you should choose me for such a confidence, I cannot imagine."

Hersington stood for a moment over her, holding her hands; very tall, very sophisticated, with an odd little smile in his eyes. "Can you not?" he asked with a caressing tone she had not heard before. "It is quite simple. You see, I trust you, Miss Trahern."

He kissed her hand swiftly, and was gone. She watched him for a long moment, before shaking herself and returning to her seat and her abandoned programme.

12

LUCY WAS BESIEGED with offers of marriage the next week from all conceivable quarters. She went to Lady Cowper's masque and refused an offer in the conservatory. She went to the Royal Academy and turned away another proposal while studying the Turners. She went on a picnic at Gravesend and deflected a gentleman over chicken in aspic. And on one memorable riding party in Richmond Park, she gainsaid several gentlemen, one-two-three, in a row like cards.

The catalyst for this sudden rash of proposals, Lucy admitted wryly, had less to do with her irresistible charms than Hersington's absence from the scene. He had taken himself off to Kentsey, suddenly, on "estate affairs," and the tonnish bloods, seeing the man they conceived their chief rival removed, hastened to take every advantage of the opportunity.

Lucy found, somewhat to her surprise, that she missed him dreadfully. They had known each other such a short while, yet no one, it seemed, could share her amusements and exasperations quite as well as he. Oh, she could tell her protectors almost anything. Natalie would make pungent comments and Almeria hilariously irrelevant ones. But neither of them, even with their best efforts, could display the intrinsic understanding that Hersington did so easily. And neither could fathom her continuing, intense uneasiness at being an impostor in the ton. It is because they have never been outside the first circles, Lucy posited. They do not know what it is to know your place in society is unassured. The earl does, bless him.

Lucy's two enemies were also far from happy. At first, they had looked with glee on her numerous tête-à-têtes with single gentlemen. But they soon realized there was no grist for their mill here. It was simply too well known that Lucy was the main prize in the Matrimonial Mart. Each time she emerged from a room, composed beside a pale-faced hopeful, their hearts sank rather than soared. The fact was that most of these encounters were gauged beforehand in the betting books at White's and Watier's and a dozen other clubs. As one bravo after another went down to defeat, her stock only rose the higher.

Nor could it be said that Lucy was capricious or heartless in her dealings with these men. She handled them for the most part gently, and always as they deserved. Those who were genuinely smitten were told kindly that they should not suit; those who obviously had mercenary concerns in mind were regaled with a story much like that she had told Freton. Clarissa had taken pains to make sure that Lucy's remark about earls gained wide currency. Far from being damaged by the rumour, Lucy was contrarily regarded as even more wealthy than anyone would have supposed.

But she was not above dealing harshly with out-and-out fortune hunters. When one down-the-wind gentleman preached passion into her ear at the Exeter Zoo, Lucy shrugged and said shortly, "Pitching it much too rum, Shriving," and left him to the tender mercies of the ostriches.

One evening, Lucy opened the whole budget to Almeria. She revealed her frustration, and her feeling that she would not marry even if she could under her delicate circumstances. "Indeed, I am not sure I wish to," she disclosed anxiously. "I have yet to meet one who moves my heart in the slightest."

They were sitting in Almeria's boudoir late after a party, addressing various wigs and falls for tomorrow's ball and other things of a like important nature. At Lucy's hesitant statement, Almeria shook her pretty shoulders and smiled at her.

"Well, I must own I am glad to hear you say that, love, for I myself find the subject of marriage, of all things, most tedious. The attentions of gentlemen are what I greatly abhor. I expect it was a great disappointment to my family, for they thought I should 'take' well—as, indeed, I did," she went on thoughtfully. "However, I found the . . . the *tendre*," she blushed, "quite discommoding. Do you know," she sat up indignantly, "a certain lord proposed to me, and then had the temerity to *kiss* me!" She blew out her cheeks.

"I found it of all things most lowering, and held no further brief for him. However, I had *accepted* him before this most ungenteel behaviour, so I thought there was no help for it. It was a settled thing until I came on a nacky way to discourage him. Only think! I left the house and stayed at a hotel that night, and did not allow my maid to accompany me! You can imagine what a kickup there was next day! And Natalie has never stopped poking at me yet. But it all righted itself, because I was not, after that, constrained to marry him—or indeed anyone! So you see, it took only a little resolution. My parents said my reputation was lost, but I cannot see why, as I stayed at the Pulteney, which even then was *all* the crack! But you take my meaning, dearest. You need not marry to please me! Indeed, not at all, if you wish it. My notion of giving you a season was only for your pleasure, at squeezing into routs and so on. You need not come to the *sticking* point, as they say. Or do they say that only about the gentlemen? Now let me see . . . well, at any rate, you needn't do any of it. So don't trouble yourself on *that* head!"

"Indeed I shan't," said Lucy, hard put not to laugh. "For I am enjoying myself quite as things are, and wish nothing further." She went to bed giggling, only wishing her friend Hersington were there to enjoy the joke.

* * *

This wish was granted the very next day. The Earl of Kentsey arrived at Staventry about the hour of two. The official hour for calls had passed and he had a good chance to see Lucy alone.

This was not at all unusual. Since Natalie had approved him, Hersington had run tame in the house and no one felt any need to chaperone Lucy while she was with him.

Lucy took in his elegant form with a glad cry (mentally noting that he was far more handsome than she had recalled), and ran to him, clasping his hands. Seating him beside her on the couch, she launched at once into her most pressing concerns.

"Oh, my dear friend, I am so glad to see you! You would not credit the week I have endured! Nothing but proposals, of a singularly ridiculous kind, and so many of them that I declare if any one so much as mentions marriage to me, I shall—I shall do something desperate! Go into strong hysterics, if necessary!"

"As bad as that?" Hersington's voice was as she remembered, low and soothing and tolerantly amused; and his eyes had the same deep brandy sparkle. "I am not unduly surprised. But since it is distasteful to you, let us by all means change the subject. I have no desire to deal with a lady in strong hysterics. Tell me, how do your *enemies* fare?"

"The Demi-Beau I have not seen this sennight, more's the thanks! As for Clarissa, a distinct coolness has grown up between us. I confess it is most amusing, for she thinks herself to be punishing me, when nothing could be more welcome than her absence. And what is more diverting, I collect she is flogging me for a crime I have never yet committed—to wit, the conquest of *your* heart!" Lucy was laughing, utterly sure he shared the joke.

He gave her a queer glance. "I wouldn't be too sure of that," he said banteringly.

Lucy coloured. "Merciful heavens, do not say so! I could

not bear it. And Almeria would be so disappointed, for she has only just given me consent *not* to marry. And for the oddest reason!

"Do but listen, Hersington," she confided, laughter in her face. "I misdoubt me I should not tell you. But it is a matter that touches you nearly. For I suspect the villain of the piece is none other than your father."

"Do tell," the earl invited, leaning towards her.

Lucy told the story with an irreverent grin, chuckling as she described how the elder Hersington's attentions had driven her aunt bag and baggage to the Pulteney.

"So she ended," Lucy said gleefully, "by telling me that she was glad I did not like kisses either, for it made us all the closer! I vow, it was all I could do not to laugh until I had left the dressing room. She was so very relieved that I was of her persuasion!"

"And are you?" Hersington asked suavely, casual in his seat.

"Why, I hardly know." Lucy looked nonplussed and embarrassed. "I scarcely have a standard by which to judge, you know. The only time I was . . . kissed. . . ." She was acutely aware that it was the earl's nephew they were talking about, although he did not know it. "It was . . . unexpected and most . . . unpleasant."

"Was it so?" asked Jasper coolly. And leaning forward, he lightly ran one tawny finger down her jaw to tilt up her chin.

There was one frozen moment when Lucy knew what he meant to do. Her eyes widened. Her pulse stopped. A dozen things went through her head. She was conscious of both shock and curiosity. Should she let him? What would it be like? An internal debate started, promising to be lengthy and end in a prim "no." But perhaps Hersington had known enough virgins—or perhaps he could read her face well enough—not to wait for the result of these mental gymnastics. He bent down and kissed her.

The kiss was simple and without overt passion. But it had a gentle, searching quality, and disordered her emotions out of all proportion to its length. To her confusion, she was sorry when Hersington dropped his hand and pulled away. Lucy emerged with eyes wide and a peachy blush creeping over her skin.

He smiled faintly, hands at his sides. "That was to give you a basis for comparison," he said softly.

Luckily—for Lucy could not imagine an adequate reply—Almeria entered the room at just this moment.

"My Lord Hersington! How very fortunate. You will *exactly* suit my purpose!"

Hiding a smile, the earl rose and bowed. "Delighted to be of service, ma'am. Pray, how can I assist you?"

"Why, by escorting us to Vauxhall, to be sure! There is to be a display of fireworks there tonight from some cause or another which I'm sure I can't recall, but it is held to be monstrous fine! And dear Lucy has never seen such a thing, whereas Natalie is feeling not at *all* the thing and *cannot* be prevailed upon to escort us. She says I could chaperone Lucy myself, and indeed," she tilted her head, "in all propriety, I *could*. It won't answer, however, for as like as not, I should lose her in a shrubbery when I was not attending. And there is such a profusion of countercoxcombs in a place such as the Gardens! I am sure I don't know how it is, but when we are with Natalie we are left quite to our own devices. Howsoever," she finished artlessly, "I believe you would be *almost* as adequate protection."

The earl replied with a grin that he should certainly do his possible. Lucy, however, still full of jumbled feelings from the kiss, murmured that Almeria must not press him. It was, she pointed out, his first night back in town. He might have other plans of greater import.

But Lucy had underrated the earl's perceptions. In a mannered voice (with a very slight rise of one eyebrow which only she could see), he gave them to understand that he was very well pleased at these plans for his disposal, and would call for the ladies about seven.

They passed the next ten minutes in aimless chitchat. At last he left, and Lucy was free to flee blindly to her room. Not that she could think very clearly there, either.

13

Lucy had grave misgivings about the evening. They lessened, however, when she saw that Tom Crowley was to be one of their party.

"I hope you shall not mind it," apologised the earl charmingly. "He was wild to go. In the event, two escorts may prove better than one," he gently teased Almeria. "For if you *do* go haring off in a shrubbery, I shall have to fetch you, you know; and it would never do to leave Miss Trahern unattended."

Almeria agreed placidly that this was so. Lucy and Hersington exchanged one look, brimful of amusement. Then Lucy, remembering, swiftly turned her eyes away.

She looked instead at Master Crowley, with some approval. The change in Crowley's habits and dress had been lasting. He was attired now in understated shades of buff and maroon. One perfect diamond stickpin graced the folds of his cravat, and his vest sported a very superior watch. His face was fresh and open, his manner pleasing. Lucy privately professed herself very well pleased in her companion. She blessed the tact that had made Hersington appoint Tom rather than himself as her escort.

The evening began very pleasantly. They first sat down to a box thoughtfully provided by my lord with champagne and ices. Lucy enjoyed looking about her at the gardens, finding them all they had been gazetted to be. When Hersington proposed a stroll after the refreshments, she was very willing. The foursome sauntered lightly in the growing dusk, making common conversation. She thought Crowley took her arm rather too meaningfully. But there *were* a lot of unsavoury characters about. She decided not to refine too much; he probably meant only to protect her.

At one point in their walk they came slap upon Beau Huston and Miss Stirlan, walking arm in arm with an abigail in tow. Lucy made the proper courtesies, blessed the new estrangement which allowed them to proceed with nothing further, and promptly forgot all about them.

But her tranquility ended when Tom suddenly started pulling on her arm and entreated her to go aside privately for a moment. What now?

She represented to him in the strongest terms that this idea was thoroughly unwelcome. When he saw that no persuasions would move her, he appealed to Almeria. He had a message for her, he whispered, of a *private* nature. From the *children*, she understood? And winked.

Hersington was studiously looking the other way. Almeria benignly waved them off, and Lucy had perforce to follow him into a dark little copse by the wayside.

When they stood there, she eyed him with narrow suspicion, not at all pleased by this chapter of events. Very composed in her pale blue muslin, she uttered coolly, "Yes? What is this message?"

"Oh, that was only a ruse," Tom said confidentially, smiling at her. "I had something of a very intimate sort to say to you. I am sure you collect my meaning, dearest divine Miss Trahern!"

Now Lucy knew what was coming. Inwardly, she sighed. How best to handle this one? Raillery?

"I do wish you will stop making a cake of yourself," she said dampingly. "You know you do not love me!"

"Ah, but I do, my sweet life! With every breath I take!" And seizing her hand, and kissing it passionately, he sank to one knee.

He made a very long speech which Lucy did not try to interrupt. She had learned that these matters were settled faster if one allowed the gentleman to have his full say. The congé could come later.

He had obviously given a great deal of thought to what he would say. It was a very involved speech, a very ardent and sincere speech, full of high phrases and flowing periods. At moments, it was even a very good speech.

It moved Lucy not one jot.

"Are you quite finished?" she asked when he had gone silent.

"No," said Tom gravely, rising and taking her arms. "There is one thing more." He pulled her towards his chest.

She twisted out of his grasp with a little chuckle. "No, no, you must not, for any consideration, kiss me again, Tom! To forgive you a second time would be beyond the bounds of even my tolerant notions of propriety!"

"But that was different!" Tom protested, crestfallen. "That was base, lustful—oh, anything you like. But between those who truly love, why . . ."

"Enough!" said Lucy. She had decided that the correct tack to take with him was benign superiority. "I don't for an instant believe that you love me. No, no!" she countered as he opened his mouth to refute this heresy. "I am aware that you have only the highest motives in suing for my hand. Indeed, I am touched and honoured. But this is not, I think, a lasting attachment."

She held up her hand at his affronted look. "In all justice, you must allow me to have my say, Tom. It is my conviction that you have been dazzled by my change of persona. It was impressive, was it not? The metamorphosis from workaday drudge to Toast of the Ton. I can understand your being bowled over by it.

"But it has blinded you perhaps to my true nature. I have not changed a whit, my friend. It is on this basis that I assure you we should not suit. You have, perhaps, forgotten that you are younger than I. This must of necessity give me an ascendency over you which you as a husband could only deplore. Once marry me, and I would revert immediately to type. I should pick, and lecture, and straighten your cravat; I should adjure you to sit up straighter and polish your top boots. I cannot think that you would like it."

She paused to let these revelations sink in. Crowley was already looking less enthusiastic.

"Furthermore, have you considered the effect on your relations? Just think of your aunt, for instance. Imagine if you will her consternation on being asked to welcome as daughter-in-law one whom she once called a menial! Good Lord. I should not want to face such a pelter! And neither, I should think, do you."

Convinced, now, but sullenly defending his position, Tom said, "Hersington didn't think so. *He* thinks it the best possible connection. Indeed, he encouraged me to this action."

"*Did* he?" queried Lucy in a sarcastic voice. "Be very sure I shall have something to say to my lord of Kentsey! But recollect that he does not know the whole of my story—as you do.

"Now," she said briskly. "I am persuaded we are in agreement, and need raise no further wind on this topic. Do, instead, make of the lie a truth and tell me how the children are."

She was enthusiastic, and Tom was by now glad to comply. He told her that they missed her dreadfully. They were every day asking after her, and adamantly asserted that no one could look after them quite the way their Lucy used. They chatted innocuously for some five minutes on this subject. Then Tom, chastened, returned her to her companions.

The earl, beyond one wise look, made no comment. To cover her trail, Lucy told Almeria that little Cecilia had been asking telling questions about the birds and the bees. Lucy composed a factual letter for Tom to deliver to her.

Involved in these machinations, she did not notice Clarissa and the Beau sneaking away from the opposite side of the coppice.

Their cups were overflowing. Finally, they had more than enough to condemn Lucy to perdition. Tom "must not kiss her again"? She had been "a menial" and had enjoyed such relations with him as to be in the habit of "straightening his cravat"? The "children"? Oh, delicious! Thank goodness they had come to Vauxhall tonight!

Lucy could not have agreed with them less. She was sizzling and simmering like a spit of bacon. All through the fireworks, she contemplated with satisfaction the rare trimming she would give Lord Hersington next time he came to call.

She did not see the earl alone for several days thereafter. He was at routs and balls, of course, but Lucy was far too busy refusing proposals to notice him. Tired of the whole project, she had begun to put it about that her affections were previously engaged. This sent the men off in short order.

Hersington eventually showed up at the house however. Lucy was in prime twig. She let him chat with Almeria inconsequentially about bonnets and Newmarket for some five minutes. Then she announced that she wished to speak to his lordship alone, at once.

Almeria threw a bright glance at them. "Oh, are you two on the outs? If you are going to quarrel, by all means do so in the garden. I cannot abide raised voices." And calmly applying herself to her tambour frame, she dismissed them.

They paced for a few moments in simmering silence. The fragrance of hollyhocks, newly planted by her own hand, was lost on Lucy. She walked with large steps, her yellow muslin skirts slashing viciously to and fro. Hersington's imperturbable elegance, as he paced beside her in a medley of ivory and beige, incensed her. The small, flickering smile on that amber face made her want to scream. How dare his hands lie so quietly on his walking cane? How dare the gold stone of his signet ring flicker harmlessly in the sun, as if he had no care in the world? Oh, she was out of patience with him.

She whirled and faced him. "I have been thinking these three days what is bad enough to say to you! I confess I have not yet plumped upon anything adequate."

"Why, what have I done?" asked Hersington, all mild innocence.

"How dare you—I say, how *dare* you, sir, set that odious nephew of yours onto me!"

"Oh, was he odious?" asked the earl in surprise. "I am disconcerted. I thought I had schooled him to be most perfectly the gentleman."

"He was all that was correct," Lucy admitted. "But it was perfectly horrid all the same! You should think shame to yourself!"

He ignored her last statement, pausing to take snuff and asking casually, "What, did he kiss you again? I had believed I trained him out of such freaks."

"You *know* that story? Why, why—" This interview was not going in the least as she had expected.

"Yes, I wormed it from him. That is why I felt you were in need of a better example of the art."

Lucy blushed. "Cad! Knowing all that, *why* would you put me in such a position? When you knew after our conversation that I could not possibly welcome his suit?"

He smiled down at her lazily. "Perhaps so that it would offer the greatest possible contrast to mine."

Lucy felt her heart beat faster. She stood very still. All the breath left her body in a rush, and the hollows beneath her cheeks took on a tantalizing curve. "Oh, Hersington," she said faintly. "Not you too?"

Easily, he took a step closer. "Yes, me too," he said with amusement. One lean hand reached up to her face. The thumb stroked her jaw just where it met her ear. His fingers slid into her hair, gently playing with the dark curls there. Very odd things were happening to Lucy's pulse. She could neither move nor look away.

"Why not, my dear heart?" he asked. He chuckled low in his throat. "Do me the justice to admit that I cannot be classed with the fortune hunters."

Never had Lucy had so much difficulty retaining her composure. Her heart was beating like a trip-hammer. All her usual thoughts of strategy for such moments had flown from her mind.

One honey-coloured hand reached around and cupped her waist, bringing her yet closer.

"It would not—my lord, you know it would not do!" she said breathlessly. Then, on firmer ground, "If you cannot be classed with the fortune hunters, neither do you belong to the ranks of the ignorant. You know that my history is—not of the most edifying."

"And you consider if I discovered the truth I should cast you off? How paltry you must think me," he replied caressingly. "Come, confide in me, dear. You know I will not mind it."

For the life of her, Lucy could not speak.

"I am perhaps more tolerant than you know," he said slyly, teasing her again. "I should have no difficulty, say, with a wife who had spent her youth selling flowers, or riding a circus horse."

He paused. "No? None of these? Well perhaps you were a free-trader, or a tavern wench. It's all one to me. Now, if you had no sense of humour, or slurped your soup at table, or rode a horse like a sack of meal—these things I would not brook in my countess!" He was laughing at her, and she was suddenly unsure. Was he making a joke of her? "But otherwise," he went on calmly, "it would make me very happy to marry you, were you seven times the tavern wench."

Now, when she was so close to surrender, Hersington dropped his hand from her waist. Along with that loss came a sudden knowledge that the maddening magic of the fingers on her cheek had somehow doubled their effect on her senses.

"That is closer to the truth than you know," said Lucy in a shaken voice. "If it were not for Natalie, for Almeria . . ." she trailed off, miserably conscious of her false position.

She looked up into his face. For a moment, she fancied she caught a deep seriousness behind those dancing brandy eyes.

"Does this mean no?"

Her hands were unaccountably clasping and unclasping in front of her. "I can't. Really I can't. You must believe me."

"Very well," said Hersington, removing the teasing hand. "I am determined to prove that I am unlike your other suitors, and take my refusal with a good grace. Come, let us talk of something else." And putting his palms behind him, he resumed pacing the flagged paths.

Lucy looked after him incredulously for a moment. Then she ran to catch up. Stunned, she listened as he began a long animadversion upon the weather. She could not find it in her to reply.

They had made the round and were returning to the house, when he looked at her with a sideways glint. "Insulted, Miss Trahern? It was uncivil in me to comply so easily, was it not? I should have fallen at your feet and gone into convulsions, promising an instant decline, I suppose. I do beg your pardon. I cannot think how I came to be so remiss."

It was all at once too much for Lucy. The tension of the last half hour resolved itself in a belly laugh.

"Indeed, it is most odious! I feel myself very slighted, especially since you are a mere earl!" she sputtered.

"That's the spirit," he said approvingly. "Give it me back in my teeth. And never fear, sweet one," he murmured, catching her hand and raising it to his lips. "We are friends, and I would have it so. But I am by no means vanquished. I shall ask again."

Then with a slight bow and an ironic twist of his eyebrows, the Earl of Kentsey left her, not to reappear for three weeks. There was much to attend on his estates, he said. He trusted she would forgive his temporary neglect.

Lucy watched him go, still as a statue. It was a horrifying moment to discover that there was no one in all the world she would rather marry.

14

OVER THE NEXT three weeks, quietly, inexorably, the bottom fell out of Lucy's social status.

It was rather frightening with what ease Miss Stirlan and Lord Huston brought a seemingly unassailable position crashing to the ground. One might—almost—admire the strategy of their campaign. They were not so foolish as to noise about what they had heard in Vauxhall. Society, to do it credit, despised an avowed eavesdropper more than any amount of lack of virtue. No, Clarissa found a more clever way to spread her news. She made her girlfriends coax it out of her.

For days she appeared at the evening balls with red-rimmed eyes (carefully done with paint) and feigned a barely checked distress every time she saw Lucy. When her friends questioned her as to what was amiss, she would say, "Nothing—nothing!" in fading accents and turn away to dab at her eyes with an already damp handkerchief (rose-water). And when they drew her aside privately and pressed her, she begged that they must not—really, they must not!—ask her any more. She had not meant to show her troubles, only it came so very hard to discover that her dearest friend—one she had *thought* her dearest friend—was no more than . . . Oh! Please do not make her tell!

But of course they did, and Clarissa gave in with a pretty reluctance, beseeching that they must not, on any account, breathe a word of this to a soul.

"It is Miss Trahern that I am so cut up about," she would

begin with a sigh. "You know, Mary, that we have been bosom beaus almost from first sight. There was that in her manner—so original, so refreshing!—that I found irresistible. I assumed, of course, that it arose from youth and high spirits. I thought none the worse of her if she occasionally went beyond the line of what was pleasing. It is her first season, after all, and she is country-bred, not knowing town ways."

Her listener would nod sympathetically at this point. And if she was inwardly pleased at what she sensed was an upcoming slight on Miss Trahern's character, she could never afterwards claim that Clarissa had not said all that was proper in Lucy's defense.

"But in the last few weeks a—an estrangement has grown between us. Perhaps you may not have noticed it."

Mary had.

"Yes, well, if you had wondered why, I shouldn't blame you. But I did not feel I could speak of it. You remember Lady Huntingdon's ball? And how Lucy disappeared for so *very* long? I was concerned, and went to seek her. I found her at last in the garden with . . . with a certain gentleman."

Clarissa was too smart to attempt blackening Hersington's name as well as Lucy's. She still held a faint hope, as well, that he might turn his eyes back in her direction.

"They were quite alone." She clenched her hands artistically, and pressed her lips as if she could say more but would not.

"It was then I began to think that Lucy was . . . loose."

There were shocked little cries and protestations here.

"Of course I did not *wish* to believe it. But it brought a certain distance between us. And then . . . Oh!" Clarissa hid her face in her hands and took a deep breath. Her voice shook.

"Last week I went to Vauxhall—to see the firework display, do you recall? I ran across Lucy's party; she was with the Earl of Kentsey, Master Crowley, and of course

Lady Staventry. We passed each other in greeting. Then as I was turning a corner, I recalled something I had meant to tell her and turned back. She was going off into the trees with Crowley."

Here she would lift her face and cry out earnestly, "I didn't mean to listen! Truly I did not! But I was concerned for her, you know. The Gardens are not entirely *safe*, and Crowley has not the nicest reputation. I was only going to fetch her, or warn her, or—I know not what. I wasn't thinking. I just saw my friend, as I thought, in danger, and I ran."

Having now set her stage, Clarissa hurried on to the really damning part of her story.

"I was on the other side of the hedge when I stopped. I could hear their voices clearly. It seemed Crowley was making a proposal in form. You may imagine my relief! I was just turning away, feeling rather silly at all my alarums. Then Lucy laughed, and said he must not kiss her *again*, for she could only forgive him once." Her voice dropped as she saw with satisfaction the affronted face before her. "And *then*," she whispered, "she told him that he would not like to be married to her, for she should behave just as she used, and be forever straightening his cravat and polishing his boots."

The listener at this point was deathly still and white. "I should not have listened, oh, I wish I had not! For next she told him that she did not believe him in love with her at all, but only dazzled by her change of identity. 'Only think,' she told him, 'how your aunt would react to the announcement that you were to wed one she was accustomed to call *a menial.*' Then she begged him to tell her how the *children* were!"

At this delicious moment, with Lucy conclusively ruined, the women would generally hug each other convulsively. Then Clarissa would sob, and say she was very sorry, she had not meant to burden her friend with such a sordid tale. But it had been cutting up her peace so and she could not, truly could not, face Lucy again!

Of course, the woman cooed, she understood.

"And you *won't* tell anybody, *will* you? For as little as I may think of Lucy now—I cannot bring myself to call her 'Miss Trahern'—she was once my friend. I should not wish to harm her, even now."

And of course the girl promised, and Clarissa evinced relief, and naturally the girl went straight out and repeated it to three other people.

It took only three or four of these interviews before no woman in society wanted anything to do with "Miss" Trahern.

Beau Huston performed a similar office for the men. He waited until Clarissa's part was firmly launched. Then one evening he showed up at his club in his most stunning rig-out. This did not, alas, include the waistcoat with coquelicot stripes. Its absence was sorely felt, and added fuel to the fires of his vengeance.

The play went on as usual for some hours. When a sufficient number of bottles had been opened that the men were ripe but not yet castaway, Beau opened fire.

"Did I hear some of you mentioning that young popinjay, Crowley?"

"Ay, he's not been to the club this sennight. But don't you go calling him names, Huston. Play and pay, that's Crowley. He's a wisty one, for a sprig."

"That's as may be. But I have heard a most diverting story about him, at all events. It makes him look a pretty fool—all of us, come to that!"

"How's this?"

"Told me a story before he bolted. In his cups, I think, else I'd never have heard."

Then he said briefly, casually, that the Mysterious Original was none other than his ordinary, whom he had passed off as a Miss for a bet.

It is easy to imagine the consternation this pronouncement engendered. Every man in the room had proposed for her at one time or another.

"Oh, it's true enough. They have several children by way of proof. Don't know where they're stowed. Heard they miss Lucy terribly, though."

"You don't say!"

" 'Od's blood!"

"Always thought there was something havey-cavey in it."

"But stay! You have not heard the cream of the jest!" said Huston sardonically. "Having seen his ladybird succeed far better than he had planned, what must Crowley do but propose for her himself! Only she wouldn't have him! One can hardly be surprised, as that nodcock has put her in the way of far better prospects. Can you wonder that Crowley posted off and hasn't been seen since?"

Some of the men thought it a capital joke. More were outraged. One gentleman, a trifle less shot in the neck than the others, nearly queered things by saying in a level voice, "Do you ask me to believe that Lady Staventry and the Duchess of Bucklass were party to such a deception? Coming it too strong, Huston. They'd never pass off a lightskirt as their niece."

Huston hid his consternation under a yawn. "Oh, I daresay she *is* their niece, in some sort. Wrong side of the blanket, you know. As to their participation . . . well, we all know what Lady Staventry is."

"She's so maggoty she wouldn't even notice the impropriety!" someone said, laughing.

A good deal of joking here. The rough part seemed over. But the same man asked, "And the duchess?"

"For a wager, perhaps?" Huston replied languidly.

"Naturally," said the questioner scornfully. "The Duchess of Bucklass is known for accepting wagers from the nephews of cits!"

However the men by this time were not to be balked of their sport. They had all felt the rough side of Natalie's tongue often enough to impute malicious motives to her.

"She's a crotchety old lass," one man grumbled. "Daresay she'd do it just to make a May game of us."

"She don't like society above half," another agreed, "for all she's been queening it for fifty years."

"I still don't believe it."

"As you wish," said Huston, shrugging. "I suggest you ask your wife. Women get wind of these things pretty fast. See if she'd welcome Miss Trahern to *her* next turnout." And he turned back casually to his play. He was satisfied. If Lucy's vouchers to Almack's weren't revoked within a week, it would be a miracle.

Wrapped in her own private misery, Lucy did not at first notice anything amiss. Hersington had left a bouquet of primroses on the morning he departed. She wore them constantly until they wilted. She drifted through the ballrooms not noticing where she was, and lost a lot of her "aunts' " money by inattention at the card tables.

When she bothered to attend at all, that is. As often as not, she pled migraine, and stayed home. She was not aware that this only fed the rumours.

Knowing what was troubling her, Natalie shrewdly left her alone. Let her brood, she thought. It might bring her to her senses. However she insisted that Lucy attend the Marquess of Lyminster's ball, the major event of the season.

Lucy sat quietly on the sidelines in misty apricot and watched the dancers. It was soothing to sit alone like this. Lately she had received no offers of marriage. Her only reaction was gratitude. She vaguely supposed that her story of a previous attachment had discouraged the remaining hopefuls. And there had not been many morning-callers, which was restful. She was able to give the house her full attention, as she had not done since the beginning of the Season. If only Hersington were here, she thought wistfully, everything would be perfect.

This would not do! She was suddenly angry with herself. She was not going to pine away and die just because she could not marry one man with honey hair and tapered fingers and a smile in his eyes. There were other things— for instance, duty to her partners. They had been uncommonly patient, these last weeks. It was time she rewarded them by a show of vivacity.

She looked down at her dance card. She blinked, looked again. It was empty. That was odd. Well, perhaps she had been more damping than she knew. She would go in to the buffet. She was hungry anyway.

Lucy filled her plate with lobster patties and jellies. How nice to be able to fill her own plate! The gentlemen generally had a knack for bringing just that one item one had hoped not to eat. That was strange, too—there were several men at the table, but not one offered to help her. In fact, she seemed to be moving in a little circle of silence. As she came up behind Sue Stratton, the girl giggled and stepped quickly away to whisper with a friend. Lucy stared at them. This was unmannerly behaviour indeed. The girls blushed and walked in the other direction.

As she turned back to the patties, perplexed, she found Lord Freton at her side.

"How very pleasant to see you, Miss Trahern. May I say how very well that dress becomes you?"

She smiled at him. "You are too kind, sir. The gentlemen have been so silent on the subject tonight that I was sure of committing a social solecism."

He gave her an odd look. "Never that, my dear. I can see you are occupied," he nodded at her plate. "But when you have appeased your appetite, perhaps I might have the honour of the next dance?"

"Why, certainly, sir. It is I who am honoured."

He chivalrously saw her back to her seat near Almeria before seeking out his partner.

Lucy ate with a good will. But she kept stealing glances at her card, where Freton's name, in flourishing letters, stood out alone.

And now she came to think of it, no one had really greeted her or come up to exchange remarks. If the gentlemen were tired of her refusals, that was one thing. But what of the ladies? She could not make it out.

It was beginning to reach her that something was wrong. She decided to see if Lord Freton could clue her.

She made him her most graceful bow when they stood up together.

"La, sir, I declare I am quite grateful for this chance to stretch my legs! It seems I have been too cold, after all, and driven away all my gallants."

"Never say so, Miss Trahern," he said gravely, uneasily.

"In truth I do not blame them," she went on lightly, watching him under her lashes, "so glum as I have been these last few weeks. Positively blue-devilled, in fact."

"Why so?"

"A friend of mine has departed for the country, and I miss him most sadly. 'Tis more than I expected. But that's over now, and I shall do my possible to be fit company."

She meant Hersington, of course. Equally, he assumed that she was regretting Crowley. He cleared his throat.

"That puts me in mind of something I have been meaning to say to you, Miss Trahern. I believe I never told you how much I appreciated the kind manner in which you refused my suit. It does you the greatest credit. I said then, and still feel, that I am proud to be counted your friend. You are a woman of honour and high principles, Miss Trahern, whatever society may say."

The look he gave her with this was so strange and full of pity that Lucy faltered on the floor. Luckily, the dance was ending and no one noticed. Freton escorted her back to Lady Staventry and left her with a punctilious bow and a gentle kiss to the hand.

The girl who had once had to fight to save space on her

card now stood at the edge of the ball with the sure knowledge there would be no further dances that evening.

"Aunt Almeria," she said quietly. "It is time we go home. My fling in society is over. They've found me out."

Back at the cottage, a roaring argument raged. Predictably, this was between Natalie and Lucy. Or more accurately, between Natalie and Natalie, as Lucy never once raised her voice.

Natalie was first angry at Lucy for dragging them away from the party so early. She had been patient (she said impatiently), but if Lucy thought she was going to put up with this milk-and-water maundering over a fellow she ought to marry and have done—

Lucy was not willing to discuss Hersington with Natalie or anyone else. She cut this tirade short.

"I left because it became clear to me that my secret is out. My career in society is finished, ma'am, and there's nothing to be done."

"In a pig's eye! What's this new megrim of yours, Lucille? Saw you m'self dancing with Lord Freton."

"He was the only partner I had all evening, Aunt Natalie."

Calmly, lucidly, she outlined the reasons for her suspicions. The dearth of morning callers. The sudden absence of offers. The lack of greetings, not only from men but ladies. No dances. The odd little scene at the supper table. "Looking back," she said thoughtfully, "I fancy there have been other events of like kind. Although I was not really attending." Lastly, and most damaging, Freton's remark that he would stick by her "no matter what society thinks."

"To me it seems signal that he admired me precisely because I turned him down," Lucy finished. "That could only mean that he thought it would have been ignoble to accept him. And what other reason could there be for *that*, save he is aware I do not belong in high society at all?"

"Make-bait," said Natalie sourly. But she was visibly

digesting this evidence. At last she said, "Nothing for it. We'll have to ride roughshod over the lot of 'em. Whatever they may think, they daren't offend us."

"Ma'am, I beg you will not!" inveigled Lucy. "Truly, I could not be less concerned. I have had my season in the sun, and it has quite satisfied me. I have no further desire to trick myself out for the dandies."

"Nonsense!" thundered Natalie. "I won't see the Staventry name sneezed at! And you're not going to do so either. We'll brazen it out. Still plenty of invitations in the card rack. We'll go to all of 'em."

"But that is just the difficulty," said Almeria, who had been waiting her chance. "We still receive cards, it is true, and for all the most *exclusive* engagements, which in course is most gratifying. But I have been puzzling my head over it this week, for it is the oddest thing, but now we have the answer: Sister, all the summons are for you and me. Dear Lucy is not mentioned once!"

Natalie was badly shaken by this piece of intelligence. She had never troubled herself over their social calendar. It was something she had no patience for, and one of the few things Almeria handled masterfully.

"Horsefeathers! Give me that!"

Almeria fluttered about the room. "Where is today's post, oh, let me see . . . no, that is the grocer's bill . . . seven pairs of kid goves at . . . ah, here's the stack. I have not opened them yet, but I am sure it is all of a piece. Only look, Nat, there is the Countess's seal on the top. Do broach that first!"

Natalie did. Her cane dropped to the floor with a clatter. She handed the missive with a shaking hand first to Almeria and then to Lucy.

It was a letter revoking Lucy's entrée to Almack's.

The three looked long at each other. For the first time in their acquaintance, even Natalie had nothing to say.

15

NATALIE AND ALMERIA sat scheming in the parlour all morning. Lucy, uninterested in these hopeless proceedings, went wandering out into the garden. She sat herself down beneath a bank of fuchsias and played with her hat.

Of course, she told herself, she did not care one whit what those posing apes thought of her. It would be very peaceful not to have to tell any more lies. She need never be tried with spurious proposals again. Especially Hersington's. She clenched her hands. Good! she thought fiercely. The man was too damnably attractive. If he had asked her again, she might have weakened. But even Hersington could not fly in the face of the entire fashionable world by marrying her. Lucy would keep house for her two strange protectresses until the end of June. Then her father would return, and they would go live in the country. They would raise cats, perhaps, and grow roses. Having reached this sensible conclusion, Lucy burst into tears.

It was some time before she noticed the clatter of arrival in front. She had a hazy notion that it had been going on for a little while. Then she heard a heavy stride, followed by the pattering of several feet. Suddenly the back door swung open. Hersington stepped into the garden, followed at some distance by Natalie, Almeria, and Tom Crowley.

The earl reached her first. He saw the crumpled handkerchief, the swimming eyes. Gently he reached down to lift her up.

"What is it, infant?" he asked, drying her eyes with his forefinger and not letting go her hand. "Does it trouble you so much to no longer be the Mysterious Original?"

His voice was so tender it nearly made her weep again. She smiled up at him tremulously. She felt so much better now he was here. "Oh, no! Not that, never that! You know yourself how much I abhorred the deception from the start." Then worried, "Did they tell you? What it was that I . . . ?"

"Be easy on that head!" he teased. "Your secret is still your own. Not that I give a snap of my fingers for your past. But here is Crowley, who thinks he knows what the rumour is. He says it is far from the truth."

"Oh?"

She turned to the rest of the company, who had now come up level with them. Crowley was blazing, his cheeks red, his riding crop slapping against his thighs. Lucy had never seen him so. "Why, he might make a man someday!" she thought in suprise.

Hersington had released her hand, and they moved to join the group.

"Now what is this story that you say is untrue?" Hersington commanded.

"We arrived in town last night," he began, breathing fast. "I stopped in at my club, you recall," he nodded to the earl, "and I heard the most revolting story! Lucy is my doxy, if you please—and I am a coxcomb who passed her off on society for a jest! And you—," he pointed to the duchess "were pleased to lend yourself to it to make fools of all the rakehells." The Duchess turned quite satisfactorily purple at such a suggestion. "And you," he told Almeria, "were so stupid you could see nothing wrong with it!"

"How did these 'facts' come out?" Hersington asked. Lucy could see him holding uproarious laughter in check. She felt much the same, and dared not look at him again.

"Huston says I told it to him while jug-bitten! Strange that *I* do not recall the incident! I cannot think that I would say such things, no matter how foxed."

"Strange indeed," said my lord musingly, "when Huston has been no great crony of yours since last April."

"Well, I am going to go see this so-dear friend," said Tom

menacingly, "and call him out! If you ladies will excuse me. . . ."

"No, we will not," said Hersington, laying a firm hand on his arm. Thomas looked daggers at him. "Your pardon, Nephew, but I believe you have not thought this through. It is Miss Trahern's reputation we are concerned with here. That will hardly be enhanced by a duel over her good name."

Tom sagged. "You are right. That would only make them whisper all the more. Damnation! Your pardon, ladies. But what's do to now?"

"Depends," said Natalie. "Where'd he get this farrago of nonsense?"

"And *why?*" wailed Almeria. "Why should Lord Huston want to harm our dear, sweet Lucy?"

"Oh, probably because I pushed him in a horsepond," Lucy replied absently.

Raucous laughter from Natalie.

"That was not very well done of you, Lucy," Almeria reproved. "Why would you serve him so?"

"He tried to kiss me," she explained.

"My! What a good idea! I wonder I did not think of it when the old lord tried to kiss me!"

Hersington glanced at Lucy, with a glint in his eye. "No doubt there was no water to hand," he suggested helpfully.

"Very true. What a pity."

"Can we stop this flummery and get to the main point?" Natalie was fulminating.

"I think I know how it happened," Lucy said slowly. All eyes turned to her. "It was that evening in Vauxhall. When Tom—you do not mind my telling this?" she asked courteously.

"N-no . . ." he said hesitantly.

She grinned at him. "I shall abridge. Mr. Crowley was so obliging as to propose to me. And I refused."

"Yes, yes," said Natalie impatiently. "What's that to the purpose?"

"I am coming to that. I told him that he should not like

marriage to me, for as I was the older I should forever be adjuring him to adjust his cravats and sit up straight as had been my way in,"—she paused—"in our previous acquaintance. And I reminded him that his aunt would not relish a connexion with,"—she was all too aware that Hersington was listening—"with someone of my background. Also," she added roguishly, "I said he must not kiss me again, for to forgive him *twice* would be beyond his deserts."

Tom's face illuminated. "And you asked about the children! Of course!"

"Oh, were there children in the rumour?"

"Yes, we have several. Did you not know?"

"Too true. What a very odd sort of female I am, to be sure. I had completely forgot," Lucy said lightly.

"I gather you have a mutual acquaintance of some youngsters?" asked Hersington, recalling her to her role.

"Oh, yes. The dearest monsters! I am quite fond of them. You must know them, for they are Tom's cousins."

"Indeed I do," he murmured. He caught Tom's eye with a quelling glance.

"These remarks could easily have been misconstrued if they were overheard. . . ."

"But they were!" exclaimed Almeria. "Surely you remember, Lucy! Huston was squiring Miss Stirlan about the park. We had only just passed them when Tom took you aside."

"Ten to one they were listening," concluded Natalie. "The bantams! Don't know why I didn't think of that Friday-faced Stirlan chit before. Bound to be in it."

"Well, now we know how it happened," said Lucy matter-of-factly. "And I must confess it's all very interesting. But what, precisely, do we intend to do about it?"

They argued over this for some hour and a half in the parlour to which Lucy had insisted they remove. She did not care a jot about her reputation, she said. So if they were going to fuss about it she might as well listen in comfort. A number of bottles of port had been gone through, though it was not yet noon, and no helpful solution reached.

"The problem you keep coming back to," she interjected at last, "is that Tom *told* Huston this story. Or so they think. We know better. But no one is going to believe otherwise."

Natalie looked flummoxed. Hersington drummed his fingers on the table.

"Perhaps he did it for a joke?" Almeria suggested hopefully. It was the first thing she had contributed. She trailed away as four pairs of eyes stared incredulously at her. "Well, gentlemen do that sometimes, you know, and I just wondered . . ."

"I think you have got it, Lady Staventry!" said Tom. "It is a joke I would never make about a lady, but if I say it was, and rag Huston about having believed it, he will look the fool indeed, to have been taken in by such a bouncer!"

"A man of his kidney would rather face a bullet than laughter any day," interpolated Hersington.

"Just so. He will be very well served!" Tom's face glowed with satisfaction.

"And Lucy's 'children'?"

"I think we can tie that all up neatly in a package," Hersington continued. "George Trahern was a friend of Sydney Bostram's, was he not? There is your cue. Some months ago, just before Lucy's come-out, all three of Maria's children became ill. Lucy very kindly consented to care for them, as their governess was also ill—"

"And so became quite one of the family," finished Natalie. "Straightening cravats means nothing in that context."

"But it made me seem almost like a servant. So naturally she would not want her nephew to marry me," Lucy put in. There were nods all round.

"Only you must make her visit at *Christmas*," Almeria urged. "For then Tom could have fobbed her off with mistletoe, and that explains the kiss!"

They all looked at her in amazement. Lady Staventry

had never come up with two good ideas at a sitting in her life.

"*You* know, Natalie," she said peevishly. "When we met Lucy, I thought it *was* Christmas, so that made me think of it."

One of those fulminating looks from Hersington.

"I never thought to be grateful for your woolliness," said Natalie dryly. "Now. We have a fine story. How do we put it about?"

She tapped her teeth with the ever-present snuffbox.

"And why should they believe it?" asked Lucy stubbornly.

"Hush, girl. We have two assets. The Staventry name and—," she looked speculatively at Hersington.

"And mine," he said promptly. "You don't think, ma'am, I intend to be left out of this adventure?"

Lucy looked rebellious. Natalie peremptorily ordered her off to prepare nuncheon.

When she returned with food, she found the foursome in very good spirits, claiming they had it all planned to a nicety.

"Never you mind how, Miss," the duchess told Lucy sharply. "Do you attend to setting Staventry house in order. We are going to have a ball. In your honour."

"Only, Lucy dear," said Almeria anxiously, "you *will* make sure there aren't any ghosts, *won't* you? I confess I could not be easy entertaining in a house full of spectres, even if I *am* to wear my Manchua satin."

"If I find any ghosts, I shall eject them," she promised firmly.

"And one thing more," said Natalie. "The ton dare not refuse us, and they will come to our ball. By that time we should have laid to rest all rumours. But just to give them the coup de grace, you and Hersington will pretend to be on the point of an engagement. He will pay you signal attentions, and waltz with you *three* times—and you shall permit it!"

"I shall not!" Lucy said mutinously.

Their schemes might have tumbled there but for Hersington. "Why, how unhandsome of you, Miss Trahern," he said, rising and approaching to stand smiling down at her. "When I distinctly told you of my great desire to rescue a damsel in distress, and it was you who dashed my previous chance to the ground. Surely you could not serve me such a turn again?"

She gazed into his twinkling eyes with a twitching mouth. "No, I suppose I could not do so. Very well, let us consider ourselves almost engaged. Though I misdoubt me I shall regret it."

"I shall engage to see that you do not," replied Hersington.

And so the battle plan was set. The next step was up to Natalie.

One fine Friday morning, Mrs. Bostram watched with misgiving as the gold-and-lavender Staventry carriage lit at her door. Her quakes were fully justified. The duchess sailed into her living room, all pennants flying, and gave her the worst half hour of her life. She reminded her of certain mistakes and indiscretions which should go nameless if she lent her support in this scheme. Then she asked after the children, and sent Almeria up to see them.

"Oh, the dear little things! I should love that!" said Almeria, whose tender heart had been troubled at being obliged to watch Natalie's bullying.

She swept into the nursery on a wave of patchouli and muslin, instantly captivating the three little termagants by asking if they would not like to assist in a scheme to help their dear Miss Trahern.

They were all eagerness. "This is how it is," said Almeria. "There are some nasty people who have told terrible lies about Miss Lucy, and now nobody likes her anymore. They will not ask her to parties, or take her out in their carriages, or *anything!*"

The children agreed that this was just too shabby. Such cawkers ought to be horsewhipped, they thought.

"No, no, we have a much better scheme," said Almeria. "We are going to play a trick on them. We'll embarrass them so much they will never be mean to Lucy again! Let me tell you how it will be."

And since Almeria's imagination was quite as active as theirs, she had soon convinced herself as well as the children.

"Good!" she said as she left. "Monday next! And don't forget, Lucy is your *aunt*. She helped you when you had the measles. But she has *never* been your governess!"

Next, unbeknownst to anybody, the duchess paid a call on Miss Clarissa Stirlan. She timed it finely when Lady Stirlan was out. She proposed, as she put it, to take the gloves off.

Miss Stirlan was not at all pleased with this proposal. She remained stubbornly silent until Natalie pulled out all stops.

"Very well, Miss," said the Dowager, rising formidably to her feet. "You are pleased to send my niece down to social ruin. I cannot stop you. But at least I shall have the satisfaction of seeing her drag you with her!" She turned as if to go.

"Wait!" said Clarissa. Her delicate face was bone-white. "What do you mean?"

"Come!" scoffed Natalie. "You know very well of what I speak. There was a certain tutor, was there not? Name, name . . . oh, Forston, or some such rot. You were all of sixteen. Of course, they caught you before you reached the border, and the matter was all hushed up. But I see no reason *I* should remain silent if *you* do not!"

Clarissa thought rapidly. It was true, she had attempted a foolish elopement some years ago. She had believed it forgotten, and after all so few people knew—but one person, telling the truth, would be enough to ruin her chances forever.

"Very well, perhaps I *did* say a word or two in certain ears! But it was only the truth! And if you wish me to cease now, I shall. It is only becoming in a young woman to cede to her elders," she said primly. Then with sudden malice, "Not that it will help your precious Lucy! The damage is done in that quarter!"

The Duchess of Bucklass regarded her much as she might a repulsive bug. "I wouldn't be too sure of that."

She pulled on her gloves and turned towards the door. "You are a misbegotten shrew," she added levelly. "I probably ought to ruin you anyway. But I shan't—if you keep a still tongue in your head. Remember that!"

And with no further amenities, she left. She stopped only once on her way home, to post a certain note with a gold crest.

16

THE MORNING SLATED for Lucy's resurrection dawned fine and blue. They had received the all-clear signal from Tom on the previous evening. He had visited White's, he said, and the story was spreading like wildfire that he had been having Huston on. "They are full of consternation at having snubbed you," he told Lucy, "and are already wondering whether they can still get out of your black books."

"Good!" Natalie had said, nodding. "Now for the ladies."

This would be somewhat more difficult, and required careful generalship. None of the conspirators breathed entirely easily until an engraved card was presented at the door on Monday morning.

"Excellent," Natalie whispered. "Now for it. Lucille, into the kitchen, and don't show your face until the signal."

Lucy had grumbled and dragged her feet through all the scheming. At last Natalie had pointed out that she would be fooling all the old biddies to the top of their bent. Wouldn't she enjoy that? Not to mention putting Clarissa Stirlan's aristocratic nose completely out of joint. Lucy had grinned and admitted that this was a consummation devoutly to be wished. After that she had entered into her part of the play with relish.

In walked the Countess Lieven, stately and disapproving. She gazed about the house, sniffed and asked suspiciously if Miss Trahern were there.

"Oh, she is about," said Almeria, waving her arm vaguely, "fixing tea or some such. I expect she will join us presently. Or is she cleaning the stillroom?" She put a finger to her chin. "I can't recall. Whatever it is, no doubt it is invaluable. I do not know how we should contrive without her, do you, Natalie?"

"No," answered the duchess. "But the countess will hardly wish to discuss domestic matters. Don't m'self. Boring things. Not to the point. Fact is," she leaned forward, "brought you here to discuss our ball. We're holding one. Staventry House. You're invited, of course. Fancy thing. Haven't done one in years. Wanted your advice about entertainment."

"*And* the ices!" Lady Staventry put in. "We want to have something completely different and *utterly* shattering. You are *just* the person to whom we thought we could most profitably apply."

The countess (who had once said, "It is not fashionable where I am not") accepted this praise as her due and began to offer exotic suggestions. The discussion passed this way pleasantly for some fifteen minutes.

But all the time Natalie's ears were at a stretch. At last she was rewarded by a knock on the door.

"Now, who could that be?" said the Duchess irritably. She opened the door with a show of surprise to Maria Bostram.

"Drat! What are you doing here?" she said ungraciously. "Have I not told you a dozen times not to call in the mornings? I am busy with the Countess Lieven."

Maria fluttered. "Oh, dear, I am so sorry, only the children *would* come and I could *not* make them stay, and what with their governess ill, and Tom saying he had promised them a treat . . ."

"Good God, are the children here too? Well, well, best let them in; otherwise they'll raise a ruckus that'll be heard clear to Carlton House!"

And in they bounced, Cecilia, Hyde, and Lindon, in

their best clothes but patently not on their best behaviour.

"Mama, Mama!" they chimed. "Oh, thank you, Mama! We have been so eager to see Aunt Lucy again!"

"I want to show Aunt Lucy my shiner!" Lindon cried. "From that great bully on Barstow Street. Wait till she hears how I milled him down!" And shouting "Take that! and that!" he danced about the room flailing at his shadow.

"Much she'll care for that," Hyde did his best to outshout his brother. "I'm going to tell her how I rode Cousin's Tom's big bruiser! Now there is a right 'un! Sound in wind and limb, beautiful stepper."

"You fell off," supplied Lindon.

"Did not! He shied into a tree branch. The *branch* knocked me off."

Cecilia, as befit a young lady, kept herself aloof from the pandemonium. She confided to Almeria that she had a question of the most *serious* nature to pose to Aunt Lucy.

"Ha, ha! Like which ribbon to wear!"

The countess looked on all this with amazement. "Who—are—these—persons?" she asked distastefully.

"Why, Maria Bostram's children, to be sure!" Almeria answered brightly. "They often come to see us."

Tom, who had popped his head in at this moment, volunteered, "Miss Trahern was asking me so often about them, I thought they ought to have a visit!"

The countess, slack-jawed, was beginning to understand. "They are—*your* children?" she asked Maria faintly.

"Why, of course!" said that lady in bewilderment. "Whose else should they be? Though I confess, I sometimes wish they were not! *I* cannot make them mind. The only person who has ever been able to do so is Miss Trahern. I have never forgiven you the iniquity of carrying her off after Christmas," she said in injured tones to Almeria.

"We've been over this before," said Natalie wearily. "Your children were quite over their measles, and a new governess had been engaged."

"And besides, it was the start of the *Season*," said Almeria in awful accents. *"Surely* you could not have expected her to miss that!"

Maria sniffed. "I should have thought her family feeling . . . her father and my husband were such great friends that—but there! The thing is done!"

The children were getting restless. *"When* can we see Aunt *Lucy?"* Lindon wailed.

"Directly," replied Tom. "Here, let us surprise her. You go hide on the stairwell, and I shall bring her out."

This idea recommended itself strongly to the children, and they quickly complied. They were unusually quiet as they waited.

"Miss Trahern!" Tom called, approaching the kitchen door. "Come out! I have something special for you."

"Half a moment. I am just now bringing the tea tray." She backed out the doors and swung around, setting the tray down with a pretty curtsey for the countess and a kind word for her other guests. She turned last to Tom.

"Well? A gift, you say? What is it?" She gave him a quizzing look. "Not mistletoe, I trust!"

Tom laughed. "No, no, not mistletoe! I could not hope to fool you in that fashion again."

"You had better not!" Lucy responded. "I have told you once and I tell you again: I should not forgive you twice for such a trick!" She wagged her finger at Tom.

But the children decided they had waited long enough. They tumbled out of the doorway, expressing their loud joy at seeing her. As coached, however, their cries were all of "Aunt Lucy." While these greetings were going on, it was left to Mrs. Bostram to explain.

"Mistletoe?" the countess asked blankly.

"My Tom! Such a bad boy! He is not my own, you know," she confided, sitting across from the Countess and taking tea. "But I have had the schooling of him since his parents died. Oh, what a trial he has been to me! Making inroads on the cellars, and gaming, and I know not what! You know what boys are!"

The countess, who did not, nodded unconsciously. She

thought she was very likely losing her mind. Never had she been obliged to sit with a party consisting of a woman of bad reputation, two eccentric crones, a young rake, the wife of a cit, and three untrammelled children. The Staventrys, she thought, had gone quite round the bend at last.

"Well, when Lucy was with us over Christmas, Tom took one of his passing fancies to her. I did not encourage it but, to make a round tale of it, he lured her under the mistletoe and kissed her. And no light kiss, either! He has since apologised, but she has twitted him with it ever after. Imagine my mortification!"

"Maria," announced the duchess, "you have bored the countess quite enough with your prattle. You may go home now. Lucille will send the children along later in our carriage." However, she tipped the woman a private wink to speak of a job well done.

Maria fluttered and flittered, very sorry, she was sure, for intruding, and stammered her way out the door.

"Mushroom," sniffed Natalie. "If it weren't for Lucille, I'd never put up with her. My apologies, Countess. Had no idea she'd push her nose in today."

Meanwhile, Lucy and Tom had been hopelessly entangled in a shouting, laughing mass of what seemed to be many more than three children. At last Lucy cried, "Enough! You have quite cut up the peace of this drawing room. I have something I particularly wish to ask your cousin Crowley, and when I have done so I am at your disposal." She hushed the yells of protest by a single raised hand. "Have done. Now go upstairs quietly, like the sensible people I know you can be, and wait in the green bedroom on the right. I fancy," she added secretively, "that you will find certain parcels there, secreted behind the curtains, if you look."

These magic words had the effect of immediately emptying the room of both noise and children.

"There!" said Lucy, crossing to the couch and sitting down. "I do apologise, your Grace. But they have not seen me in so long, you see. They are such excitable little things." She turned to Tom before the countess could reply. "Tell me, Mr. Crowley, how fared our little joke?"

"Oh, famously!" the young man said enthusiastically. "You should have seen Huston's face when I told him I was ragging him! At first he would not believe it was a mock-up! His face is full of egg today at White's, I can tell you."

"Well, he is very finely served!" said Lucy. "I do not for a moment regret it."

"What is this famous joke? Do pray share it," the Countess said archly.

"It is not very edifying," said Lucy doubtfully.

"Missish nonsense," said Natalie. "I'll tell you. Our niece had a score to pay with Huston. So she got Tom here to tell the Beau a Banbury tale about her being a woman of easy virtue, with a string of children. And he swallowed it whole, the fool. When Tom put him right, he made sure it was in front of all of White's. I was never more diverted."

"Except that it redounded," said Almeria sadly. "For Huston told *all* the gentlemen this tale, and *they* believed it too."

"I expect he was angry with me," said Lucy fairly. "After all, I did throw him in the horsepond."

"You . . . threw . . . him . . . in . . . ?" The countess was getting a glazed look.

"When he tried to kiss me against my will," Lucy explained kindly.

"I see," that august lady said faintly.

But, "That is not funny, of course," Tom said. "The story hurt Miss Trahern. I am sorry about that part of it."

"Well-a-day!" Lucy shrugged charmingly. "Don't tease yourself, Tom. I have been besieged with fortune-hunters since the first night of my debut. These three weeks of silence have been in the nature of a holiday. I am almost sorry to see them ended."

"Oh, Lucy, do not say so!" Lady Staventry squeaked. "Why, you must not—you would not think of—"

"Calm yourself, Aunt," said Lucy, laying a fond hand over hers. "I shall do the pretty at our ball, be it ne'er so tiresome. But now," she rose, "I must go to the children. They will be quite impatient for me by this time. I hope you will excuse me," she said smoothly to the countess. "To have those imps rioting in the drawing room again is what I am persuaded you will not at all wish."

The Countess assented. With eager tread, Lucy ascended the stairs. She could hardly wait to see the children again! She had so much to tell them.

Meanwhile, Tom had been waved out the door, and the ladies were once again discussing the forthcoming ball. Here the countess felt herself back on firm ground. She hardly blinked an eye now at hearing that the grand affair was to be in Lucy's honour.

As she was going, Natalie said casually, "Oh, by the by. We received the oddest letter t'other day, revoking some vouchers at Almack's. I expect it was sent here by mistake, as the unfortunate's name happens by coincidence to be Lucy."

"Oh, of course." The countess looked at her own handwriting and gulped. "Yes, indeed," she said haughtily. "I know just who this was for. Thank you for telling me of it. That secretary! But there. You know what hired help is these days."

And she rushed off to Lady Cowper's; full of news, out of breath, and feeling unaccountably as if she had just been run over by a carriage.

17

LUCY'S REENTRY INTO society was just as carefully crafted as the rumour-quashing campaign. Natalie helped with this, but the masterstrokes were Lucy's.

For some days after the countess's visit, no one from Staventry House appeared in public. At first this was seen as an admission of guilt. Then the news began to trickle round that as high a source as Lieven scoffed at the stories. Suddenly, the Staventry silence took on a different aspect. Were they offended? Were they angry? Would they—heavens forfend!—not invite one to their grand ball? It did not bear thinking of! One must right accounts directly! Accordingly, a throng of morning callers besieged the little gatehouse. But all were turned away on the pretext that the party preparations were all-consuming. This only increased the worry.

Tension was high when at last one night the ill-assorted trio swept into Almack's in a blaze of diamonds and velvet and cerulean silk. This magnificence applied only to the older ladies. Lucy was dressed quite simply, in an ivory muslin with gold velvet trimmings that brought out her warm brown eyes. This simplicity also purposely enhanced the notion that her innocence had been unfairly reproached.

The three were instantly surrounded by sycophants. They had been so sadly missed! Had they been ill? Were they quite recovered? Almeria said yes, the most shocking thing, dear Lucy had contrived to twist her ankle while supervising the opening of the House. And naturally she could not go to parties that way. So they had stayed home with her.

Where Lucy could not go, they had no wish to go either, remarked Natalie pointedly.

They sailed on majestically through the room. It was noted that, while the women were gracious, their answers were short and not very warm. One of the few exceptions to this coldness was their treatment of Hersington, who had escorted them in. This raised brows too. *Hersington* was still with them? The rumours *must* be wrong! The earl, for all his sudden succession to the title, was still of the very first circles. He would never knowingly countenance a social climber. It also spurred Lucy's old swains to new heights of determination.

Once around the room went the royal progress (with Lucy saying very little) and then her aunts deposited her on a little gilt chair, adjuring her to have a care to herself. They would look to her later, they said. Not to check her behaviour, which they knew to be irreproachable, but to satisfy themselves that she was not straining herself. Did she truly not mind it? For they were promised to Lady Winton at cards.

"Not the least in the world; you will see it shall do very well. For I have Hersington here to amuse me, and Crowley to run my errands, and there is also our faithful Lord Freton. If I truly cannot brook the tedium, the earl will call me a chair, I'm sure."

This little tableau was naturally witnessed by Lucy's old court, who were eagerly assembling behind her aunts awaiting a chance to flatter her. They noticed their exclusion from Lucy's entertainment programme. It put them on their mettle. These gentlemen rushed forward at once on the aunts' departure, soliciting her hand for the dance, asking if she would like some lemonade or cakes, wanting to hold her fan, fetch her shawl, and offering every other service possible to a young woman who was perfectly healthy and not in the least lonely.

They were destined for disappointment. First they discovered that Lucy had not brought a card because she did not intend to dance. Yes, she assured, her ankle was healing well. However, the doctor did not feel she should risk it at dancing. The night of their own ball on Saturday would be quite soon enough. Oh! Had so and so not received an invitation? She was quite sure she had intended to send one . . . she should have to look into it. All with a compassionate smile which left the unfortunate to wonder if he had been cut.

This was an impression that Lucy had schemed to produce. Not a single card had yet been sent, for all that the ball was a Topic all over town. Tomorrow, the cards would be delivered by hand, as if she had suddenly relented and decided to forgive the beneficiary after all. Lucy well knew that the relief would contribute to the mood of her party—and that not one would tell a living soul he had almost been left out.

But though Natalie had approved these strategic plans with their small dash of revenge, she had worried over Lucy's emotional reactions to her renewed social status. The girl was angry—with good reason—and if she snubbed these people just when they were ready to recant, all might come to naught. There had been no way to control her actions. Natalie had not even tried. She had said merely, "Not a time to get on your prunes and prisms, girl," and left Lucy, with some misgiving, to make up her own mind.

So here was Lucy being welcomed back by the ton with open arms. She thought it a very great bore. In addition, she was angry. How dare all these toadeaters expect to return to her good graces just for the asking! But she was an adult and she believed in manners; she was gracious to everyone. However, her politeness was absentminded and automatic. It was obvious to everyone that she paid heed only to the Earl of Kentsey and, to a lesser extent, Tom Crowley and Lord Freton.

Uneasily the men milled about. Drifting away when she had nothing to say to them. Drifting back hoping she would change her mind. Only to find themselves outside the barrier set up by Hersington and Trahern, which no one could breach for more than a moment at a time.

One gentleman tried lightheartedly to scold Hersington for monopolising Miss Trahern. "On the contrary!" he replied with maddening coolness. "I am acting at the behest of her aunts!"

"Besides which," Lucy said in support of him, "I am so much more comfortable charging Hersington with my little commissions. He is quite one of the family by this time."

This made other men very anxious indeed. They muttered and glanced at each other and sidled away, to return again later.

Meanwhile, Lucy was having a marvellous time. She found herself glad for the fiction her aunts had built. After all, Hersington was the only person who, despite evidence, had not believed ill of her. He had been the only disinterested person willing to help her. Crowley and her aunts did not count; they had known the truth. Hersington was the only friend, in fact, that she had in London. She found herself loving him even more.

And she was, for the first time, enjoying an evening in Almack's.

As soon as Lucy sat down, one deaf dowager remarked in stentorian tones, "You see, I told you it was all a hum! She's as like to the duchess as she can stare. Only look at that nose!" Those around Lucy fidgeted and coughed, pretending they had not heard. Lucy felt a cynical little smile curving her lips, and looked sideways to find a similar one on Hersington's. From that moment, she began to enjoy the evening.

With cunning beyond her wont, she made a point of

being especially sweet to Clarissa Stirlan. She knew it would irritate her.

Clarissa had of course come to claim her share of Lucy's recognition. Having graciously withheld her damaging comments about Lucy for over a week, she felt entitled to a portion of the reflected glamour, if not outright gratitude. She came up dripping pretty protestations and breathing envy that turned to delight when she heard of Miss Trahern's indisposition.

"You cannot dance? But my dear, what a pity!" she cooed. "It is very much too bad, for you have been out of circulation so long! I vow, it seems a positive age since I have seen you on the floor!"

Lucy countered this sugary malice with some of her own. "Oh, have I not been dancing? Truly I had not noticed. Oh, dear! I should not have said so—what a blow to my gallants! But you see, I was so very moped while my friend the earl was out of town; I vow I cannot recall a thing about those weeks! If I did *not* dance, it is a mercy. I should surely have trodden on my partners' toes most dreadfully!"

This was a fine little poser, offering various messages. It could be taken to mean that she had not missed anyone and did not care for their opinion. Clarissa took it so, and it made her furious. So Lucy had not even noticed her fall from grace, had she? Hmph! It took much spice out of the triumph. Then again, it could also mean, "I have forgotten. All is forgiven." One hoped so.

But what it definitely *did* mean was that Hersington was beginning to consolidate his gains with her. The men redoubled their efforts, but without much hope.

At one point, Lucy expressed a desire to take a turn around the room. A dozen gentlemen immediately offered to do the honours.

"No, no!" she chided, shaking her curls at the foremost of them. "Your appearance is sheer poesy, my dear sir, but were my ankle to fail me enroute, rather than suffer your waistcoat to be rumpled, I believe you would drop me! Hersington will do it better. His elegance is of a very plain sort."

So they travelled the circumference of the room slowly, she leaning on his arm and pretending occasionally to limp.

He raised an eyebrow at her. "Well? How like you London's second welcome to the Original?"

She grimaced. "As insincere as the last, and more hypocritical. At least the tabbies are not watching me so this time! I was used to feel they expected me to do something outrageous every moment."

"Not *expected*," he quizzed her. "*Hoped*. Only think what it must be for them with nothing to do but sit and watch. An evening with no indiscretion committed is to them an evening lost!"

"And yet they disapprove," Lucy objected.

"One can be entertained by what one dislikes." Then he screwed up his face, let his hands shake, and spoke in a gravelly voice. "Mary—Mareee! Look at that one, will you? She batted her eyelashes at Manningtree. D'you think she's loose?"

Lucy, getting into the spirit of this, said in a trembling tone, "I shouldn't wonder at it! She's only worth ten thousand pounds, after all. And her mother's a blonde."

"Do tell! Blondes are not at all the thing these days. We shall have to cut her dead," Hersington replied. "Thank heavens *my* girl has more conduct. She . . . Lisa! *Lisa!* What are you doing! Come here this instant! Young lady, what were you doing with your hands in the punchbowl? It's not mannerly."

"And what's more, it dries the skin," added Lucy severely. But she could contain her mirth no longer. Standing there in full sight of the ton, they laughed and laughed till Hersington was obliged to put an arm around her to support her.

"Oh! Oh!" she gasped at last. "I shall never make a dowager. I see too much that is laughable in the world!"

"A severe drawback," Hersington agreed, his chuckle modulating down to the slow smile that made her spine tingle. "Do you know," he reminded her softly, "that you are standing quite brazenly on your 'bad' ankle?"

"Why, so I am!" she said unrepentantly. "Let us continue our circuit of the room." She had not taken many steps, however, before she stopped and stared at a particular couple on the dance floor. She tugged the earl's sleeve excitedly. "Hersington, look!"

It was Huston and Clarissa. They were gliding across the floor: both blonde, overdressed, and spiteful. They were also both ostracised. Society, which had eaten up their slander the week before, now blamed them for the snub they were receiving from the Staventrys, and shunned them. After Lucy had taken the wind out of her eye earlier in the evening, Clarissa had retired to a corner. There Huston, similarly cast out, had joined her. They murmured darkly about two-faced people who did not appreciate the brave bearers of Truth. Soon they found themselves so much in agreement that their association became a positive pleasure rather than an enforced refuge.

"I collect you mean your erstwhile tormentors," the earl replied to Lucy's exclamation. "They do make a handsome couple," he said. "And they are really remarkably alike in both character and fortune. Is it so surprising that they should waltz together?"

"My lord," she told him in mock disgust, "I may not make a very *good* dowager, but you would not do *at all!* You have never even noticed that this is the *third time* those two have partnered each other. What's more, each one was a waltz!"

"My word," said the earl, much struck. "Do you think there will be an 'interesting announcement' from that quarter soon?"

"I would bet my sacred honour on it. If we do not see a notice in the gazette inside a week, I shall—I shall—I don't know what I shall do! What think you of that?"

He looked at the couple again, and then at the glowing girl beside him. The girl whom they had almost ruined. And who was now, effortlessly, but without any loss of either pride or graciousness, making her way back to a position she obviously deserved.

A grave smile flickered over his face. "I think," he said, "it will serve them richly right. Theirs is a marriage made in hell."

18

LUCY'S BEHAVIOUR AT Almack's established the pattern for all the days that followed. She appeared at each important festivity, politely but firmly rebuffed all her aspiring suitors, and paid nearly exclusive attention to Hersington.

She found herself unexpectedly grateful for Natalie's insistence on the "engagement" pretence. It allowed her to largely ignore those people whose behaviour she had always detested. And it allowed her to be constantly close to the man she never pretended—at least to herself—not to love.

She loved his hands and his walk and the way he would lower his eyelids and smile. She loved his voice and the way his arm would sometimes brush hers as they sat side by side. She loved—and was embarrassed by—the breathless feeling when he helped her into a carriage or off a horse, and held her just a moment too long, just a bit too close. He had exchanged the perfunctory hand kiss for a kiss on the wrist, just touching the skin between her glove and wrist. It sent strange flashes right up to her shoulder.

But more than all, she loved his sense of humour. It marched with hers. She never found something ridiculous but she could turn to him and see the same realisation on his face. They played "The Dowager Game" until it was honed to a fine science. They played it in different characters. Once she would be Lady Jersey and he the Countess Lieven. Another time she would be Lady Prewlitt-Howes and he Lady Cowper. They would pick particular debutantes of unimpeachable reputation and make jades of them on the basis of an eyelash or badly stitched reticule. They would replay specific balls and shred the stodgiest members there. But Lucy claimed that she had the earl beaten to flinders, because she had made the first correct prediction. Lord Huston and Clarissa Stirlan announced their intentions in print the day before Lucy's ball.

Hersington made a moue. "What a pity. You had said if they didn't get roped you shouldn't know what you had done. I had a plan for your penance. You were to have married a mere earl." And he said no more, but allowed the matter to drop.

Lucy could not let it rest, however. That night, alone in her bed, she stared distractedly at the ceiling, chasing her thoughts.

She was in love with him. No question about it. It was the first time for her, but she rather doubted that it was temporary. Her love might fade, but only with time and great pain. This would never occur again.

Whether Hersington loved her, she did not know. At times it seemed he did, and then at times . . . Some moments he would draw perturbingly near, and look down into her face, with his eyelids dropped in that languid, sensual way—and then tweak her nose and make a jest, or return a handkerchief she had dropped, as if it were of no moment. Who could tell? Perhaps it was only the pretence, the game they were both playing, to fool the world into thinking them engaged.

Sighing at her canopy, Lucy admitted that such a thought depressed her. Yet was it likely that he loved her? How could he? Why should he?

And even if he did . . . Lucy sternly reproved her heart's leaping at this thought. Even so, what of it? Could she marry the Earl of Kentsey?

Lucy twisted and buried her face under the bedclothes. No. No, she could not. She ignored the stabs of pain and shored up her logic once more. It would not be right for her to wed the earl. She was far beneath him socially.

To be fair, she argued on, I don't think he would care. He is a lovely, an extraordinary man; I cannot believe such superficialities would weigh with him. But even supposing he loved me, and my status made no difference . . . For a moment she felt happy, then dropped her head onto the pillow again. Even if. She still must not marry him. It would be one case for him to accept such a wife. But once her background was a matter of public record, which it assuredly must eventually be . . . ? Could she bear to see him ostracised from the only world he knew, the world in which he moved with ease even while recognising its absurdities? She turned over uneasily. No. No. She could not do that to him. Not to Hersington. She bit her lips and tried to pretend that the wetness trickling slowly down her cheeks was damp from an open window. She did not know whether she wanted this exquisite, torturous courtship to go on forever, or if she wanted her father to come home and rescue her. She wondered which was better: to start the yearning now and get it over? Or to see him, to see him, to see him—just a few more times.

That was Friday. Saturday was the night of the ball. No one, looking at Lucy as she stood to receive her guests, could have guessed the slow, sweet poison flowing through her veins.

Her dark curls tumbled past tiny, pearl-pocked ears to swan-white shoulders. These were bared by a daring gown of heavy, silver-gray satin that sighed when she curtsied. The sleeves were slashed to show quantities of heirloom lace. The silvery, moonlike colour of the dress gave Lucy a sparkling quality. And it had another effect as well.

This was a very adult dress. Satin. Low-cut. There was even a diamond bracelet. This was not the dress of a debutante. This was a gown for . . . an engaged woman.

Everything had been orchestrated for this impression,

even to Hersington's early arrival and his stance very near the entrance—almost, but not quite, part of the receiving line. It was also significant, the matrons told each other knowingly, that this entertainment was being held in Staventry House proper. That seemed an unmistakable sign that Miss Trahern was soon to set up household.

The mansion glittered and shone as it had been built to do. Lucy was proud of it. It had taken enormous work and organisation, even with plentiful servants, to prepare the house for entertainment on a grand scale after twenty years' closure. She felt, as to style, she had nothing for which to blush. She was particularly pleased with the circulating goldfish pond in the supper room and the flowering lilac trees on the colonnade.

She had felt some last-moment trepidation about the part she was to play with Hersington. "It's all very well to start such a deception," she told Natalie. "But what when the necessity for it is finished? What when I disappear again with my father?"

"Nothing simpler," barked Natalie. "Jilt him. We put it about that you threw him over for higher game. Posted off to the Continent with a Spanish duke, somesuch."

"Yes, I suppose that would answer," said Lucy slowly. "I cannot like it, all the same. I would not wish to make Hersington look the fool."

"Such hobgoblins!" chided the duchess. "His idea, heh? His offer? All right then. Accept it gracefully. All this potheration over nothing! You are giving me the migraine. Feed the cats and go change your clothes!"

Lucy laughed and complied. It was good to know that some things never changed.

At first the ball went just as she expected. She was asked for every dance, but cried off from all, citing her duties as hostess. However, she condescended to dance with Hersington. Then a minuet with Crowley. Then a waltz with Hersington. A country dance with Freton. And then Hersington again.

Since each of these dances was spaced at least an hour apart, the evening was considerably advanced when her third time with the earl occurred and the eyebrows began to rise. Lucy glanced around as she finished the figure and found all eyes covertly upon them.

Hersington whispered in her ear. "Now," he said. "Now is the time for the obligatory moonlight walk in the garden that will finish the business."

She drew away from him somewhat. "You surely can't mean—?"

"I have the duchess's express order. If we do not do so, a public announcement will be expected tonight. However, if we slip off, it will seem we have come to a private understanding."

"I see. Very well then," she sighed as he steered her towards the corridor to the terrace, "let us finish the last act of the comedy."

Opening the door to the park, he threw her a sideways glint.

"Do you know, you are a most unconvincing lover, Miss Trahern. I do not believe I have ever had so much difficulty obtaining a tête-à-tête before."

If you only knew, she thought. If you only knew how badly I want to be in the garden with you, and how I fear it. Aloud, she said lightly, "Ah, but you must remember I am to jilt you. One cannot expect too much of a jilt, I collect. Natalie has decided it all, precise to a pin."

He tucked her arm in his and began to walk with her towards the flower garden. Scents of jasmine and rose floated to her in the night, and the tang of fresh-mown grass. She heard the soft shush of the stream as it emptied into the small lake. The pines threw dark stripes over everything, dappled by silver patches of moon. Hersington strode beside her, his face sculpted to bone and mystery in this light, his hair a silvery waterfall.

His voice came to her deep and familiar. "Ah, yes, the invaluable Duchess of Bucklass. As fine a strategist as I should care to meet. Have you never wondered, Miss Trahern, what she and I said to each other that day we were closeted so long?"

"Why yes, of course." Lucy was mildly surprised at the choice of topic. Relieved that it was not more personal. "But it would have been ill-bred of me to ask. So I didn't."

"Discreet Miss Trahern," he chuckled gently. "We were talking about you." They had stopped under an arched trellis. The scent of honeysuckle came to her, piercingly sweet. "And what was said?"

"She asked my intentions toward you. I told her." He paused. She could see his face clearly now. He was smiling, and the mild teasing note never left his voice. But about the eyes was something strained and sober. "She advised me that you had a lot of goosish notions in your bonebox." Lucy giggled. "And that the first time I offered for you, you would undoubtedly refuse. However she also said," and here he gently clasped her elbows and drew her closer, "that if I were any sort of man, I would ask again."

All levity had left his voice now. It became as intimate and caressing as the hands that slid up her arm to stroke her bare shoulders. "I am asking again, dearest. I want you to marry me and live with me always. Will you?"

The words were so simple. Yet every syllable fell with undeniable sincerity. Lucy was caught in the dilemma she had most feared. And how, how, how could she think with his arms around her, so close she could feel his chest rise and fall as he breathed?

She tried. She took a shaky breath. "My lord, you cannot mean it. You are—jesting with me—surely?"

One hand moved up to trace the back of her neck. She closed her eyes and shivered. He leaned toward her and his words were honeyed fire in her ear.

"I was never more serious in my life. I love you, Lucy. I will never love anyone else. Can you, in all honesty, say the same is not true for you?"

"My lord, I cannot—I must not—please do not ask me!" Her voice and body alike were quivering badly.

"Nevertheless, I will have my answer," he murmured. His clasp dropped to her waist and tightened; the hand at her neck moved to her jaw. He brought her face, all unresisting, to his and kissed her.

It would have been too much to expect that Luct would not respond. She did, heartily and thoroughly, making up in enthusiasm what she lacked in skill. It was a very long moment indeed before Hersington could bear to let her face slide slowly away between his fingers. When he did look down into her wide liquid eyes, gazing so intensely back up at him, he saw with shock that she was crying.

"Oh, my dear," he moaned, and gently urged her to the nearby bower. He made her sit, and tenderly wiped the tears, which kept on falling. "What is it, sweetling? Did I frighten you? I did not mean to press you, only . . ." he was kneading her hands, and his voice was thick and shaken. "I had to know. I had to know if you, too . . ."

"Well, now you know," she said in a tight, forlorn little voice. "And it doesn't make the slightest difference. I cannot marry you." Unconsciously, she had torn her handkerchief in half. She was still weeping; silently, slowly, without stopping.

With infinite care he drew her against his shoulder. He made soothing sounds and patted her as if she were a child. She no longer resisted. She let her head rest against his chest and clasped her hands round his waist and sighed. Let her have this. This at least. There would be years enough alone.

"Why can't you marry me, sweetheart?" he asked reasonably.

"It would not be fitting," she mumbled into his coat. "You are of too high a station for such as me."

He rubbed her back in slow circles. "Nonsense, my dear. You have manner and style and address enough for two.

What care I for the rest?" When she did not reply, he tried again. "Come, am I then such an ogre? What is this terrible past that you dare not reveal to me? I can hardly believe it so very bad." Here the calming hand moved to the back of her neck. "Knowing you as I do." He dropped a kiss on her head. "Loving you as I do."

She sat up suddenly and said with desperation, "But you don't understand! I am an impostor! Those two women are not my aunts at all!"

He smiled at her with singular sweetness. "No, how can you say so? When you look so very much like them!"

Lucy made some smothered exclamation, before he went on, tilting her chin up with one hand. "Only look: two eyes, one forehead, two cheeks, one nose," touching each feature as he named it. "Quite a remarkable resemblance indeed. Two lips . . . two beautiful, irresistible lips," he murmured, and kissed her again.

For a moment she was quiescent, molding pliantly into his embrace, answering to the lips that questioned and sought and devoured. But from somewhere, she found the strength to pull away. She exiled her hands to her lap and clenched them. In a voice with a ragged semblance of calm, she said, "Hersington, you do not understand the case at all. True, you were always aware that I was not what I seemed. Now it appears you even know that I was not related to my protectors. But there is something even they do not know. My lord, to tell you who I am is beyond my power. Even I do not know that."

"What do you mean?" His face was as intent on her glimmering form in the moonlight as if his whole life hinged on this moment. Which it did.

"My father you know as George Trahern. As do I. But that is not the truth. He told me once that he changed it when he was very young. What the name was from which he felt it incumbent to flee, I do not know. I never have. So you see, my lord earl, I could be anybody. A lot of the possibilities are vile beyond imagining. Only consider what would happen to you if we married, and then such a fact came to light about the woman you had made a countess. Hersington, you may snap your fingers at the fashionable world now—but that is because you have it. You do not know what it is to be . . . outside. I do. And I will not have it for you."

Desperately, the earl played his last card. Always, always, he had been so sure that someday Lucy would confide in him. That when she did, and he laughed at her fears, she would lay them to rest and give herself to him. Now he saw her slipping away, for principles, ethics, considerations, none of which was going to fill the hole in his heart as he grew old alone. "What if—" he began hoarsely. Then stopped, gripped her hands tightly between his own, and went on. "Supposing I knew all your past—all the things you've done that make you feel ineligible, all your true relatives—and I didn't care?

"For I don't, my love. Surely you must know it doesn't matter to me. Would it then set your mind at rest? Would you then consent to marry me?"

She drew a deep breath and said with finality, "No, my lord, I would not."

He saw the resolve in her face and knew he had lost. Should he have told her earlier all he knew about Miss Trahern, the governess? What use when she would only say the knowledge would not protect him from being cast off by society?

All that was left to him was to end with dignity, He faced it. He bowed his head. He inhaled and said bleakly, "So there is nothing to be done."

"No." Her voice was a whisper of wind on a long, vast desert. A desert which they would have to walk alone.

They rose by tacit consent and walked back towards the house; in their pain more separate and apart than they had ever been.

Just beside the lake he stopped her. "I will not trouble you again. I shall go back to Kentsey. And try to learn—

though it is impossible—to forget. But tell me once, for the lonely years—Lucy, was it true? Do you love me?"

He had never used her Christian name before. His voice was an ache.

"Oh, yes, Hersington—so much!" she said brokenly. Then, irresistibly, she snatched his palm and passionately imprinted a kiss there. And ran wordlessly down the path, as if all the demons of hell were after her.

== 19 ==

LUCY STEPPED BACK inside the corridor to find the duchess waiting. This latter took one look at her white, pinched face and snapped, "Refused him again, did you? Nincompoop! I'll have a word to say to you on that head! But for the nonce go tend to Almeria. Something's frightened her. She's wandering about distracted, can't make heads nor tails of it. You go find out. I'll see to the guests. Cover for you both. They're leaving, y'know. Good thing. Saw that fubsy-faced you're wearing, cat would be out!" She rustled disdainfully off toward the grand staircase.

After some fifteen minutes of searching, Lucy located Almeria. Lady Staventry was wringing her hands, walking up and down a little back staircase, and pacing round and round in circles on the landing. The activity did not appear to be calming her mind. Nor, since this staircase had not been part of Lucy's cleaning programme, did the hem of her mantua gown derive much benefit.

When Lucy touched her shoulder, Almeria gave a squeal and whirled around. "Oh! Lucy dear, it is you! You gave me *such* a fright. And I am ever so glad to see you—oh, no, I am not! For I had forgot that it is all your fault. Yes, you are to blame, and after you *promised*. But it's all one. I should *never* have let Natalie badger me into holding a ball here, for what do the decorations and the spacious size of the rooms and the gleaming appointments and—and—all of that! I say, what do they *signify*, if one must as a consequence be frightened out of one's wits and hide on a potty old staircase just to be *safe?*"

Lucy had never seen Lady Staventry so vexed. In her own childish way, she was obviously quite angry. Lucy put an arm around her waist and walked with her in her manic course: up the stairs, fast; down the stairs, slow. Round and round the landing. A stop to wring the hands. Up the stairs again.

Meanwhile she talked soothingly. "I would not for worlds have disappointed you so, Aunt. But I am baffled. What is it I have done? What has so cut up your peace?"

"Why, you *swore* most *faithfully* that you would rid the house of every ghost before I set foot in it. And I believed you—and truly, at first, it seemed you had done the business, for there were no spectres *anywhere* that I could see; and none of the guests complained either, so I must suppose the receiving rooms to have been quite wholesome. And then!" Almeria stopped tragically on the landing and flung up her hands. "What must you needs do but go gallivanting out in the garden and stay an *unconscionable* length of time—and now we have a ghost again! Soon we shall probably have a whole raft of them! There will be no dealing with them!" She glared at Lucy and put her hands on her hips.

Lucy took Almeria's hands with an expression of contrition and said, "You are right! I have been most remiss not to have seen to it. Where did you see this bogey?" Lucy had a shrewd suspicion it was either a flapping curtain or a lost party guest.

"Well, I had gone down to the small front parlour. We had it fitted for a tiring room, you remember, for ladies who wearied of dancing or gentlemen who wanted a cigar? The music made my head ache so, and I wanted to nibble on a sweet. Well, as I was there, this fellow wandered in—no, he did *not* wander! He *drifted!* For all the world as if he had no direction and no feet. And he was *not* dressed for a party. His clothes and his hair were all pale and floppy. He started floating around the room looking at this and that and paid me no heed at all but looked *right* through me—then sat down at his ease and started drinking the sherry! So *naturally* I knew he was a ghost! Are you going to get rid of him?" she finished anxiously.

A great light had dawned on Lucy. She put a hand to her forehead. "Oh, Lord—Papa! But he *would* arrive tonight, and in just that fashion! I must go to him at once."

She sped off leaving an indignant and bewildered Almeria behind. "What has come to Lucy? Claiming her father is a ghost! Of all the starts!" She shook her head and continued pacing.

Meanwhile, Lucy's mind was in a pother. She had, of course, written to her father, telling him only: *Through a series of circumstances too tedious and complicated to relate, I have come under the protection of two remarkable and powerful old ladies: The Lady Staventry and the Duchess of Bucklass. They take good care of me, and we are all most fond of each other.*

Knowing her father, Lucy fancied he had paid little attention at the time. But when he returned to England, he had pulled out her letter, seen the name "Staventry," and looked no further. Having obtained the direction of Staventry Place, it would be just like him to wander in as if he owned it, without announcing himself to the butler or sending a card, and settling down to drink the sherry!

But why, oh, why of all nights tonight? Lucy had known the day must come when she would be taken from her engagingly bizarre "aunts," and be deposited in some cottage somewhere. Worse still, to be taken from Hersington, never to see him again. But to have the one follow so hard on the heels of the other—it gave her an almost physical pang. Or perhaps she was being optimistic? Mr. Trahern's early return might mean his venture had failed, and she would need to work again. Most likely in London. And be obliged to meet Clarissa in the park one day as she was airing her charges? Good God, what a notion! Unbearable!

This was all vapours, however, until she saw the man

himself and heard where matters stood. And to do her credit, Lucy really loved her maggotty old father. Under all these roiling worries was an uncomplicated joy at the thought of seeing him again.

She opened a little green door and entered the room. There stood her father, with his back to her, pottering with a clock.

George Trahern was, as Almeria had stated, a "pale, floppy" man. He was tall, lean, and light-coloured, with formless clothes that fluttered about him like feathers and hair that flapped untidily on his head like an abandoned nest. He had clever, long-fingered hands, a round and jovial but somehow otherwhere face, and eyes that tended to fade as one looked at them. His lapels were always ash-specked, his shoes down-at-heel. But he loved children (for whom he always kept string in his pockets), played a mean game of cards, and although of no use as a source of common sense, he was astonishingly brilliant on some ten or twelve topics which very few people in the world understood at all.

Lucy tiptoed up to him—he was still absorbed in springs and wires—and kissed him softly on the cheek. "Hello, Father," she said gently. "Welcome back."

George Trahern turned his head slightly and kissed the air where she had been a moment ago. "Oh, hullo, Lucy. Glad to be back. Look at this!" He straightened and held up an unidentifiable piece of metal. "Such a rare clock I've not seen this age . . . and it's shamefully neglected. Shamefully. "Well," he sighed, wiped his hands, and set it carefully down, "that's the nobility for you."

His voice was as she remembered, a meandering combination of mild wonderment and mild complaint. George Trahern had never quite gotten into the way of ordinary living. "I must say," he went on as he sat and helped himself to another glass, "this is a very odd sort of place you've fallen into. I'm not scolding, mind, but it does seem there are some strange sorts of people here. The servants are a confused lot. Didn't seem to know their business. At last they sent the housekeeper in to me. I suppose she must have been, that is. Odd sort of menial. Dressed all in satin, very pretty too, but fifty if she's a day. Tricked out to the mines, in fact, which made no sense at all for one of her station. Did she show me to a room? Offer to find me supper? Tell me where to locate you? No. She stared at me, went quite white, ordered me on no account to touch the comfits, and ran from the room! Perhaps I am not up to snuff on these matters," Mr. Trahern went on on bewilderment. "But it does not seem to me to be behaviour calculated to put a guest at his ease!"

Lucy smiled and patted her father's arm. "Oh, Papa, what a welcome you have had, to be sure! That was not a servant at all, but Almeria. She thought you were a ghost, which explains her unusual behaviour. As for the satin, we have got a party on tonight, you see. The servants are all busy with that. I expect there was no one at the door to attend you."

"Ah, that explains it." He crossed his legs, and seemed disinclined to say anything more for a while. Lucy soon found herself fidgeting. Now that her charade was almost at an end, she suddenly felt a need for her father's approval.

"Papa, did . . . did you think it excessively . . . strange in me? To stay here I mean? After I left the Bostram's?"

"Oh, no," said Mr. Trahern comfortably. He was fiddling with the cuckoo's inner workings again. "I myself would never want to stay in a place where they treat their clocks like this. . . ." A little pop! and he removed a rusted nail with a grin of satisfaction. "There. That's got it! But if you are happy, here," he continued, "that's all I care for. By all means, remain as long as you like."

Lucy's brows puckered. It was not like her father to approve a situation which involved accepting charity. Unless . . .

"Papa," she began hesitantly. "I had quite thought that when you returned we should set up household together.

This does not sound to be your plan. Does it mean that your venture in America was—well, unsuccessful? I would naturally not wish to be a burden to you if you were unable to support me. . . ."

He turned around at last. "No, no, my dear. Nothing of that nature. My little scheme worked famously. One might even say we are very well set up now." He chuckled comfortably. "I know you think me a mutton-head when it comes to money matters. But even I am not so sap-skulled as not to realise that without my sensible Lucy to manage me I should soon be blown up at Point-Non-Plus! The long and short of it is that I have retained a trustee. According to him, we need never trouble our heads again about such things."

"Oh, Papa!" She ran across to him and hugged him. "I am so *very* proud of you! I always knew you could do it! If only Mama could be here!"

All of a sudden the inventor looked embarrassed. "That is precisely the difficulty, my dear, and why I should not mind your remaining here. You see . . ."

He got no further. The door swung open and hit the wall with a impatient snap. The Duchess of Bucklass stood majestically in the opening. Her voice was something between a laugh and a growl.

"As I thought. Well, George? Speak up, man! Been fifty years. Haven't you got a greeting for your little sister?"

20

Lucy was never quite sure of what happened next. It seemed to her that the room spun crazily around. When it stopped, she was sitting on the couch with a tumbler of brandy. She had a vague impression of sharp cross-questioning about the past going across the room. But when at last she opened her eyes, it seemed that the topic had moved to memorable boxing matches of the last twenty years.

Her father and her aunt—my God, her aunt!—were laughing at each other. George was saying, "And then one of the audience—robust fellow, hat over his eyes, never knew who—started yelling that Mendoza had been cheated, and a mill started, the referee came up—and damme if this stranger didn't give the ref a leveller such as I've never seen! Beautiful science, but more bottom than sense, I always thought. Clapped him in jail, shouldn't wonder."

"No they didn't," cawed Natalie, in great good humour. "I know who that pugilist was, and you're looking at her!"

"Good God!" His eyes went wide, and then he clapped her on the back. "So you grew up all right and tight, petticoats and all! Almost makes me sorry I left home!"

Lucy sat up slowly, half offended by their enjoyment. She felt as if someone had removed Britain from underneath her feet and replaced it with some other island. It hardly seemed a time for levity. "Excuse me," she said fuzzily. "Perhaps I belong in Bedlam. But I rather thought you indicated a while ago . . . that you were brother and sister? Or did I imagine it?"

Her father looked at her in bemusement. "Well, naturally, my dear. I assumed that was why you had chosen to stay here. Blood's blood, and all that, and you were in mighty queer stirrups . . . although how you had smoked my disguise after all these years I could not fathom. Do you mean to say you *didn't* know? That you thought you were accepting charity? But no. In course Natalie must have told you."

"Natalie did *not* tell me," said Lucy in a hard voice, fixing her with a stare. "And I should like to know why."

The Duchess shrugged. "Could hardly tell you what I wasn't sure of myself. Suspected. Only suspected. Your father sounded too much like that will-o'-the-wisp brother of mine for coincidence. Besides. That nose of yours. Just like mine."

Lucy choked.

"Are you all right, girl?"

"Quite. Do continue," she said faintly.

"Know what you're thinking. High ropes again. All that time believing you weren't an heiress. Weren't well born. Weren't fit to marry. Wrong. All of it true. Could have married anybody. Should have married Hersington. Told you so. Didn't listen. The more fool you."

It was beginning to sink in. Lucy was everything the ton had believed her to be, everything she had been ashamed of lying about. Now that her father had triumphed, she was even an heiress in her own right. She could even have these two wonderful ladies as her aunts. But she could never have Hersington, because she had driven him away. She had told him "Never." He would not ask again.

With a shaking hand, she emptied her glass. "I think," she said, "I need another brandy."

Natalie was no fool, however. As soon as she had parted from Lucy she went hunting for his lordship. She caught him just as he was letting himself out a back door.

"One moment," she commanded. "Got an errand for you."

His shadowed face was expressionless in that light. "I am yours to command, of course."

"Lucille gave you your notice to quit, did she? Wait, don't speak." As he moved uneasily. "Obstinate chit! Don't blame you for planning to give up. But." She paused, cocking a head. "One fact she don't know. Crucial one. Bound to find out tonight. May change everything. Willing to try?"

"Ma'am." Something inflexible in that cultured voice. "She has given me her final answer. As a gentleman, I would not dream of pressing her further."

The Duchess tapped her foot. "You're as stubborn as she. Perfect match. Pity. Well, I wash my hands of you. But I warn you—"

"About that favour?" His voice was smooth and polite and icy cold.

"Hem. Puppy! Have it your way, then.

"Almeria's had a fright. Lucy's father arrived tonight"— she noted with satisfaction his barely perceptible start— "and Almeria got a maggot into her head that he was a ghost because he was all in white. She's wandering around the house like a spirit herself. I've got to get back to the guests. I'd take it kindly in you if you'd contrive to calm her down and then bring her to the front parlour. I'll join you there as soon as I can. But don't leave her till then, mind!" This in case Lucy preceded her. "Will you do it?"

"With great pleasure," he said, bowing, and handed her back to her post by the stairs.

This explains the emergence of Hersington into the parlour just as Lucy was finishing her second brandy.

Almeria was sheltered in the crook of his arm, looking as adorable and undersized as a kitten beside a St. Bernard. In contrast to his hollowed, restrained face, hers was bright-eyed and expressive. Her anxious eyes darted from face to face.

She shrank into his chest when she saw George Trahern. "Are you *sure* it is not a ghost?" she whispered.

"Not a bit of it," he soothed. "It is merely Miss Trahern's father, back from America."

He was studiously not looking at Lucy as he seated Lady Staventry beside her on the couch.

Lucy glanced at him once, hunger and pain washing across her face. Then, thinking quickly, she spoke loud enough for Hersington as well as Almeria to hear.

"Indeed, it is not a ghost, though I can see how you might have thought so. For you see, there is a remarkable thing we have just discovered. Do you remember that older brother you told me about, the one who left so many years ago and simply never returned? You will hardly credit it, but it appears that he is none other than my father! He never died at all! And here he is!"

"Oh, my," was all Almeria's comment. She looked at the interloper with rather more dismay than less.

But Hersington gazed at Lucy for one brief, flashing instant, and what she saw on his face made her shiver. It was as if all the suns of the world had come up at once to dwell in his eyes.

She blushed firecely, and looked away, towards her father. "Your attention, if you please!" she announced crossly. Everyone was looking at her now. "If I understand what has passed in this room, there is much to be explained. I am very distressed to find that I have been laboring all my life under a misapprehension about my own identity! And I would like to know," —she let out her breath explosively—"*why?*" She turned to her father. "*Why* did you leave in that cavalier fashion? And why did you change your name? I quite thought—forgive me—that it was because of some scandal. And once having left, married, and produced a child, why did you never tell me or my mother? Did I not deserve the truth?"

"Ah." Her father recrossed his legs, smoking his pipe, very much at his ease. (*I am going to scream*, thought Lucy).

"As to the name change, that is elementary. I did not

wish to be traced. Later, I did not tell your mother because . . . we were very happy, but I daresay she would have preferred a more . . . conventional style of living. Had she known it was in my power to give it her . . . I should have ended in exactly the trap I had sought to escape. You are in the right of it, however, to imply that I should have informed you. I am afraid, my dear, that after so many years, it simply slipped my mind. I was only seventeen, you know, when I left."

He seemed all at once to truly notice Almeria. "I say, that is the housekeeper that treated me so shabbily. What is she doing here? This is a private family conference, you know, miss. You ought not to be here."

At last Almeria roused herself with an insulted shake. "Oh! Now I *know* you are my brother George! You are as odious as ever!" (Lucy noticed the earl's shoulders shaking at this point, and hastily looked away to preserve her own countenance.) "A housekeeper, indeed, when I cannot even wash a dish without breaking it!" She seemed to think this a strong recommendation in her favour.

"So you are Almeria?" he said curiously. "That stands to reason." He addressed Natalie. "We always said she should turn into a beautiful ninnyhammer. Remember? And only look. We were right." George, no more than Natalie had ever understood the social graces. The vague pleasure in his voice showed that he was entirely unconscious of the insult.

But Almeria had not yet begun. "Well, if *you* are my brother *George*," she said waspishly, "I have a bone to pick with you! Yes, and have had anytime these fifty years! What sort of trick was it to leave us when you *knew* I was the next in line for inheritance? I had to take all the money—and although money is generally very useful, *especially* when one wants to buy things, it almost made Lucy hate me! I should rather never own a groat than make Lucy angry!"

Lucy squeezed her hand, and Hersington gave her a quick look.

"Yes, and what is more, I was courted by dozens of

horrid little toads, and had stupid fellows *kissing* me! Plus estates and trust funds and servants to manage and all manner of flummery which makes my head spin and gives me nightmares *besides* ruining my card game—and it is all your fault! In my books, in short, you are the most complete cad!" She crossed her arms and assumed a look as close to bellicose as she would ever come.

Trahern looked taken aback at this attack. "My dear sister, I am most sincerely sorry! If I had realised your sentiments, I should certainly have taken you with me. For that is precisely why I shabbed off myself. *I* did not want to manage estates and go to state dinners and prose on with politicians and wear scratchy formal clothes. Of all things, I abhor pomp!"

"Oh, I, too!" she agreed eagerly. "I am quite of a mind with you, and if that is why you left, then naturally I must forgive you.

"And Lucy dear, you must understand too. For after all, you never liked the fuss and were forever making excuses against too much consequence. I recall, if you do not, that you hid in the buttery when Manningtree came to call! And he brought the prettiest posies, too! Nor would you let us present you at one of the drawing rooms. So please, you musn't be cross with our brother. He has just come back from the Colonies, after all, after months and months of battling with monsters and heathens and rebels and—and things," she waved her arms vaguely. "It would be very ungracious in you to wash his head for him now!"

Grinning, Lucy dropped a kiss on her head and sat down. "You are in the right of it, ma'am. It would not do at all. Nor how can I be angry when this revelation has truly made you my aunt at last?"

"Oh, my, it has!" cried Almeria, astonished. They embraced.

They pulled apart to find George going on mildly as if there had been no interruption. "If you do not like pomp," he was remarking, "I fail to see why you live in this mausoleum. If one believed in ghosts, this would certainly be the place one might reasonably expect to find them."

"Indeed!" said Almeria. "I shall *never* be induced to give a party here again. No matter," she looked at the duchess darkly, "how *sensible* it may seem. But in fact, we do not reside here, but in the cozy little gatehouse which you may recall. It is just down the drive, remember?"

He nodded. "I am glad to have the clock explained . . . I recall the gatehouse quite well," he added reminiscently. "It has a lovely secluded attic that I always thought would do nicely for a laboratory. . . ."

"We can easily fit it out as one, if you like," Almeria put in. "I am sure that if we asked Lucy . . ."

Her father coughed and looked at Lucy apologetically. "That is just what I have been meaning to say. I love my daughter, of course, and in other circumstances would be pleased to reside with her. But I do not, in fact, intend to remain long in England."

Lucy glanced an enquiry. "Oh?"

He fidgeted. "When you said you wished your mother could be here it put me in mind . . . my dear, your mother and I had a happy life. But it has been some years, you know . . . and while I was in America I met a widow."

"And you would like to remarry." Lucy was beginning to see.

"Yes. You do not mind it?"

"No. I am very happy for you. And now that you have money, we can always visit, can we not? It is not as if we shall be separated forever."

"Quite." But he seemed as if there was something he would still like to say.

Natalie forestalled him. "Lucille can live with us indefinitely, of course. Happy to have her."

"I appreciate that, of course, but forgive me if I say it will soon cease to be suitable. It is time," he said earnestly to Natalie, "that my daughter was married. I am come over to England expressly to find a husband for her."

This shocked the ladies into silence. After all their efforts!

He went on in his unheeding way. "Though I don't know how I am to do that. I am so long out of society that I have lost the way of it. I wish there were some easier manner of doing the thing," he fretted.

He swivelled rather wistfully toward Hersington. "I say, you look like a rather nice chap. I don't suppose," he asked hopefully, "that *you* would like to marry my Lucy?"

Lucy froze in her seat.

"As a matter of fact," said Hersington casually, "I would."

Lucy's father looked at her. She could only nod breathlessly.

"Oh, good, that's settled!" said Trahern with childish pleasure at a difficult task avoided. "Tell me, sir, as a matter of formality, could you give me your name and . . . and so forth?"

Lucy was trying so hard neither to laugh nor cry that she did not at first follow the trend of the conversation. Having mastered her emotions, she heard her father say mildly, "Hersington, eh? I knew a Hersington once. Nice fellow. Strange taste in women, as I recall,"—she and the earl exchanged a now-familiar glance—"but otherwise the best of good fellows. I remember a son . . . Justin, was it? Brown-haired. You can't be he."

"My brother is unfortunately deceased," Hersington said levelly. "Nevertheless you may recall me."

Lucy sat up and took notice.

"Do you recollect a foundry in Soho? I put a greasy piece of cog in your pocket, ruining it beyond repair. You apostrophised me as a raging scapegrace, and predicted an early death on the gallows." He was smiling, relaxed, standing with his hands in his pockets. Lucy crooked her brows. He had not told her they had ever met. What was going on? Her father's next words jolted her.

"Then you must be little Jasper! What a pleasant surprise! And how glad I am that my predictions were quite off. Otherwise we should not have had this happy solution to our difficulties, should we?"

Lucy was paralysed in her seat. A final revelation had come to her.

Little Jasper. *Little Jasper!*

She rose suddenly. "You will excuse us, father," she said shakily. "But if we are to be wed, there are some details to be worked out."

"Of course, of course," he waved benignly. "But I say, Lucy, if *Almeria* is not the housekeeper, who is? I don't like to be a trouble. But I've travelled a long way, you know, and it's nearly morning—not to put too fine a point on it, I'm devilish sharp-set!"

Lucy was immediately all concern. "Oh, Papa, I am so sorry! *I* am the housekeeper! In the excitement of your arrival I had quite forgot. Leave me alone to order the servants while Hersington joins me in the garden. Five minutes' time," she shot at him meaningly. Then she gave her father a hug, and rustled out. Hersington followed shortly afterward.

It remains only to be noted that some two minutes later a kitchen maid, very distressed, came in to speak to Natalie. She didn't wish to contravene Miss's orders, she was sure—but was she *really* to boil the cats in an omelette for breakfast?

21

LUCY FLOUNCED OUT to the garden and stood with crossed arms, tapping her foot. Fortunately for the coming interview, it was now growing light. Unfortunately, to Lucy's irritated mind, it bid fair to be a beautiful morning. She thought it churlish of the yard to be so fresh and poignant, the bushes to throw such piquant shadows, the air to be full of blossom scent. It was not at all helpful, Lucy thought crossly, in maintaining her anger.

And maintain it she must. Lucy's earlier surprise and joy at her new status had given way to pique. It was not enough that her own father was not who she had thought, that her aunts had concealed their identities, that even she was an entirely different person than she had always supposed—no, all this was not enough! Hersington must needs trick her too! Crowley's "other uncle," indeed! Grrr! It was too much to be borne. She would be pleased to ring a peal over him! But it was hard to hold to such a resolution with the birds carolling "love, love, love, love, love!" all around.

Clearly, thought Lucy sourly, they have never been exposed to such a comedy of errors. They had never been advised, for instance, that they were worms, and later had someone say, "So sorry. A slight error. You are, in fact, birds."

The absurd thoughts her anger had brought her failed her at this moment, and Lucy giggled. That was naturally the moment when the Earl of Kentsey appeared on the garden path.

He was sauntering elegantly towards her—*sauntering!*, Lucy thought indignantly—and the new-risen sun made a nimbus of his hair. He approached slowly, hands in pockets, jewels winking on his vest. His lean, lithe form and the carved and shadowed contours of his face had not changed a whit over the turmoil of the last hours, except for a certain relaxation about the mouth. He looked, in that moment, achingly beautiful. Lucy was incensed.

The earl stood over her with that lazy, good-humoured smile she knew so well. His voice was an amused drawl. "So, my dear? When do we read the banns?"

"What makes you think I am going to marry you?" Lucy asked with a curl of her lip.

Hersington's reply was reasoned and even, although a smile lurked in the back of his eyes. "When we spoke of this matter some hours since," he reminded her gently, "you gave me to understand that your only objection was your lack of a solid identity. Since this obstacle has now been removed, I feel you are in honour bound."

"I will not marry you!" she snapped. "You are entirely unsuitable!"

"Pray, why?" he asked with a singularly maddening smile.

"You!" Lucy exploded. She whirled around, shook her fists, and began stomping towards him menacingly. "You! You! You ought to be horsewhipped!"

"I?" he feigned surprise.

She pounded her fist twice for emphasis. "You are Uncle Jasper!"

"Why, so I am," he agreed amiably. "I do not see what there is in that to make me ineligible."

"You lied to me! You said you were not he!"

"I don't think so," Jasper said judiciously. "I recall saying that I knew him better than anyone, but did not espy him at present. Since I could hardly see myself across the room, there was in fact no falsehood involved."

"It was trickery," insisted Lucy, pacing up and down before him.

"True." He showed no sign of contrition. In fact, the earl was enjoying the sight of a flushed, dishevelled Lucy trying to trounce him. Her eyes were bright, and one dark curl had twined charmingly round her ear. He found her entirely delectable.

"You could have told me!" she accused, a little plaintively.

"I could have, I suppose. But I could not think of a graceful way to approach the reigning debutante and say, 'By the by, I am the man who used to pay your wages.'" He watched her fondly as she pouted at this logic and searched for another line of attack.

"I should have smoked you long ago! I might have guessed who you *really* were!"

"Certainly you might," he supported affably. "It was singularly dim of you not to have done so."

"It was there all along! I even had a description! 'Uncle Jasper' is not the only thing the children call you, you know."

Hensington was smiling openly now. "I fancy not. Would you care to tell me what other names they applied to me?"

Lucy's anger was fast running out against his determined affability. She looked down as she tried to call the epithets to mind, and did not notice Hersington creeping up on her.

"Well, they said you were a top-of-the-trees," she began in almost normal tones.

"Did they?" he asked caressingly.

"Yes. And a Corinthian, a great gun, up to every rig and row in town."

As she recalled the children's slang, Lucy had begun to grin. Hersington thought this a strategic moment to put his arm around her waist. He felt her quiver.

She looked up at him a bit tremulously, but with an imp of mischief in her face. "Unlike your nephew, whom they called a curst basket-scrambler. Oh, and you are clutch-fisted, if you please."

"That sounds like Maria," commented Jasper, tilting up her chin and smiling. "Shall I tell you what the children say of *you?*" he teased gently. "The first day I arrived, I was informed in no uncertain terms that you were a trump. At least that was Lindon's opinion. Hyde averred that you were no such thing, as females couldn't be."

"Did he?" she said rather breathlessly. For Hersington had touched his lips to her forehead as she spoke. And then, abandoning all manners, he ignored her question and proceeded to kiss her quite ruthlessly, and not at all like a man who intends to let his beloved move off to the country to raise cats.

The earl raised his head at last. Now very sure of his welcome, he could afford to hold her loosely in the circle of his arms, smiling down at her and joking lazily. They had all the time in the world. As casual as he looked, however, Lucy could feel the power and tension in that lean body.

He went on as if they were finishing any casual conversation. "You, however, may call me anything you wish, so long as you also call me 'darling'."

Lucy wrinkled her nose at him. "I shall call you an odious tyrant!"

" 'Darling,' " Jasper prompted.

"You are an odious tyrant, darling," replied Lucy meekly. And just to show how thoroughly she held him in contempt, she kissed him again.

This conversation went on some time. While it was lacking in intellectual stimulation, both parties seemed to find it thoroughly satisfactory.

"We must be married soon," Hersington said at last in a shaken voice.

"Soon," Lucy agreed.

He kissed her again, on the neck this time. "Shall we publish the banns tomorrow, and marry as soon as possible?"

Lucy made a sound that could have been taken as assent.

"From Staventry House?" He kissed her shoulder.

Lucy roused herself. "Oh, I think not. Almeria would be so upset. But stay, Hersington!" she said with excitement.

"Jasper," he reminded softly.

"Jasper," she repeated shyly. "My dear, what of this? Clarissa and the Demi-Beau are to be married in a few weeks. Suppose we steal their thunder and make our wedding the very same day?"

Hersington, nibbling on her fingers, seemed much struck. "That's a capital idea. In fact, I shall even award it the highest form of praise. It is what Almeria would call 'the nackiest notion.'"

"Oh, do let's go tell her," said Lucy eagerly, tugging his hand.

Hersington held the little palm firmly and pulled Lucy back against his chest.

"Later," said the Earl of Kentsey. "Just at present, I have a notion even nackier than that."

From her subsequent actions, it can only be inferred that Lucy quite agreed.

If you have enjoyed this book and would like to receive details of other Walker Regency romances, please write to:

Regency Editor
Walker and Company
720 Fifth Avenue
New York, N.Y. 10019